Paul Auster's
CITY
OF
GLASS

Script Adaptation:
PAUL KARASIK AND
DAVID MAZZUCCHELLI

Art:
DAVID MAZZUCCHELLI

AVON BOOKS  NEW YORK

D1529279

Neon Lit: Paul Auster's City of Glass is an original publication of Avon Books. This work has never appeared in graphic form. Any similarity to actual persons or events is purely coincidental.

AVON BOOKS
A division of
The Hearst Corporation
1350 Avenue of the Americas
New York, New York 10019

Copyright © 1994 by Bob Callahan Studios
Published by arrangement with Bob Callahan Studios
Library of Congress Catalog Card Number: 93-91005
ISBN: 0-380-77108-X

Neon Lit Editor: Bob Callahan
Neon Lit Design: Art Spiegelman
Neon Lit Avon Books Senior Editor: Robert Mecoy
Neon Lit Production: Anne Marie Spagnuolo, Eileen O Malley Callahan,
    Leslie Jackson. Map of Ireland: Leslie Jackson.

First Avon Books Trade Printing: August 1994

AVON TRADEMARK REG. U.S. PAT. OFF. AND IN OTHER COUNTRIES.
MARCA REGISTRADA, HECHO EN USA.

Printed in the USA

ARC 10 9 8 7 6 5 4 3 2 1

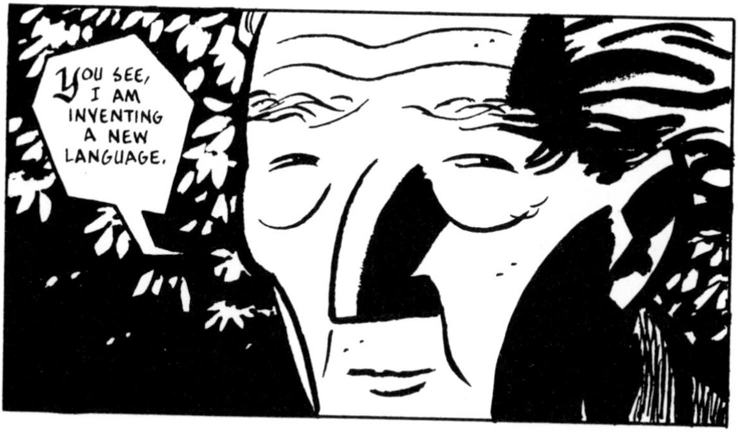
YOU SEE, I AM INVENTING A NEW LANGUAGE.

WRONG NUMBER

The music of historic change is now heard in some of the most exciting works of contemporary crime fiction. These days, sophisticated writers turn to the comparative simplicities of crime fiction to help spell out the essential unease of our age. In this regard — and as our own leading example — Paul Auster's *City of Glass* appears to us today as an unfinished, perhaps ultimately unfinishable diagram for some bold, new and experimental symphony. In a book such as *City of Glass,* we leave forever the honorable worlds of a Dashiell Hammett or a Raymond Chandler, and enter into a far darker, more complex domain.

In Dashiell Hammett's world, decent, tough-minded individuals called private detectives still succeed in restoring the social order, by redressing the crime of sin. In Auster's era — our own era — crime is inherent: it can't be reversed. And the social order will not be restored, for it never existed in the first place. In the new city, both the criminal and the detective have been assigned a fate before the book even begins, a fate in which no easy sense of a lost Eden can possibly be regained. Everything here is shadows. This is a world in which only a neon literature might actually obtain.

The sound of shattered glass, and the sight of jagged edges, is at the very center of word and picture driven crime fiction. The old logics simply no longer calculate. "Commit a crime," *Real Clue Comics* told us, as early as in 1948, "and the world is made of glass." In Paul Auster's city, we are driven back beyond even Hammett and Chandler to the still earlier genius of a Sir Conan Doyle. Compare, for example the role of deductive reasoning in both Auster and Doyle. With Doyle, deduction is everything. With Auster, the clarity of pure reason becomes a vast, still musically interesting highway which, if pursued too rigorously, can only lead straight into the loony bin.

Turn, if you will, to one of the crowning moments in this book — the moment when Auster's sleuth, Daniel Quinn, finally confronts his own Moriarty, Peter Stillman's unknown and ultimately unknowable Father. The men meet in a park-bench setting on Riverside Drive in the city of New York. As in Doyle, both men are hunch-makers, note-takers, code-breakers, reason's scientists — but, in this city at least, such artful habits of mind won't do either man any damn good. The darkness is there to engulf them. Everywhere, the shadows extend.

The question therefore is not whether Paul Auster is a crime writer, anymore than it is whether Daniel Quinn is a real crime detective. Both the author and the character have, in fact, fallen into this world at random, and both will choose the patterns of crime detection to tran-scend the darkness which both know intuitively stands at the heart of the post-modern condition. Quinn's journey will fail. For showing us this world in its exactness, and in its limitations, Auster, quite clearly, may claim a win.

In the end, this new neon literature is the literature of individual human obsessiveness. It assumes silently that when no convincing social order can be established, the individual personality itself will start to unhinge. Its ancestors are thus not Hammett, Chandler, or Doyle; but Poe, Dostoyevsky, and perhaps James M. Cain. This new literature makes the point, rather decisively, that, in such a violent and irrational world, it is not surprising when the deeds of serial killers are taken as hideously precise omens of the true nature of our age.

And here, finally, is where we make our own shift into this landscape. In the hands of Paul Karasik, who first found the right rhythms, and David Mazzucchelli, who has brought these rhythms to form, we move past the speed of sound to the actual speed of light in order to capture the switches which occur throughout the fall in, and out, of human intellectual abstraction. A final lamp light lit against the darkness? A shadow, after all, is still a sign.

The tension between the absolute geometries of the minds of Stillman and Quinn, and the absolute randomness of the world which will rise up and swallow them, cannot be rendered any more exactly than it has been in this singular act of picture fiction, the first Neon Lit edition of Paul Auster's *City of Glass*.

— Bob Callahan

                    It was a
wrong number that
started it...

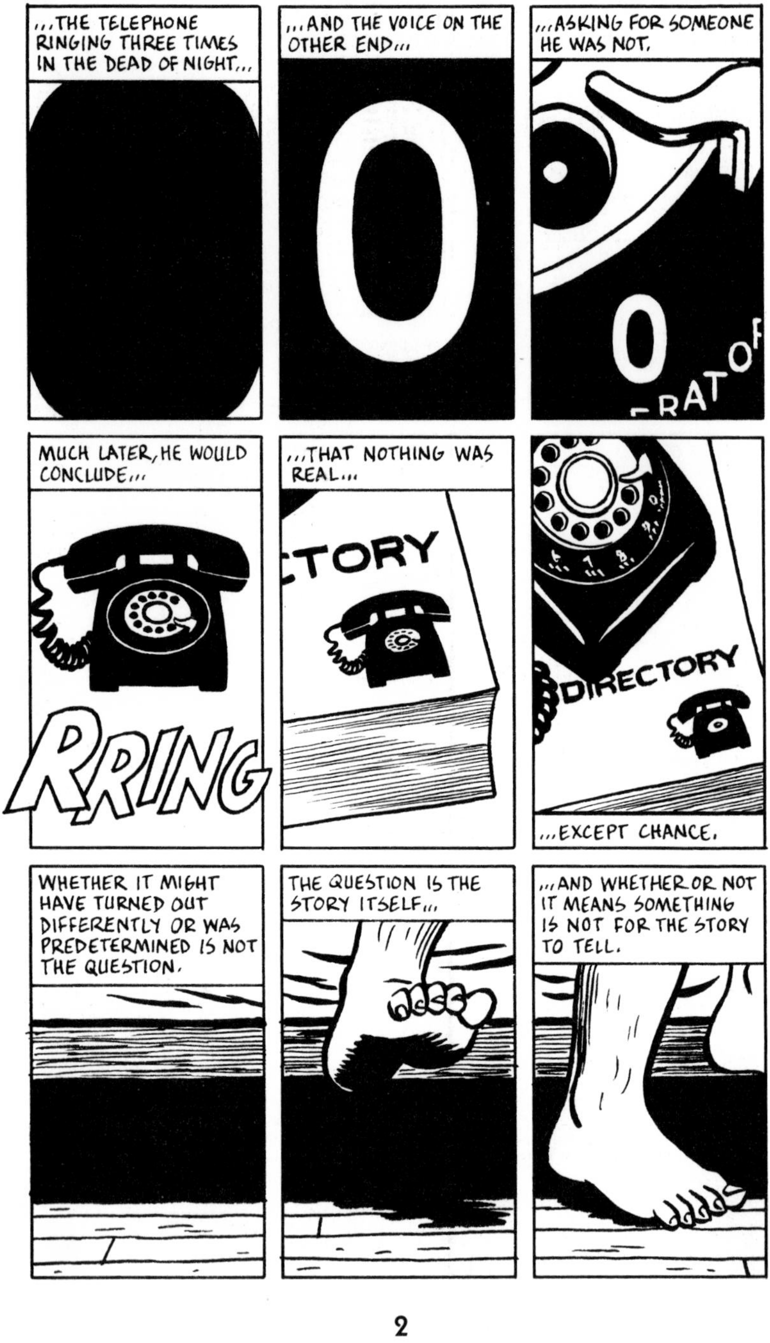
...THE TELEPHONE RINGING THREE TIMES IN THE DEAD OF NIGHT...
...AND THE VOICE ON THE OTHER END...
...ASKING FOR SOMEONE HE WAS NOT.
0
MUCH LATER, HE WOULD CONCLUDE...
RRING
...THAT NOTHING WAS REAL...
CTORY
DIRECTORY
...EXCEPT CHANCE.
WHETHER IT MIGHT HAVE TURNED OUT DIFFERENTLY OR WAS PREDETERMINED IS NOT THE QUESTION.
THE QUESTION IS THE STORY ITSELF...
...AND WHETHER OR NOT IT MEANS SOMETHING IS NOT FOR THE STORY TO TELL.

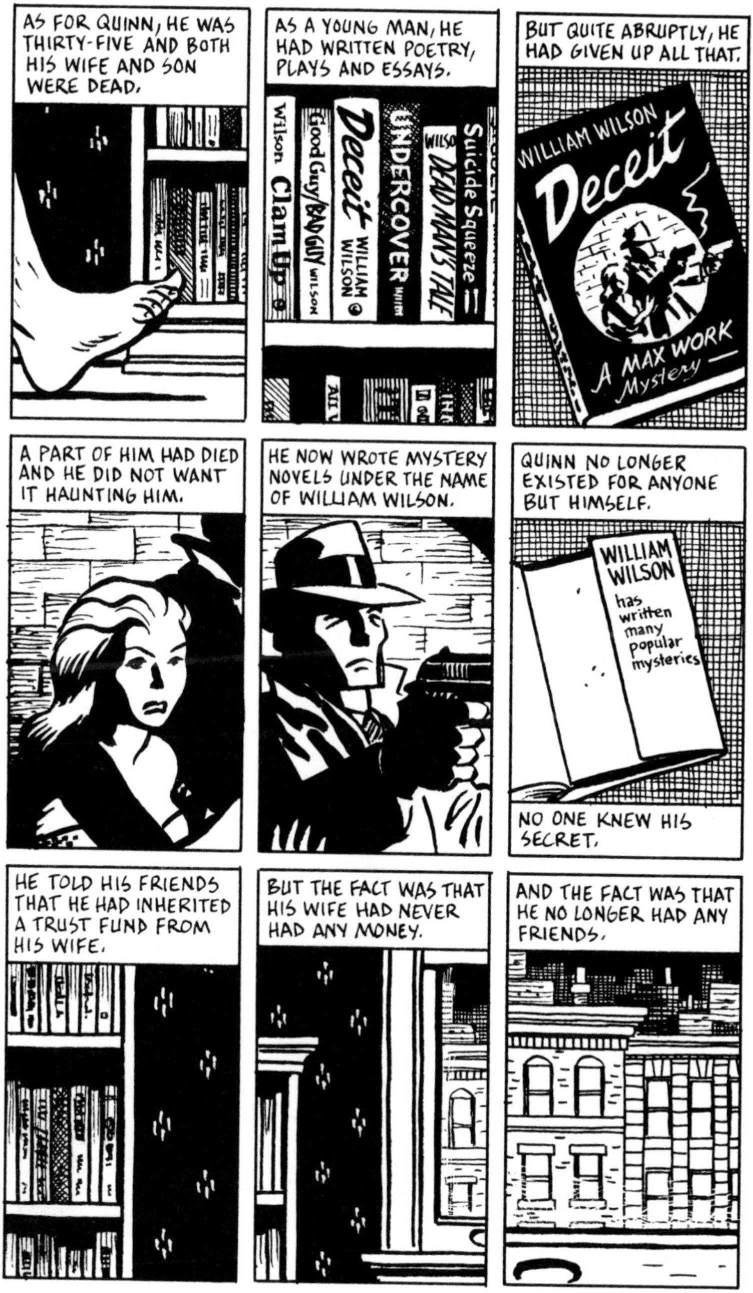
AS FOR QUINN, HE WAS THIRTY-FIVE AND BOTH HIS WIFE AND SON WERE DEAD.
AS A YOUNG MAN, HE HAD WRITTEN POETRY, PLAYS AND ESSAYS.
Wilson Clam Up
Good Guy/BAD GUY WILSON
Deceit WILLIAM WILSON
UNDERCOVER
WILSON DEAD MAN'S TALE
Suicide Squeeze
BUT QUITE ABRUPTLY, HE HAD GIVEN UP ALL THAT.
WILLIAM WILSON
Deceit
A MAX WORK Mystery
A PART OF HIM HAD DIED AND HE DID NOT WANT IT HAUNTING HIM.
HE NOW WROTE MYSTERY NOVELS UNDER THE NAME OF WILLIAM WILSON.
QUINN NO LONGER EXISTED FOR ANYONE BUT HIMSELF.
WILLIAM WILSON has written many popular mysteries
NO ONE KNEW HIS SECRET.
HE TOLD HIS FRIENDS THAT HE HAD INHERITED A TRUST FUND FROM HIS WIFE.
BUT THE FACT WAS THAT HIS WIFE HAD NEVER HAD ANY MONEY.
AND THE FACT WAS THAT HE NO LONGER HAD ANY FRIENDS.

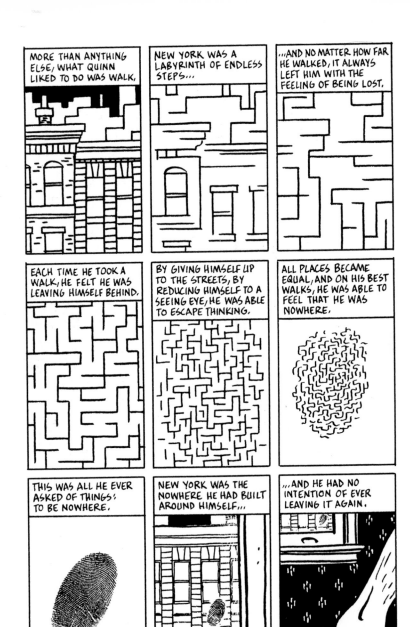

MORE THAN ANYTHING ELSE, WHAT QUINN LIKED TO DO WAS WALK.

NEW YORK WAS A LABYRINTH OF ENDLESS STEPS...

...AND NO MATTER HOW FAR HE WALKED, IT ALWAYS LEFT HIM WITH THE FEELING OF BEING LOST.

EACH TIME HE TOOK A WALK, HE FELT HE WAS LEAVING HIMSELF BEHIND.

BY GIVING HIMSELF UP TO THE STREETS, BY REDUCING HIMSELF TO A SEEING EYE, HE WAS ABLE TO ESCAPE THINKING.

ALL PLACES BECAME EQUAL, AND ON HIS BEST WALKS, HE WAS ABLE TO FEEL THAT HE WAS NOWHERE.

THIS WAS ALL HE EVER ASKED OF THINGS: TO BE NOWHERE.

NEW YORK WAS THE NOWHERE HE HAD BUILT AROUND HIMSELF...

...AND HE HAD NO INTENTION OF EVER LEAVING IT AGAIN.

4

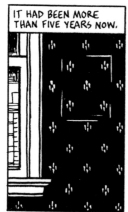

IT HAD BEEN MORE THAN FIVE YEARS NOW.

HE DID NOT THINK ABOUT IT VERY MUCH ANYMORE.

EVERY ONCE IN A WHILE, HE WOULD SUDDENLY FEEL WHAT IT HAD BEEN LIKE...

...TO HOLD THE THREE-YEAR-OLD BOY IN HIS ARMS,

IT WAS AN IMPRINT OF THE PAST LEFT IN HIS BODY.

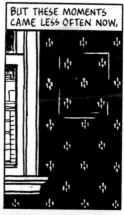

BUT THESE MOMENTS CAME LESS OFTEN NOW.

HE HAD CONTINUED TO WRITE BECAUSE IT WAS THE ONLY THING HE FELT HE COULD DO.

RRIN—

YES?

THERE WAS A LONG PAUSE.

5

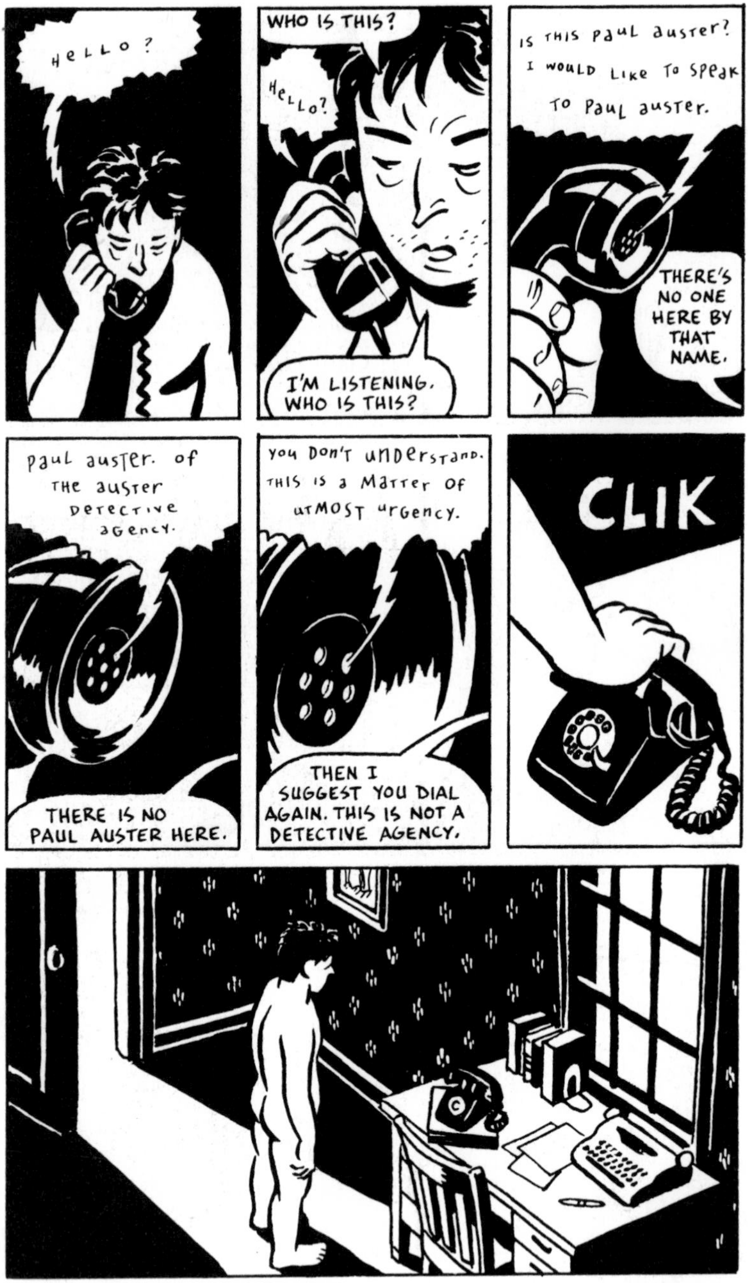
HELLO?
WHO IS THIS?
HELLO?
I'M LISTENING. WHO IS THIS?
IS THIS PAUL AUSTER? I WOULD LIKE TO SPEAK TO PAUL AUSTER.
THERE'S NO ONE HERE BY THAT NAME.
PAUL AUSTER. OF THE AUSTER DETECTIVE AGENCY.
THERE IS NO PAUL AUSTER HERE.
YOU DON'T UNDERSTAND. THIS IS A MATTER OF UTMOST URGENCY.
THEN I SUGGEST YOU DIAL AGAIN. THIS IS NOT A DETECTIVE AGENCY.
CLIK

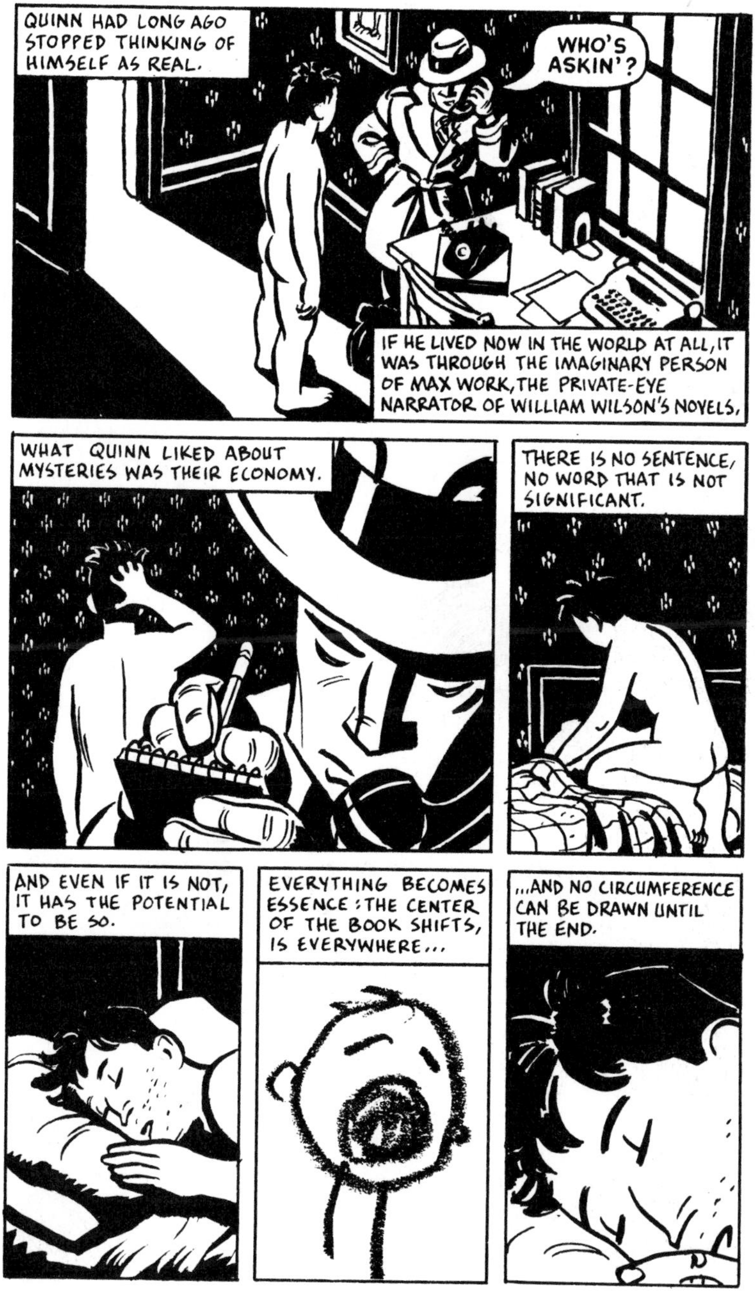
QUINN HAD LONG AGO STOPPED THINKING OF HIMSELF AS REAL.
WHO'S ASKIN'?
IF HE LIVED NOW IN THE WORLD AT ALL, IT WAS THROUGH THE IMAGINARY PERSON OF MAX WORK, THE PRIVATE-EYE NARRATOR OF WILLIAM WILSON'S NOVELS,
WHAT QUINN LIKED ABOUT MYSTERIES WAS THEIR ECONOMY.
THERE IS NO SENTENCE, NO WORD THAT IS NOT SIGNIFICANT.
AND EVEN IF IT IS NOT, IT HAS THE POTENTIAL TO BE SO.
EVERYTHING BECOMES ESSENCE: THE CENTER OF THE BOOK SHIFTS, IS EVERYWHERE...
...AND NO CIRCUMFERENCE CAN BE DRAWN UNTIL THE END.

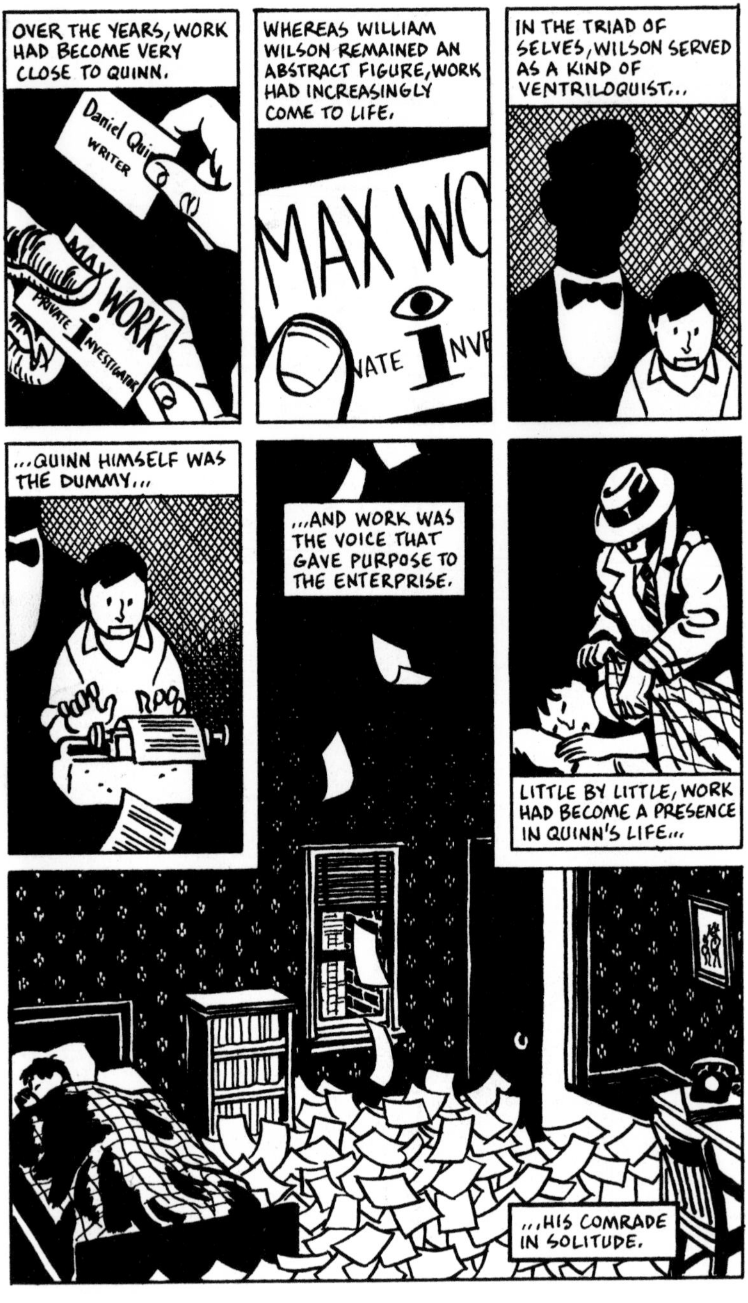
OVER THE YEARS, WORK HAD BECOME VERY CLOSE TO QUINN.
Daniel Qui
WRITER
MAX WORK
PRIVATE INVESTIGATOR
WHEREAS WILLIAM WILSON REMAINED AN ABSTRACT FIGURE, WORK HAD INCREASINGLY COME TO LIFE.
MAX WO
VATE INVE
IN THE TRIAD OF SELVES, WILSON SERVED AS A KIND OF VENTRILOQUIST...
...QUINN HIMSELF WAS THE DUMMY...
...AND WORK WAS THE VOICE THAT GAVE PURPOSE TO THE ENTERPRISE.
LITTLE BY LITTLE, WORK HAD BECOME A PRESENCE IN QUINN'S LIFE...
...HIS COMRADE IN SOLITUDE.

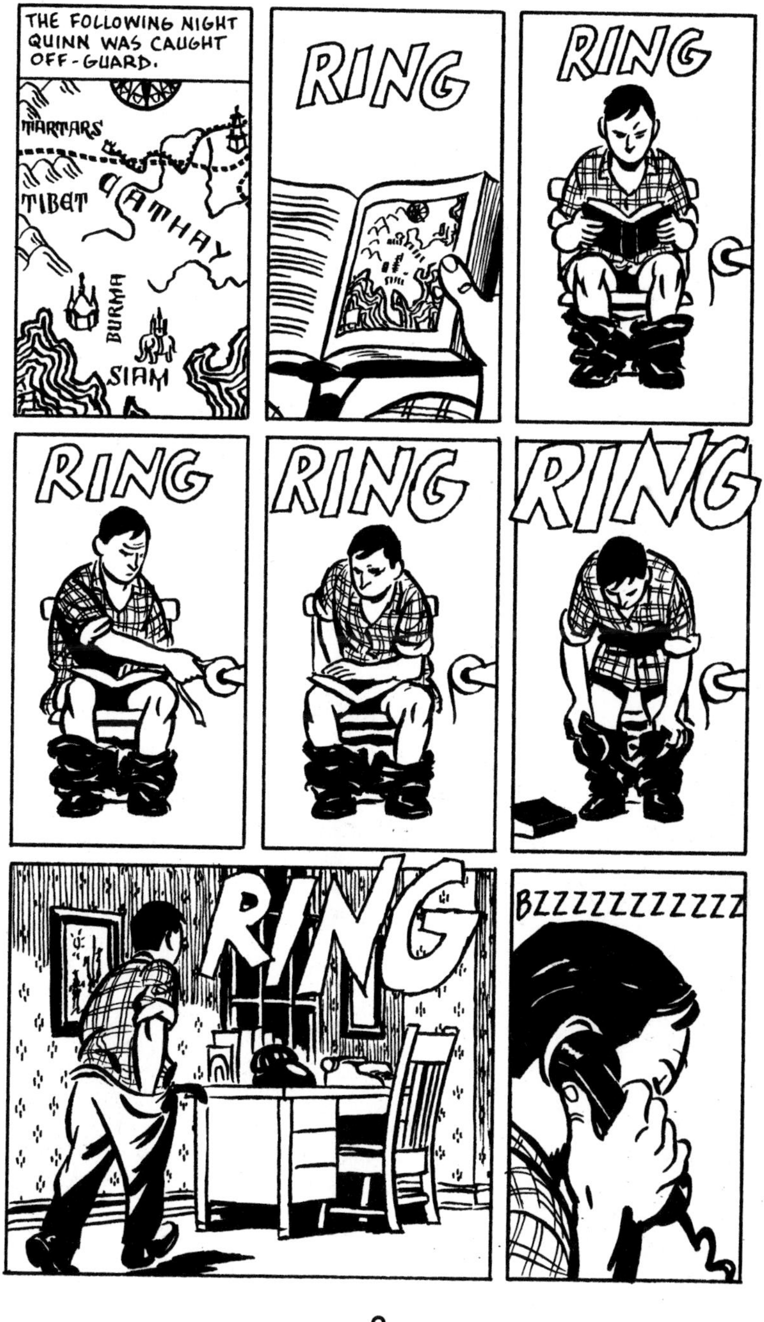
THE FOLLOWING NIGHT QUINN WAS CAUGHT OFF-GUARD.
TARTARS
TIBET
CATHAY
BURMA
SIAM
RING
RING
RING
RING
RING
RING
BZZZZZZZZZZZ

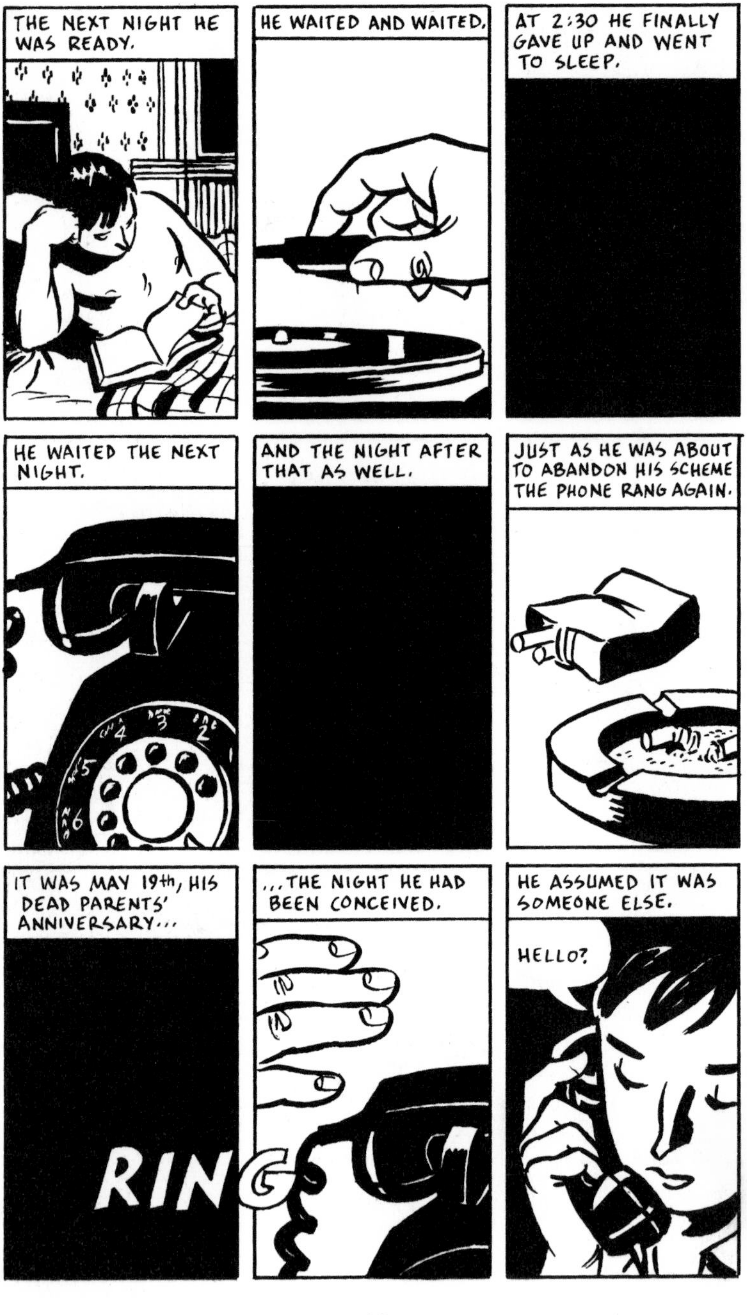
THE NEXT NIGHT HE WAS READY.
HE WAITED AND WAITED.
AT 2:30 HE FINALLY GAVE UP AND WENT TO SLEEP.
HE WAITED THE NEXT NIGHT.
AND THE NIGHT AFTER THAT AS WELL.
JUST AS HE WAS ABOUT TO ABANDON HIS SCHEME THE PHONE RANG AGAIN.
IT WAS MAY 19th, HIS DEAD PARENTS' ANNIVERSARY...
...THE NIGHT HE HAD BEEN CONCEIVED.
RING
HE ASSUMED IT WAS SOMEONE ELSE.
HELLO?

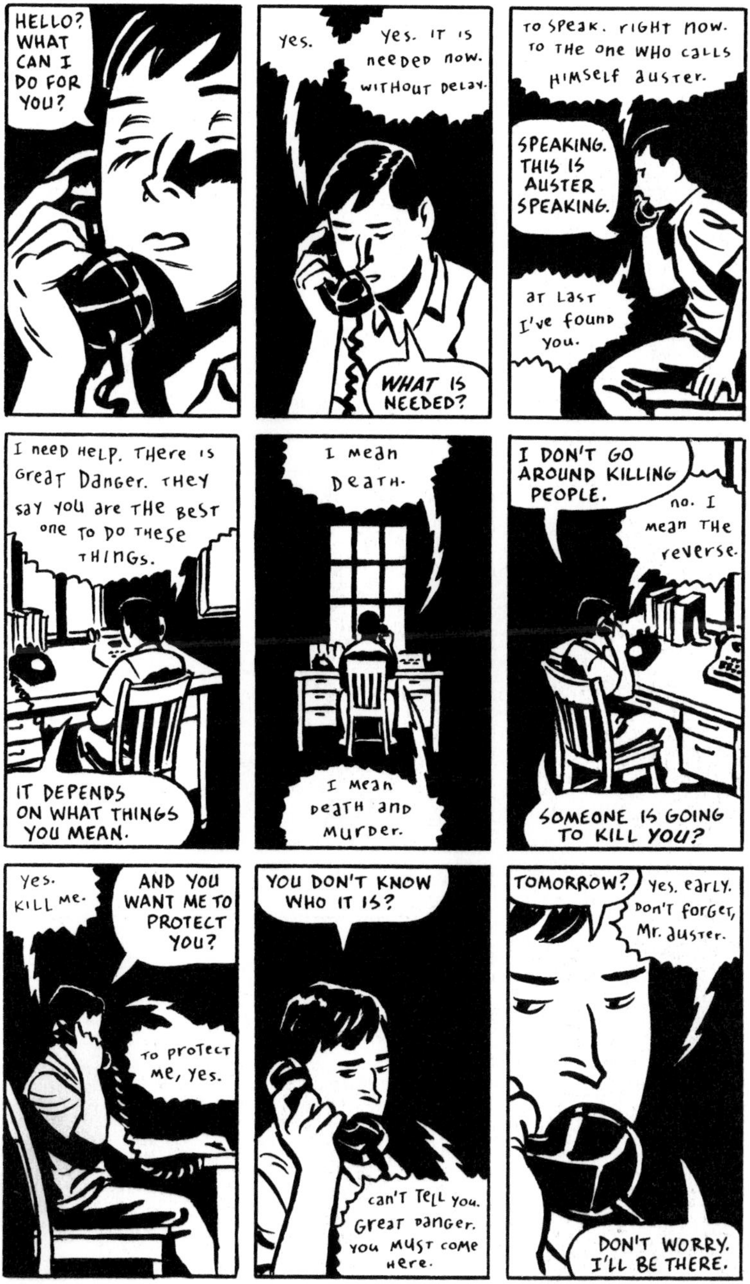
HELLO? WHAT CAN I DO FOR YOU?
yes.
yes. IT IS needed now. WITHOUT DELAY.
WHAT IS NEEDED?
TO SPEAK. RIGHT NOW. TO THE ONE WHO CALLS HIMSELF AUSTER.
SPEAKING. THIS IS AUSTER SPEAKING.
AT LAST I'VE FOUND YOU.
I NEED HELP. THERE IS GREAT DANGER. THEY SAY YOU ARE THE BEST ONE TO DO THESE THINGS.
IT DEPENDS ON WHAT THINGS YOU MEAN.
I MEAN DEATH.
I MEAN DEATH AND MURDER.
I DON'T GO AROUND KILLING PEOPLE.
NO. I MEAN THE REVERSE.
SOMEONE IS GOING TO KILL YOU?
YES. KILL ME.
AND YOU WANT ME TO PROTECT YOU?
TO PROTECT ME, YES.
YOU DON'T KNOW WHO IT IS?
CAN'T TELL YOU. GREAT DANGER. YOU MUST COME HERE.
TOMORROW?
YES. EARLY. DON'T FORGET, MR. AUSTER.
DON'T WORRY. I'LL BE THERE.

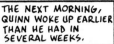

THE NEXT MORNING, QUINN WOKE UP EARLIER THAN HE HAD IN SEVERAL WEEKS.

I SEEM TO BE GOING OUT.

BUT IF I AM GOING OUT...

...WHERE EXACTLY AM I GOING?

W 107 ST

ONE WAY

12

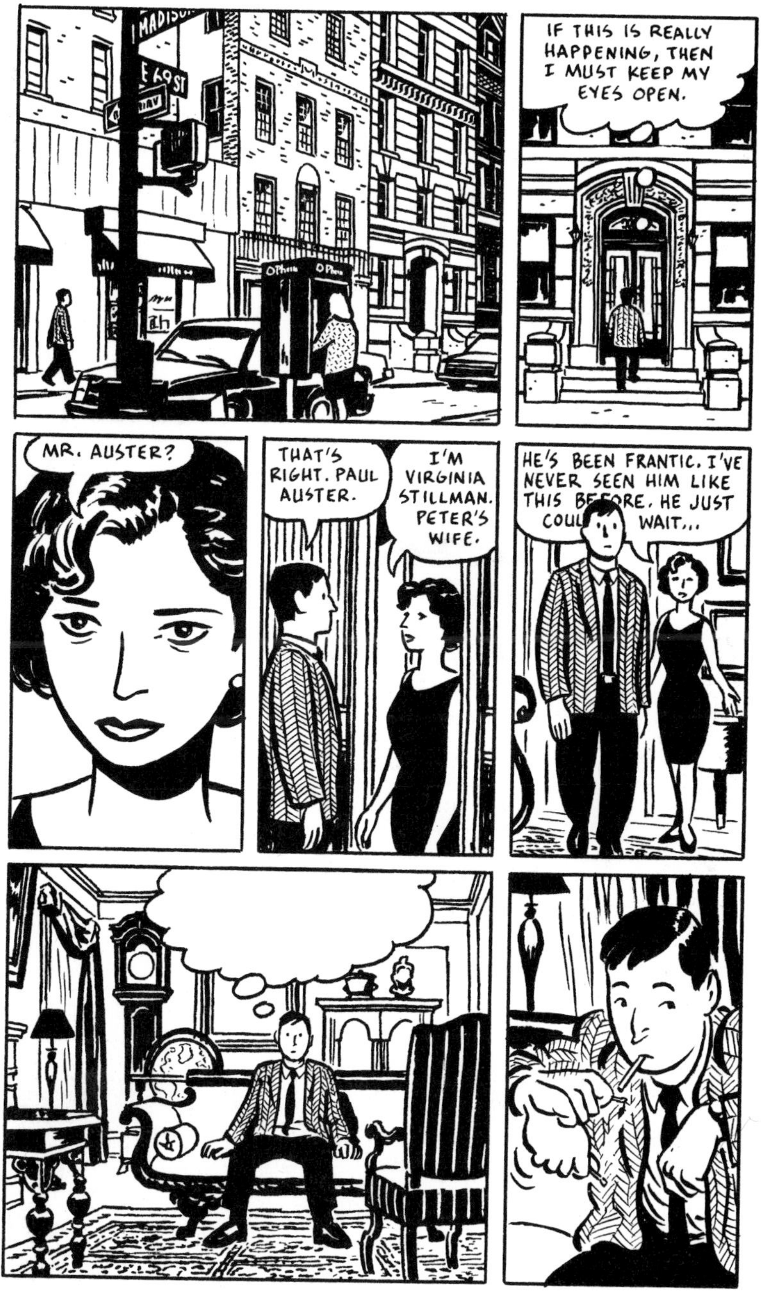
MADISO
E 69 ST
IF THIS IS REALLY HAPPENING, THEN I MUST KEEP MY EYES OPEN.
MR. AUSTER?
THAT'S RIGHT. PAUL AUSTER.
I'M VIRGINIA STILLMAN. PETER'S WIFE.
HE'S BEEN FRANTIC. I'VE NEVER SEEN HIM LIKE THIS BEFORE. HE JUST COUL WAIT...

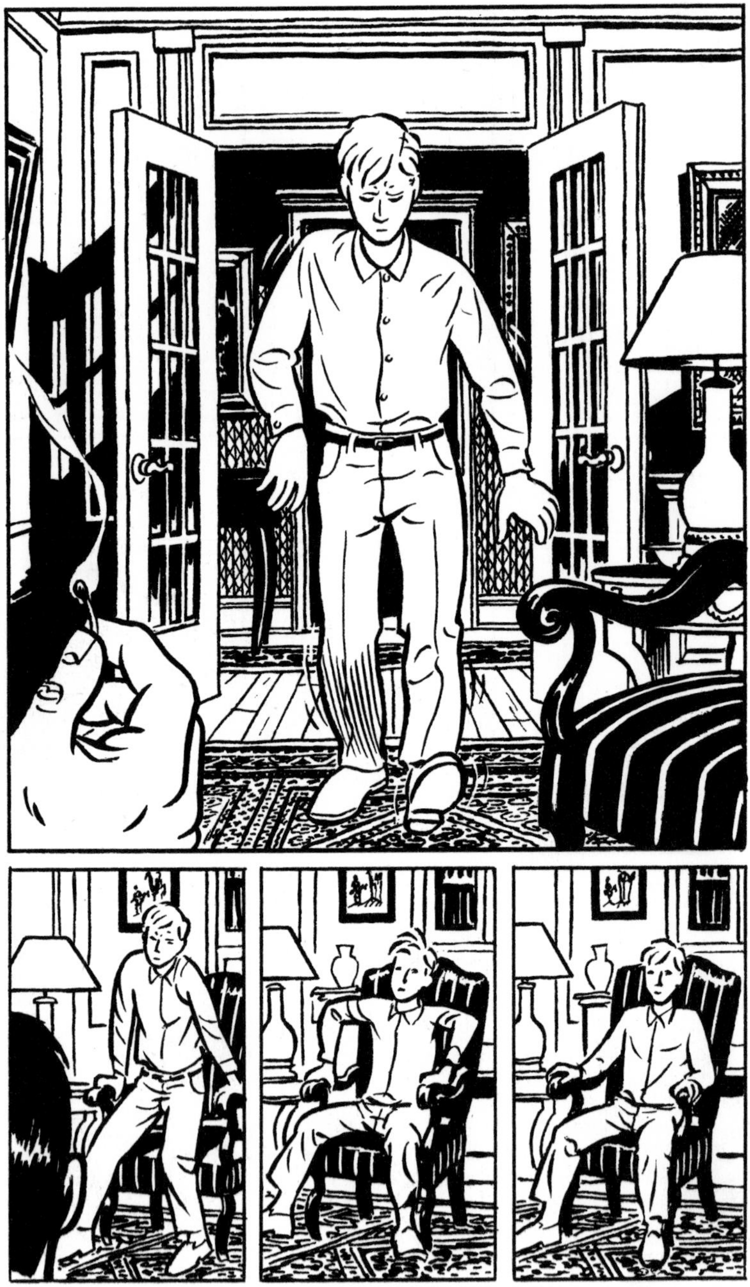

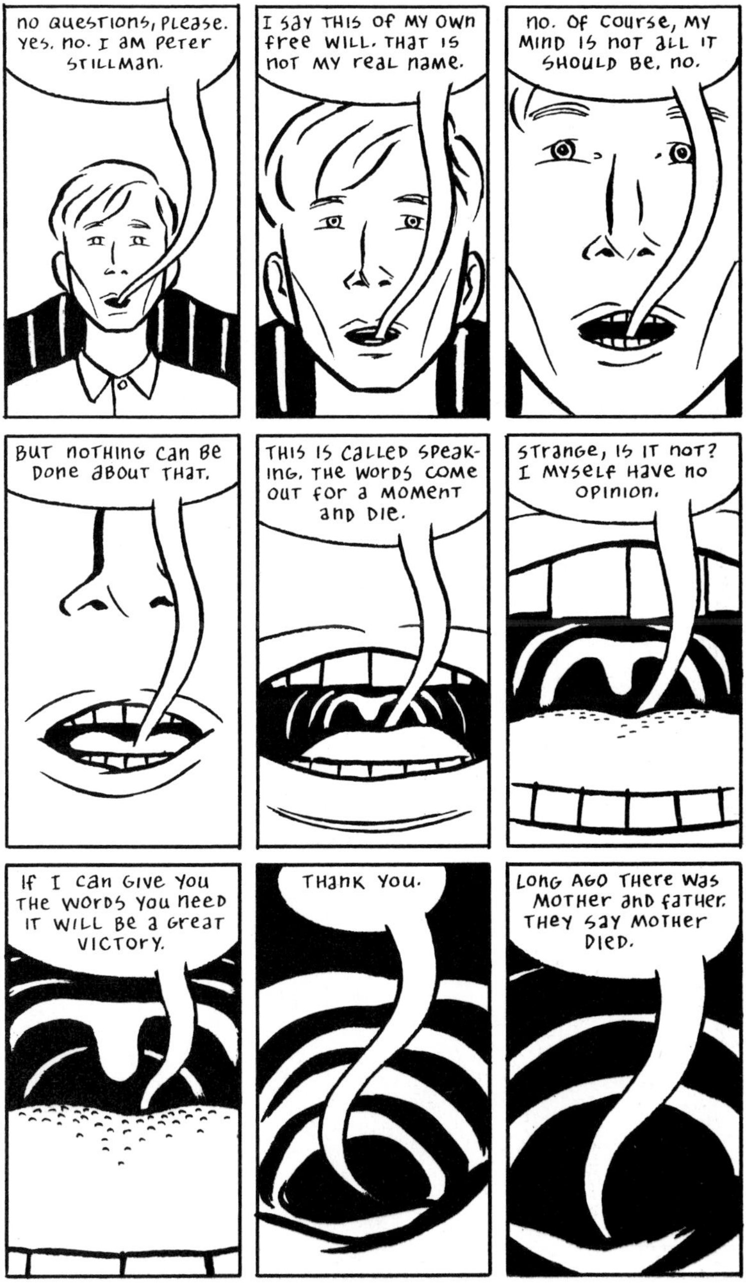
NO QUESTIONS, PLEASE. YES. NO. I AM PETER STILLMAN.
I SAY THIS OF MY OWN FREE WILL. THAT IS NOT MY REAL NAME.
NO. OF COURSE, MY MIND IS NOT ALL IT SHOULD BE. NO.
BUT NOTHING CAN BE DONE ABOUT THAT.
THIS IS CALLED SPEAKING. THE WORDS COME OUT FOR A MOMENT AND DIE.
STRANGE, IS IT NOT? I MYSELF HAVE NO OPINION.
IF I CAN GIVE YOU THE WORDS YOU NEED IT WILL BE A GREAT VICTORY.
THANK YOU.
LONG AGO THERE WAS MOTHER AND FATHER. THEY SAY MOTHER DIED.

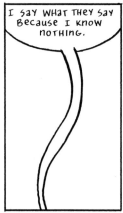

I say what they say Because I know nothing.

There was this. Dark. Very Dark. As Dark as very Dark. They say: that was the room.

not even a window. poor Peter Stillman. and the BOOM, BOOM, BOOM, the caca piles, the pipilakes. excuse me. anymore.

There was MUSH food in the HUSH Dark room. He ate with his hands. excuse me. I mean Peter Did.

I am Peter Stillman. That is not my real name. thank you.

My real name is Mr. Sad. What is your name, Mr. Auster? Perhaps you are the real Mr. Sad, and I am no one.

What Did Peter Do in that room? no one can say. Some say nothing.

as for me, I think that Peter could not think. Did he Blink? Did he Drink? Did he Stink?

Ha Ha Ha. excuse me. sometimes I am so funny.

16

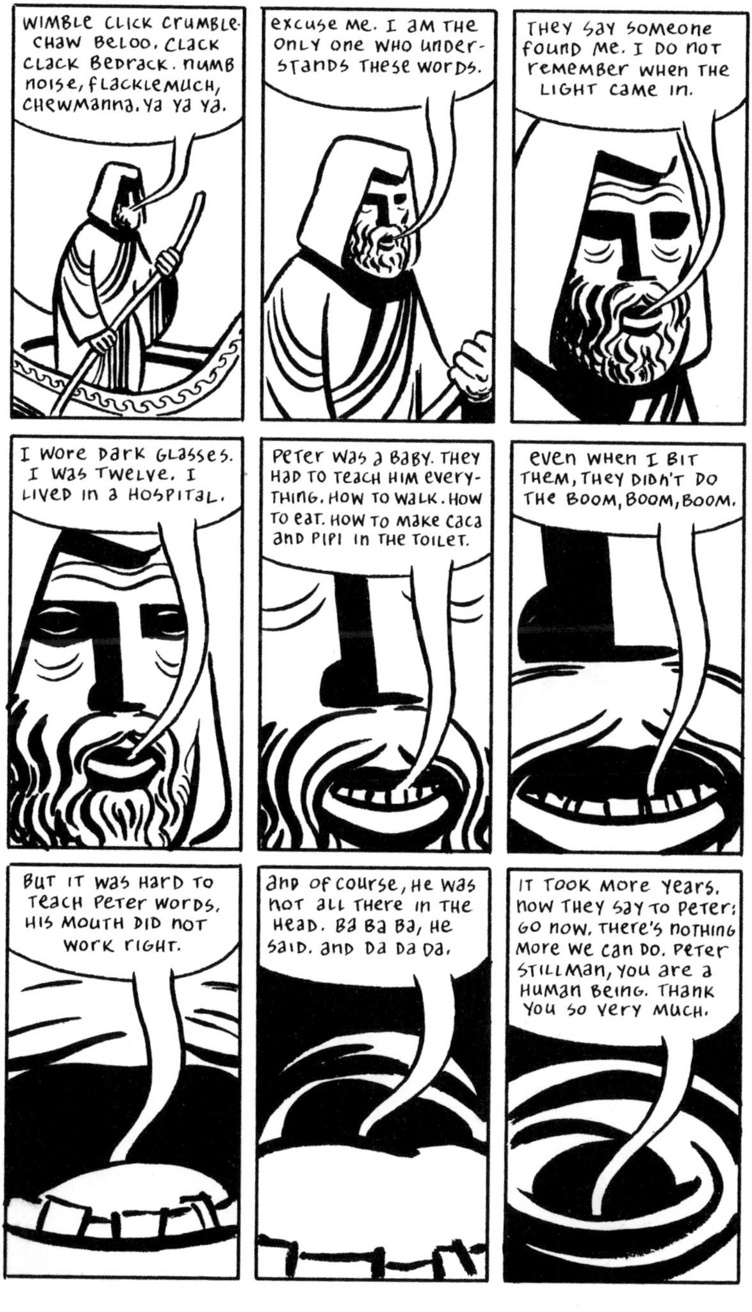
WIMBLE CLICK CRUMBLE-CHAW BELOO. CLACK CLACK BEDRACK. NUMB NOISE, FLACKLEMUCH, CHEWMANNA. YA YA YA.
EXCUSE ME. I AM THE ONLY ONE WHO UNDER-STANDS THESE WORDS.
THEY SAY SOMEONE FOUND ME. I DO NOT REMEMBER WHEN THE LIGHT CAME IN.
I WORE DARK GLASSES. I WAS TWELVE. I LIVED IN A HOSPITAL.
PETER WAS A BABY. THEY HAD TO TEACH HIM EVERY-THING. HOW TO WALK. HOW TO EAT. HOW TO MAKE CACA AND PIPI IN THE TOILET.
EVEN WHEN I BIT THEM, THEY DIDN'T DO THE BOOM, BOOM, BOOM.
BUT IT WAS HARD TO TEACH PETER WORDS. HIS MOUTH DID NOT WORK RIGHT.
AND OF COURSE, HE WAS NOT ALL THERE IN THE HEAD. BA BA BA, HE SAID. AND DA DA DA.
IT TOOK MORE YEARS. NOW THEY SAY TO PETER: GO NOW. THERE'S NOTHING MORE WE CAN DO. PETER STILLMAN, YOU ARE A HUMAN BEING. THANK YOU SO VERY MUCH.

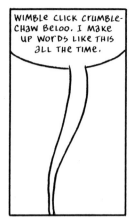

WIMBLE CLICK CRUMBLE-CHAW BELOO. I MAKE UP WORDS LIKE THIS ALL THE TIME.

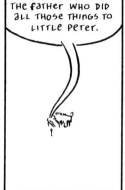

YOU ARE WONDERING: THE FATHER WHO DID ALL THOSE THINGS TO LITTLE PETER.

THEY TOOK HIM TO A DARK PLACE. THEY LOCKED HIM UP AND LEFT HIM THERE. HA HA HA. EXCUSE ME. SOMETIMES I AM SO FUNNY.

THIRTEEN YEARS, THEY SAID. A LONG TIME. BUT I KNOW NOTHING OF TIME.

I AM NEW EVERY DAY. I AM BORN WHEN I WAKE UP IN THE MORNING, I GROW OLD DURING THE DAY, AND I DIE AT NIGHT.

FOR THIRTEEN YEARS THE FATHER WAS AWAY. HIS NAME IS PETER STILLMAN TOO. STRANGE, IS IT NOT? THAT TWO PEOPLE CAN HAVE THE SAME NAME?

WE ARE BOTH PETER STILLMAN. BUT PETER STILLMAN IS NOT MY REAL NAME. SO PERHAPS I AM NOT PETER STILLMAN AFTER ALL.

THIRTEEN YEARS, I SAY. OR THEY SAY. I KNOW NOTHING OF TIME.

TOMORROW IS THE END OF THIRTEEN YEARS, THAT IS BAD.

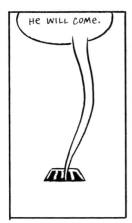

HE WILL COME.

THE FATHER WILL COME. AND HE WILL TRY TO KILL ME. THANK YOU. BUT PETER LIVES NOW. YES.

I AM MOSTLY A POET THESE DAYS.

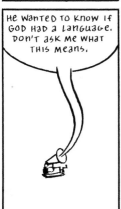

I AM A RICH MAN. I DO NOT HAVE TO WORRY. YOU BET YOUR BOTTOM DOLLAR.

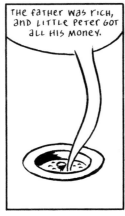

THE FATHER WAS RICH, AND LITTLE PETER GOT ALL HIS MONEY.

THE FATHER WAS PERHAPS NOT REALLY BAD. HE HAD A BIG HEAD. THERE WAS TOO MUCH ROOM IN THERE.

HE WANTED TO KNOW IF GOD HAD A LANGUAGE. DON'T ASK ME WHAT THIS MEANS.

THE FATHER THOUGHT A BABY MIGHT SPEAK IT IF THE BABY SAW NO PEOPLE. WHAT BABY?

PETER KNEW SOME WORDS. THE FATHER THOUGHT MAYBE PETER WOULD FORGET THEM. AFTER A WHILE.

THAT IS WHY THERE WAS SO MUCH BOOM BOOM BOOM. EVERY TIME PETER WOULD SAY A WORD HIS FATHER WOULD BOOM HIM.

PETER LEARNED TO KEEP THE WORDS INSIDE HIM. THE WORDS MADE NOISE IN HIS HEAD AND KEPT HIM COMPANY.

THAT IS WHY HIS MOUTH DOES NOT WORK RIGHT.

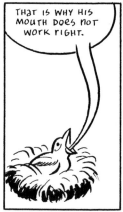

PETER CAN TALK LIKE PEOPLE NOW. BUT HE STILL HAS OTHER WORDS INSIDE HIS HEAD. THEY ARE GOD'S LANGUAGE.

THAT IS WHY PETER LIVES SO CLOSE TO GOD. THAT IS WHY HE IS A FAMOUS POET.

EVERYTHING IS GOOD FOR ME NOW.

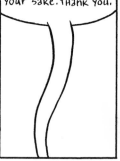

WHENEVER I ASK, MY WIFE GETS A GIRL FOR ME. THEY COME UP HERE AND I FUCK THEM.

POOR VIRGINIA. SHE DOES NOT LIKE TO FUCK. PERHAPS SHE FUCKS ANOTHER.

MAYBE IF YOU ARE NICE TO HER SHE WILL LET YOU FUCK HER. IT WOULD MAKE ME HAPPY, FOR YOUR SAKE. THANK YOU.

20

I KNOW THAT ALL IS NOT RIGHT IN MY HEAD. 	AND IT IS TRUE, YES, AND I SAY THIS OF MY OWN FREE WILL. 	THAT SOMETIMES I JUST SCREAM AND SCREAM. 
FOR NO GOOD REASON. 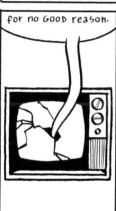	BEST OF ALL, NOW, THERE IS THE AIR. 	YES. AND LITTLE BY LITTLE I HAVE LEARNED TO LIVE INSIDE IT. 
FOR NOW I AM PETER STILLMAN. THAT IS NOT MY REAL NAME. 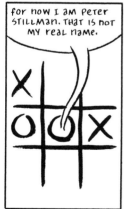	I CANNOT SAY WHO I WILL BE TOMORROW. 	EACH DAY IS NEW, AND EACH DAY I AM BORN AGAIN. 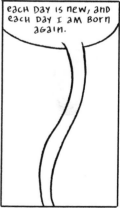

21

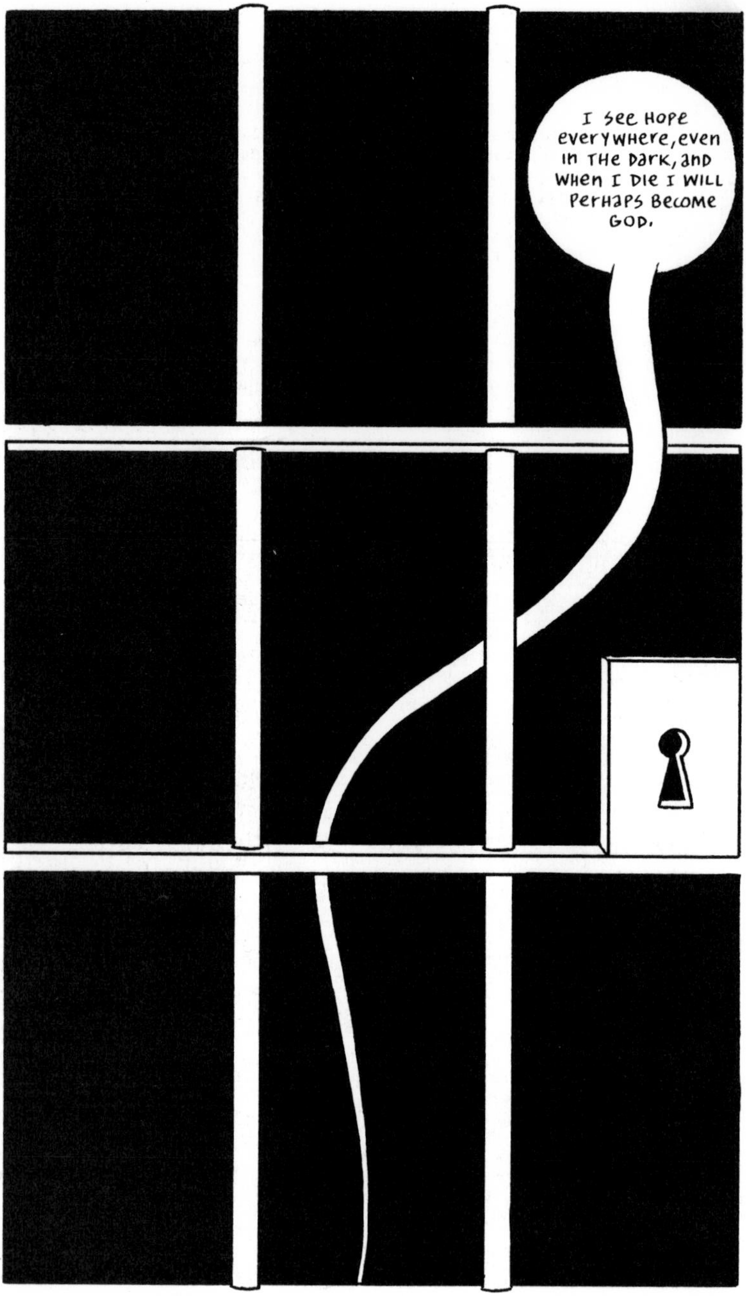
I see hope everywhere, even in the dark, and when I die I will perhaps become God.

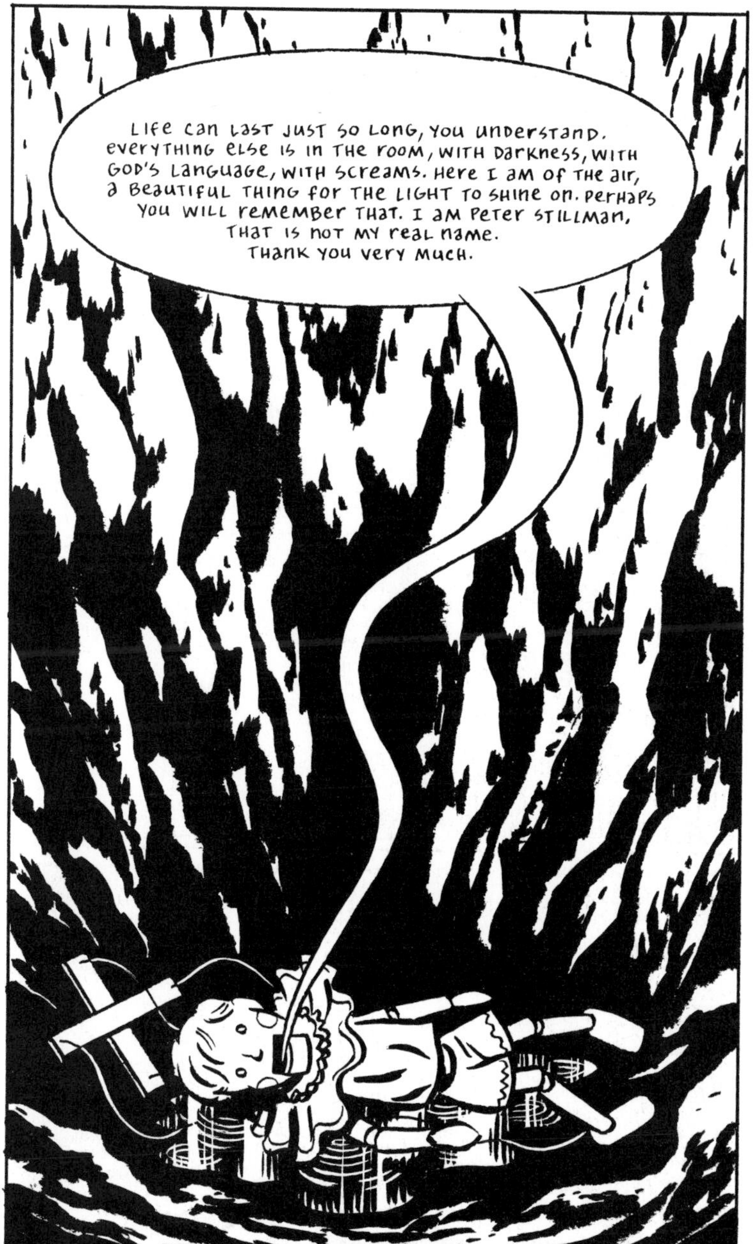
LIFE CAN LAST JUST SO LONG, YOU UNDERSTAND. EVERYTHING ELSE IS IN THE ROOM, WITH DARKNESS, WITH GOD'S LANGUAGE, WITH SCREAMS. HERE I AM OF THE AIR, A BEAUTIFUL THING FOR THE LIGHT TO SHINE ON. PERHAPS YOU WILL REMEMBER THAT. I AM PETER STILLMAN, THAT IS NOT MY REAL NAME. THANK YOU VERY MUCH.

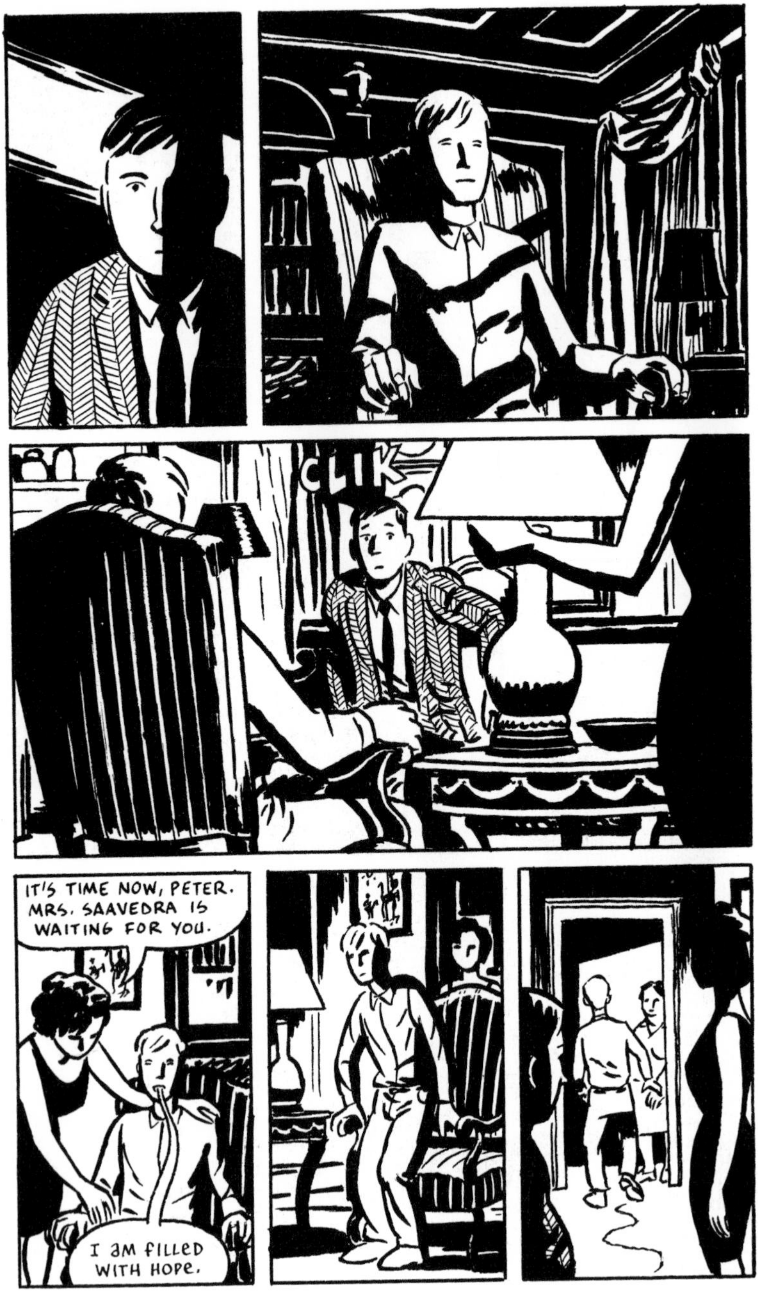
CLIK
IT'S TIME NOW, PETER. MRS. SAAVEDRA IS WAITING FOR YOU.
I AM FILLED WITH HOPE.

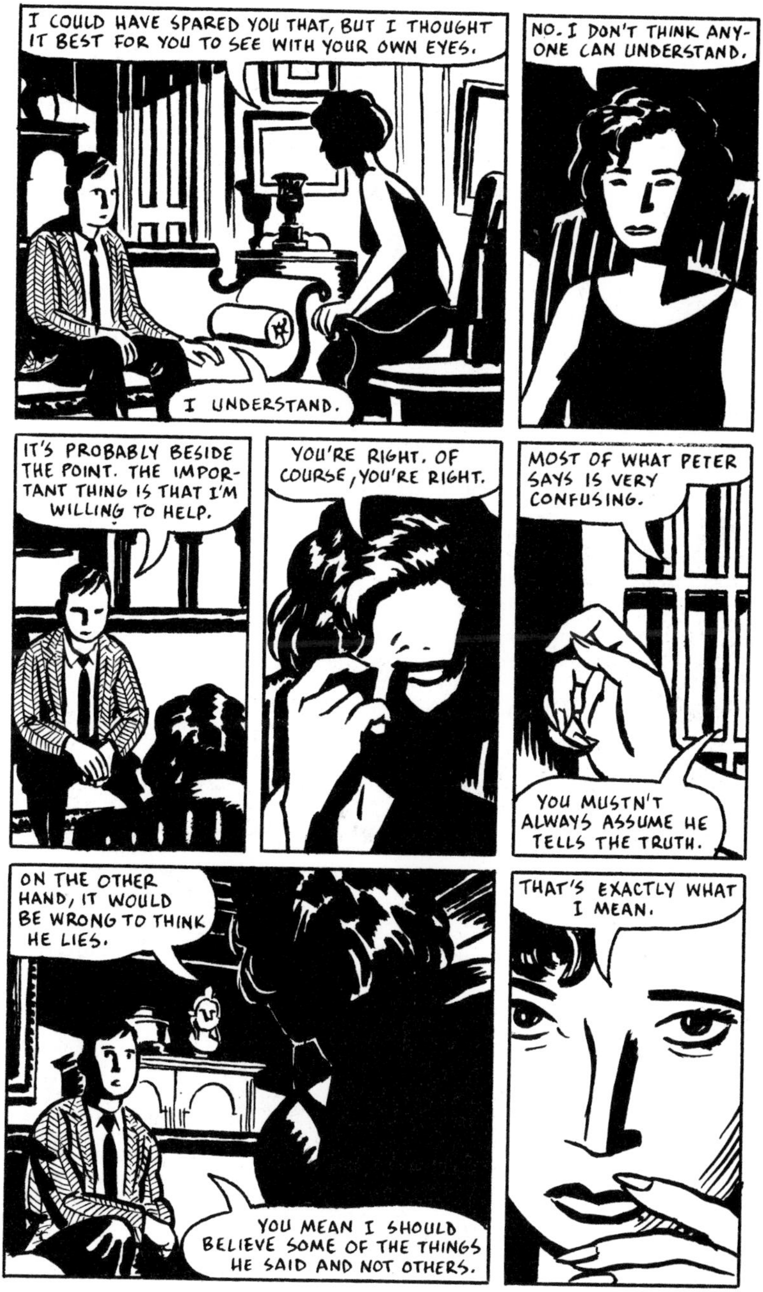
I COULD HAVE SPARED YOU THAT, BUT I THOUGHT IT BEST FOR YOU TO SEE WITH YOUR OWN EYES.
I UNDERSTAND.
NO. I DON'T THINK ANYONE CAN UNDERSTAND.
IT'S PROBABLY BESIDE THE POINT. THE IMPORTANT THING IS THAT I'M WILLING TO HELP.
YOU'RE RIGHT. OF COURSE, YOU'RE RIGHT.
MOST OF WHAT PETER SAYS IS VERY CONFUSING.
YOU MUSTN'T ALWAYS ASSUME HE TELLS THE TRUTH.
ON THE OTHER HAND, IT WOULD BE WRONG TO THINK HE LIES.
YOU MEAN I SHOULD BELIEVE SOME OF THE THINGS HE SAID AND NOT OTHERS.
THAT'S EXACTLY WHAT I MEAN.

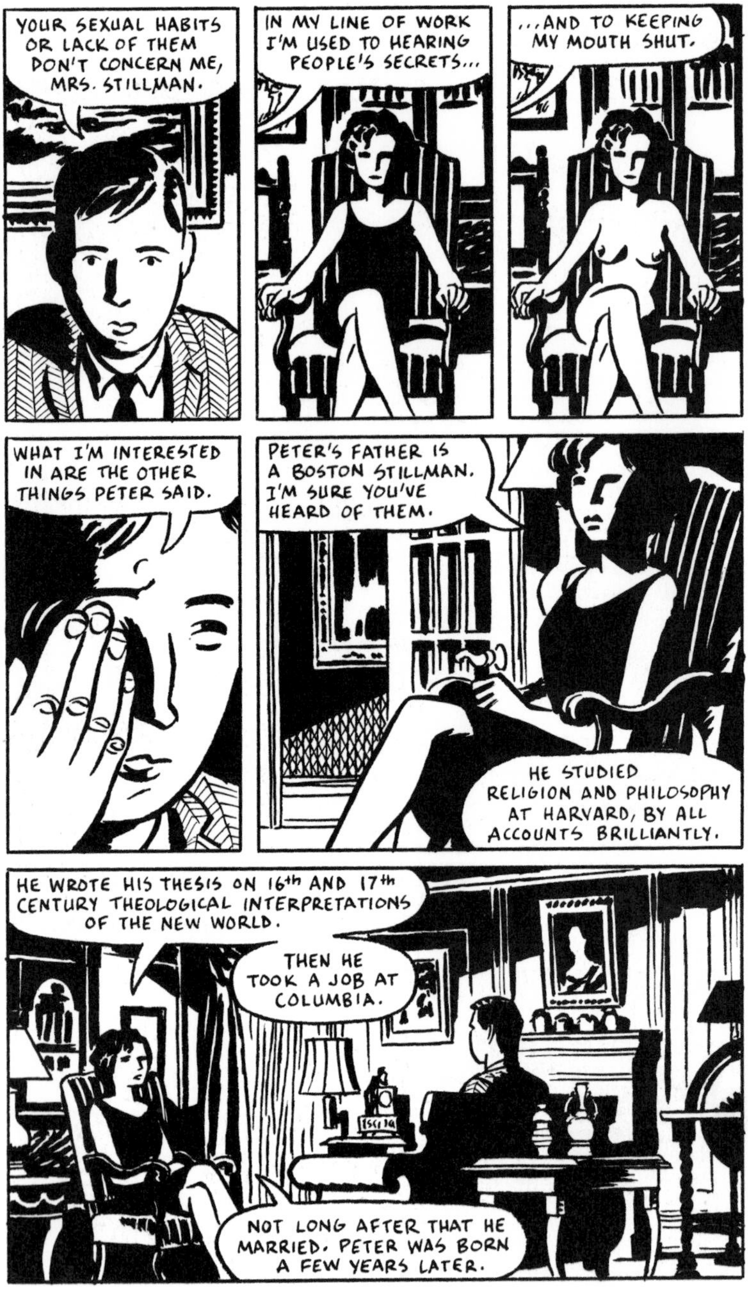
YOUR SEXUAL HABITS OR LACK OF THEM DON'T CONCERN ME, MRS. STILLMAN.
IN MY LINE OF WORK I'M USED TO HEARING PEOPLE'S SECRETS...
...AND TO KEEPING MY MOUTH SHUT.
WHAT I'M INTERESTED IN ARE THE OTHER THINGS PETER SAID.
PETER'S FATHER IS A BOSTON STILLMAN. I'M SURE YOU'VE HEARD OF THEM.
HE STUDIED RELIGION AND PHILOSOPHY AT HARVARD, BY ALL ACCOUNTS BRILLIANTLY.
HE WROTE HIS THESIS ON 16th AND 17th CENTURY THEOLOGICAL INTERPRETATIONS OF THE NEW WORLD.
THEN HE TOOK A JOB AT COLUMBIA.
NOT LONG AFTER THAT HE MARRIED. PETER WAS BORN A FEW YEARS LATER.

"STILLMAN'S CAREER WAS PROSPERING. HE RE-WROTE HIS DISSERTATION INTO A BOOK."

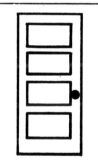

"THEN PETER'S MOTHER DIED."

"PETER WAS TWO, A PERFECTLY NORMAL CHILD. A NURSE WAS HIRED TO CARE FOR HIM."

"AFTER SIX MONTHS STILLMAN FIRED HER."

"HE RESIGNED TO DEVOTE HIMSELF FULL-TIME TO HIS SON."

"THEN HE DROPPED OUT OF SIGHT."

"HE STAYED ON IN THE SAME APARTMENT, BUT HARDLY EVER WENT OUT."

"I THINK HE BEGAN TO BELIEVE SOME OF THE FAR-FETCHED RELIGIOUS IDEAS HE HAD WRITTEN ABOUT."

"IT MADE HIM CRAZY, ABSOLUTELY INSANE."

"HE LOCKED PETER IN A ROOM, COVERED THE WINDOWS..."

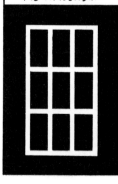

"...AND KEPT HIM THERE FOR NINE YEARS."

1960
1961
1962
1963
1964
1965

"IMAGINE IT, MR. AUSTER. NINE YEARS."

"AN ENTIRE CHILDHOOD SPENT IN DARKNESS, WITH NO HUMAN CONTACT EXCEPT AN OCCASIONAL BEATING."

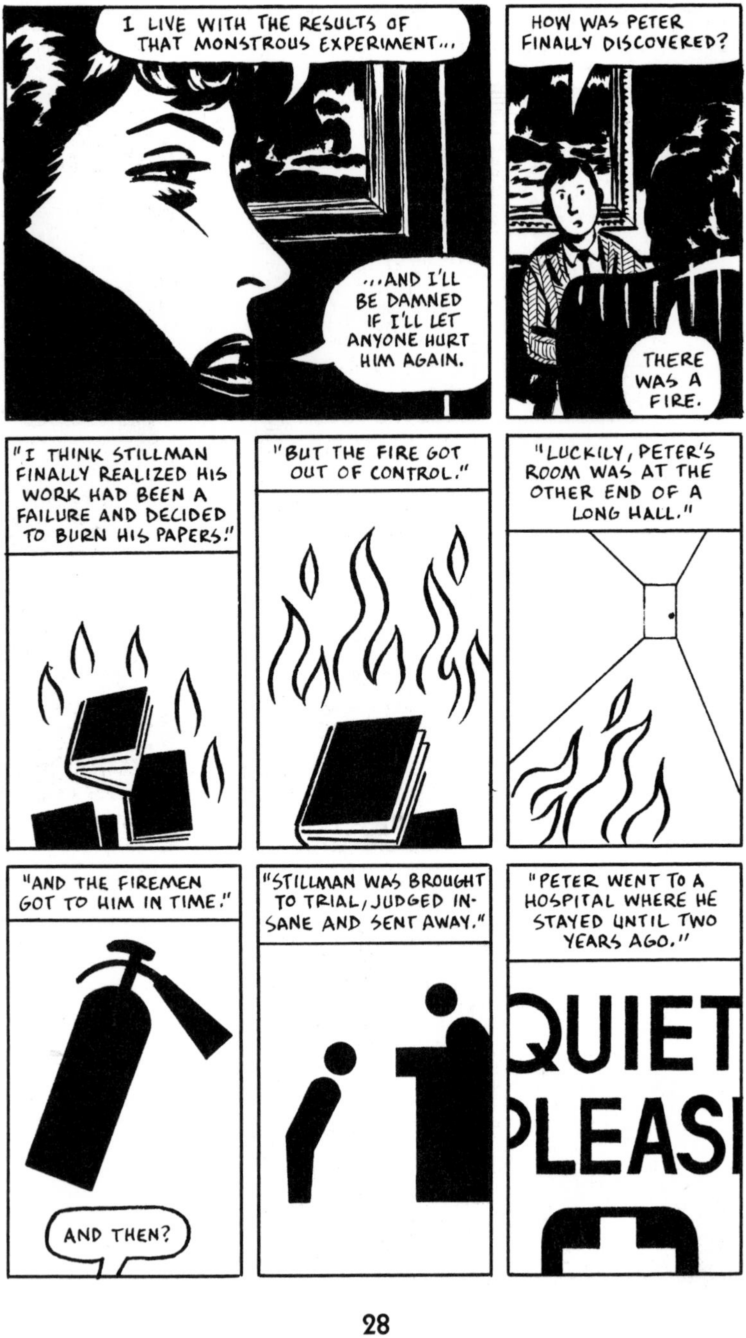
I LIVE WITH THE RESULTS OF THAT MONSTROUS EXPERIMENT...
...AND I'LL BE DAMNED IF I'LL LET ANYONE HURT HIM AGAIN.
HOW WAS PETER FINALLY DISCOVERED?
THERE WAS A FIRE.
"I THINK STILLMAN FINALLY REALIZED HIS WORK HAD BEEN A FAILURE AND DECIDED TO BURN HIS PAPERS."
"BUT THE FIRE GOT OUT OF CONTROL."
"LUCKILY, PETER'S ROOM WAS AT THE OTHER END OF A LONG HALL."
"AND THE FIREMEN GOT TO HIM IN TIME."
AND THEN?
"STILLMAN WAS BROUGHT TO TRIAL, JUDGED IN-SANE AND SENT AWAY."
"PETER WENT TO A HOSPITAL WHERE HE STAYED UNTIL TWO YEARS AGO."
QUIET
PLEAS

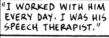

"I WORKED WITH HIM EVERY DAY. I WAS HIS SPEECH THERAPIST."

I DON'T MEAN TO PRY. BUT HOW EXACTLY DID THAT LEAD TO MARRIAGE?

TO PUT IT SIMPLY, IT WAS THE BEST WAY TO GET PETER OUT OF THE HOSPITAL.

WASN'T THAT AN ENORMOUS SELF-SACRIFICE?

NOT REALLY.

I WAS MARRIED ONCE BEFORE — DISASTROUSLY.

AT LEAST WITH PETER THERE'S A PURPOSE TO MY LIFE.

STILLMAN IS BEING RELEASED TOMORROW. HE'LL BE ARRIVING AT GRAND CENTRAL.

AND YOU FEEL HE MIGHT COME AFTER PETER?

"TWO YEARS AGO HE SENT PETER AN INSANE LETTER,"

"HE CALLED HIM A DEVIL BOY, AND SAID THERE WOULD BE A DAY OF RECKONING."

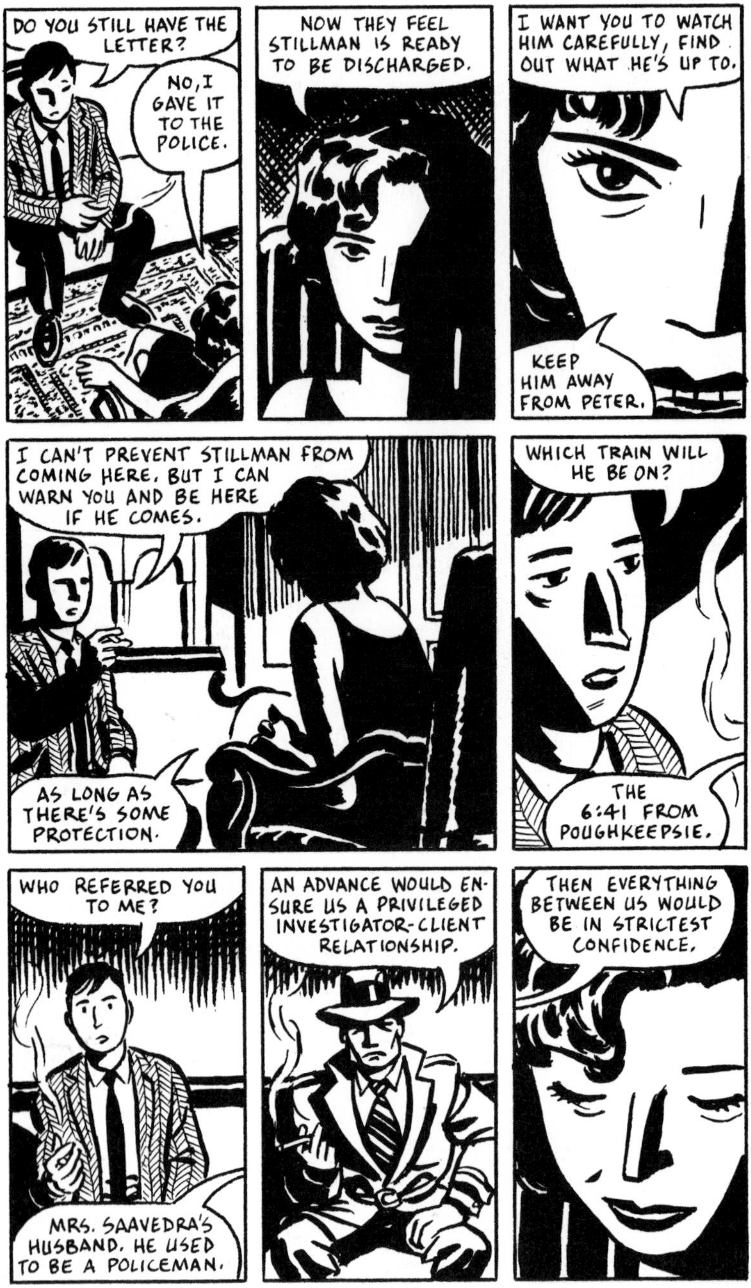
DO YOU STILL HAVE THE LETTER?
NO, I GAVE IT TO THE POLICE.
NOW THEY FEEL STILLMAN IS READY TO BE DISCHARGED.
I WANT YOU TO WATCH HIM CAREFULLY, FIND OUT WHAT HE'S UP TO.
KEEP HIM AWAY FROM PETER.
I CAN'T PREVENT STILLMAN FROM COMING HERE. BUT I CAN WARN YOU AND BE HERE IF HE COMES.
AS LONG AS THERE'S SOME PROTECTION.
WHICH TRAIN WILL HE BE ON?
THE 6:41 FROM POUGHKEEPSIE.
WHO REFERRED YOU TO ME?
MRS. SAAVEDRA'S HUSBAND. HE USED TO BE A POLICEMAN.
AN ADVANCE WOULD ENSURE US A PRIVILEGED INVESTIGATOR-CLIENT RELATIONSHIP.
THEN EVERYTHING BETWEEN US WOULD BE IN STRICTEST CONFIDENCE.

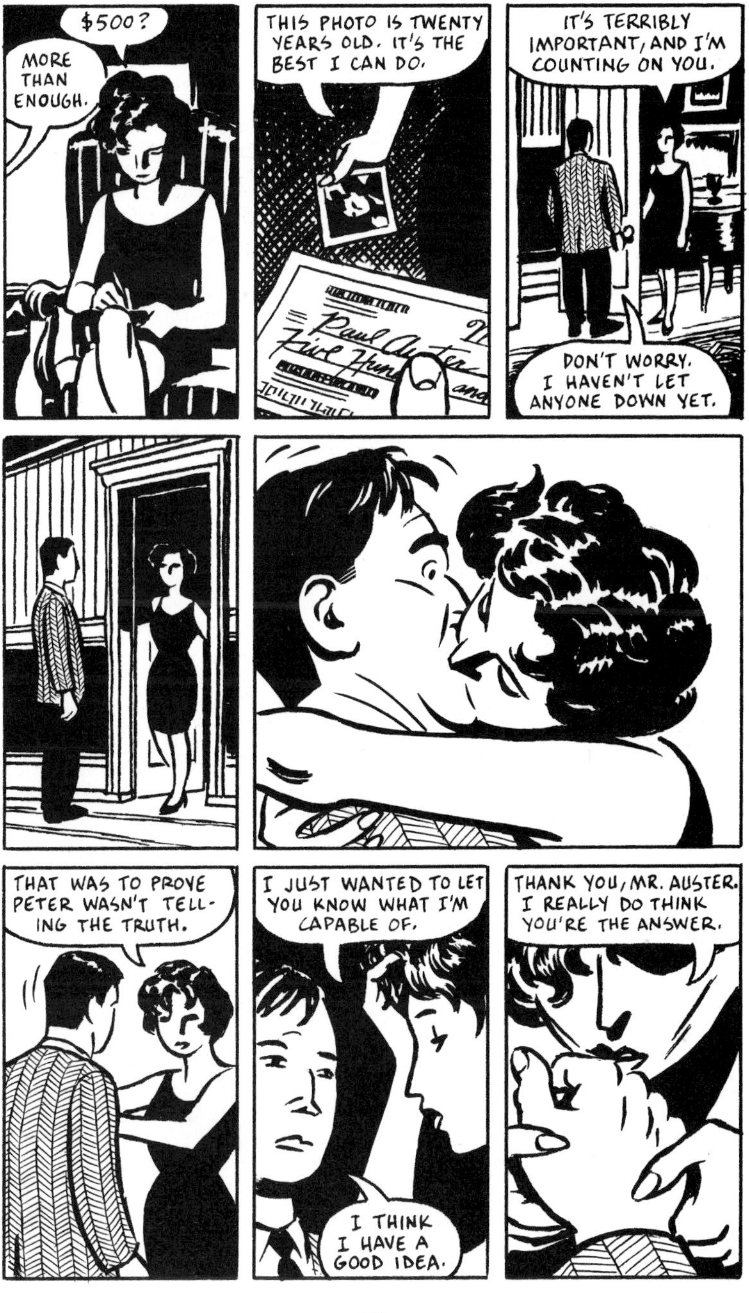
$500?
MORE THAN ENOUGH.
THIS PHOTO IS TWENTY YEARS OLD. IT'S THE BEST I CAN DO.
Paul Auster
Five Hun
IT'S TERRIBLY IMPORTANT, AND I'M COUNTING ON YOU.
DON'T WORRY. I HAVEN'T LET ANYONE DOWN YET.
THAT WAS TO PROVE PETER WASN'T TELLING THE TRUTH.
I JUST WANTED TO LET YOU KNOW WHAT I'M CAPABLE OF.
I THINK I HAVE A GOOD IDEA.
THANK YOU, MR. AUSTER. I REALLY DO THINK YOU'RE THE ANSWER.

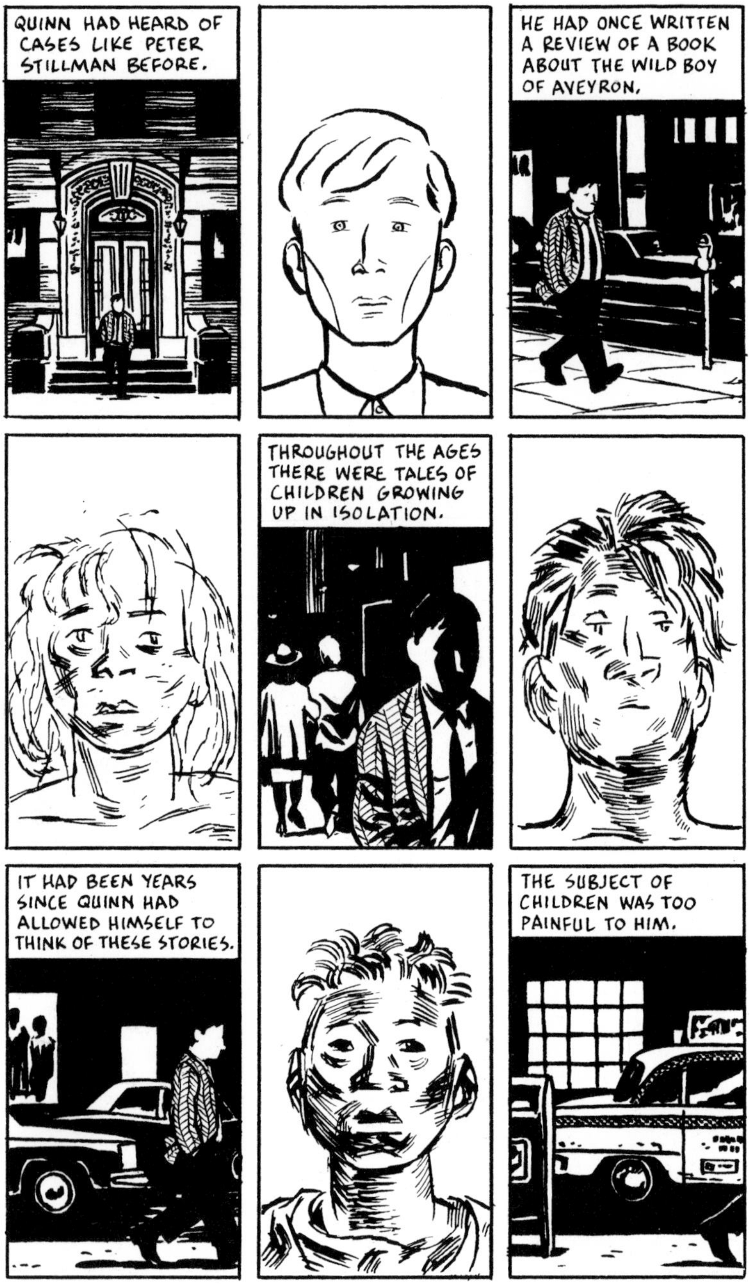
QUINN HAD HEARD OF CASES LIKE PETER STILLMAN BEFORE.
HE HAD ONCE WRITTEN A REVIEW OF A BOOK ABOUT THE WILD BOY OF AVEYRON.
THROUGHOUT THE AGES THERE WERE TALES OF CHILDREN GROWING UP IN ISOLATION.
IT HAD BEEN YEARS SINCE QUINN HAD ALLOWED HIMSELF TO THINK OF THESE STORIES.
THE SUBJECT OF CHILDREN WAS TOO PAINFUL TO HIM.

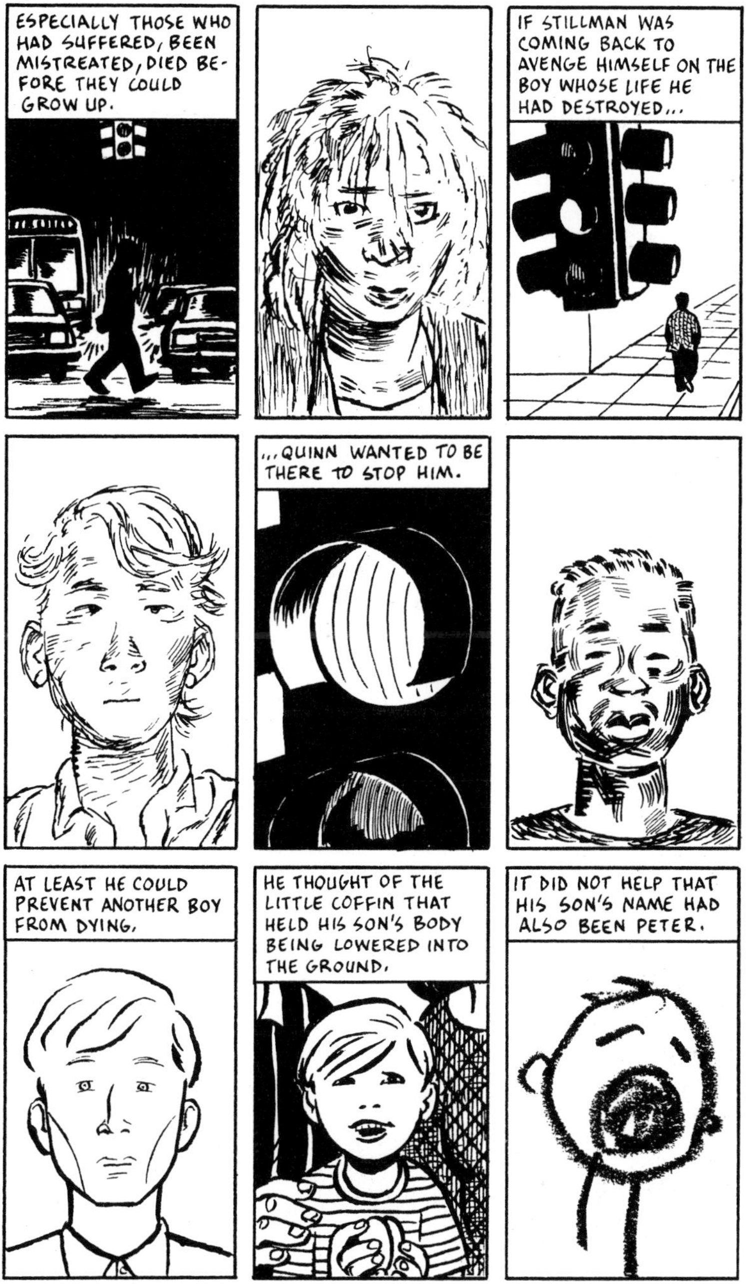
ESPECIALLY THOSE WHO HAD SUFFERED, BEEN MISTREATED, DIED BEFORE THEY COULD GROW UP.
IF STILLMAN WAS COMING BACK TO AVENGE HIMSELF ON THE BOY WHOSE LIFE HE HAD DESTROYED...
...QUINN WANTED TO BE THERE TO STOP HIM.
AT LEAST HE COULD PREVENT ANOTHER BOY FROM DYING.
HE THOUGHT OF THE LITTLE COFFIN THAT HELD HIS SON'S BODY BEING LOWERED INTO THE GROUND.
IT DID NOT HELP THAT HIS SON'S NAME HAD ALSO BEEN PETER.

QUINN WONDERED IF PETER SAW THE SAME THINGS HE DID...

...OR WHETHER THE WORLD WAS A DIFFERENT PLACE FOR HIM.

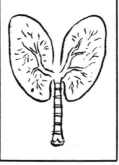

AND IF A TREE WAS NOT A TREE, HE WONDERED WHAT IT REALLY WAS.

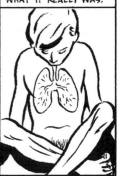

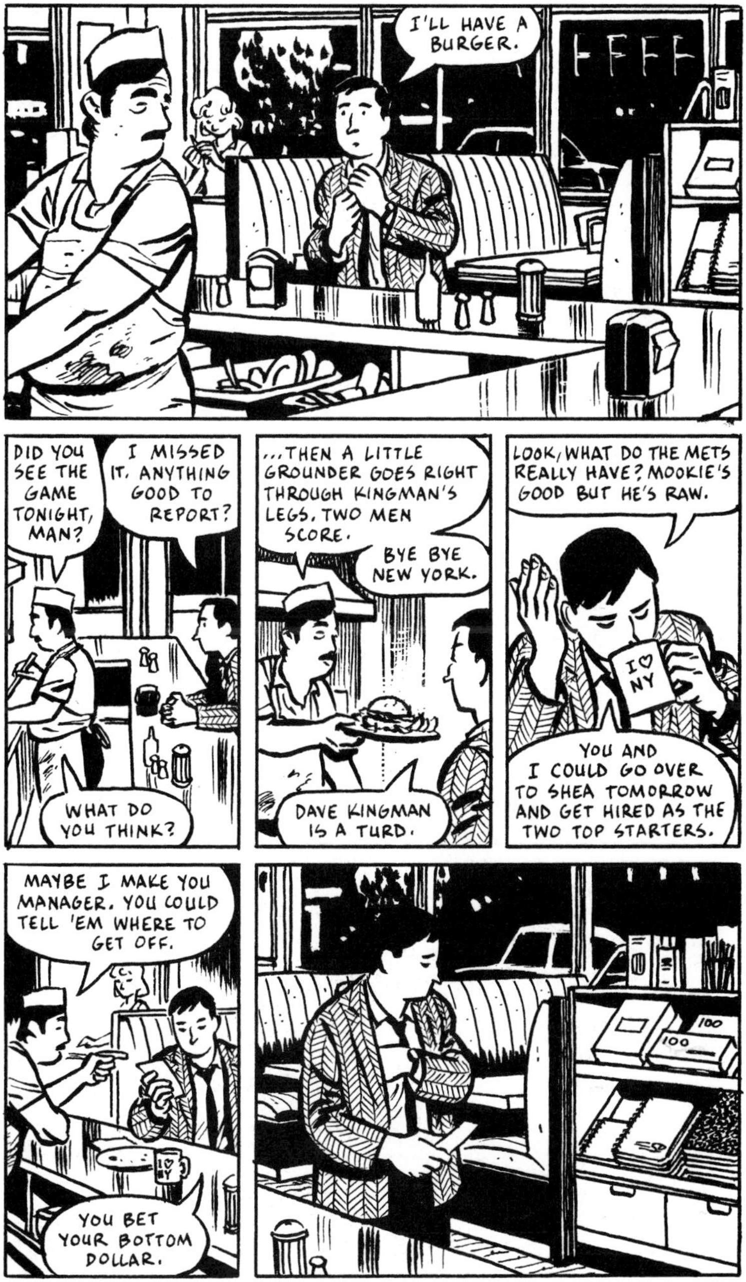
I'LL HAVE A BURGER.
DID YOU SEE THE GAME TONIGHT, MAN?
I MISSED IT. ANYTHING GOOD TO REPORT?
WHAT DO YOU THINK?
...THEN A LITTLE GROUNDER GOES RIGHT THROUGH KINGMAN'S LEGS. TWO MEN SCORE.
BYE BYE NEW YORK.
DAVE KINGMAN IS A TURD.
LOOK, WHAT DO THE METS REALLY HAVE? MOOKIE'S GOOD BUT HE'S RAW.
I ♡ NY
YOU AND I COULD GO OVER TO SHEA TOMORROW AND GET HIRED AS THE TWO TOP STARTERS.
MAYBE I MAKE YOU MANAGER. YOU COULD TELL 'EM WHERE TO GET OFF.
YOU BET YOUR BOTTOM DOLLAR.
100
100

QUINN USED A TYPE-
WRITER ONLY FOR
FINAL DRAFTS.

HE WAS ALWAYS ON
THE LOOKOUT FOR
GOOD NOTEBOOKS.

WITH THE STILLMAN
CASE, HE FELT A NEW
NOTEBOOK WAS IN ORDER.

IN THAT WAY, PERHAPS,
THINGS MIGHT NOT GET
OUT OF CONTROL.

THIS NOTEBOOK WAS
SPECIAL —

— AS IF ITS UNIQUE
DESTINY WAS TO HOLD
THE WORDS THAT CAME
FROM HIS PEN.

HE HAD NEVER DONE THIS
BEFORE, BUT IT SOMEHOW
SEEMED APPROPRIATE TO
BE NAKED AT THIS MOMENT.

IT WAS THE FIRST TIME
IN MORE THAN FIVE
YEARS THAT HE HAD PUT
HIS OWN NAME IN ONE
OF HIS NOTEBOOKS.

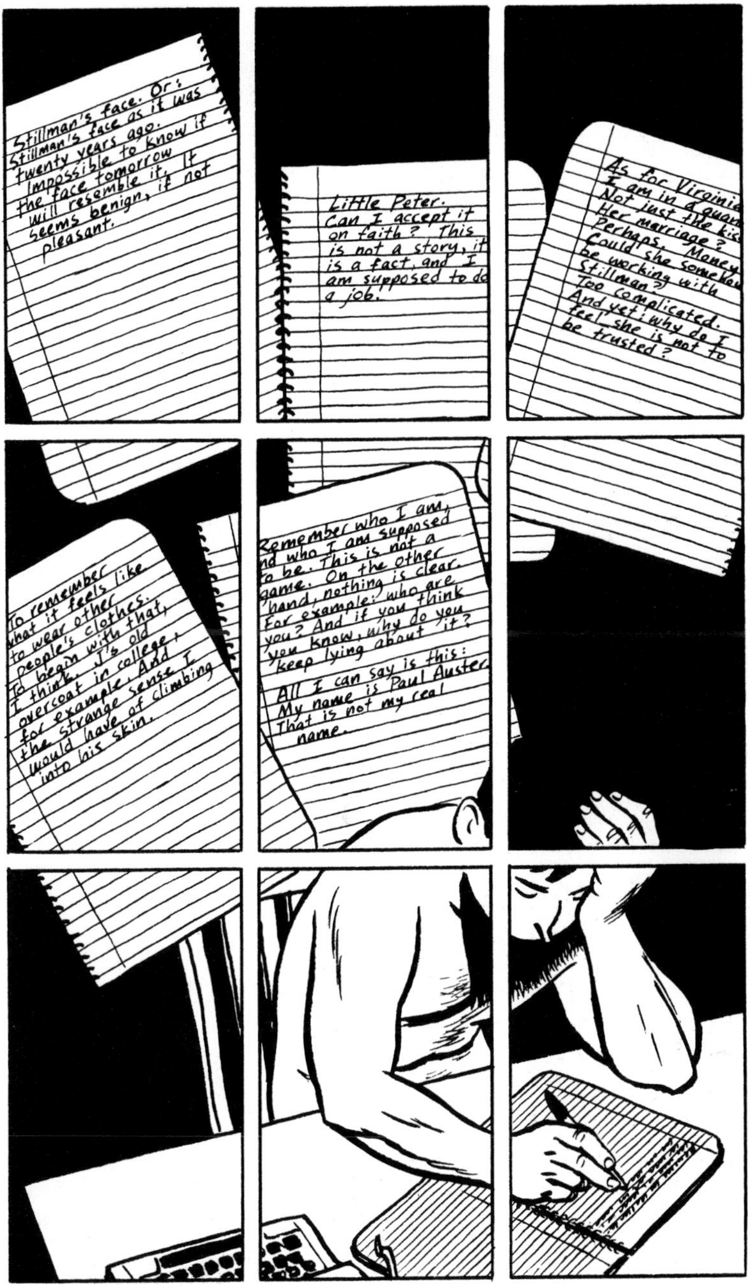
Stillman's face. Or: Stillman's face as it was twenty years ago. Impossible to know if the face tomorrow will resemble it. It seems benign, if not pleasant.
Little Peter. Can I accept it on faith? This is not a story, it is a fact, and I am supposed to do a job.
As for Virgini
I am in a quan
Not just the ki
Her marriage?
Perhaps. Money
Could she somehow
be working with
Stillman?
Too complicated.
And yet: why do I
feel she is not to
be trusted?
To remember what it feels like to wear other people's clothes. To begin with that, I think. J's old overcoat in college, for example. And the strange sense I would have of climbing into his skin.
Remember who I am, nd who I am supposed o be. This is not a game. On the other hand, nothing is clear. For example: who are you? And if you think you know, why do you keep lying about it?
All I can say is this: My name is Paul Auster. That is not my real name.

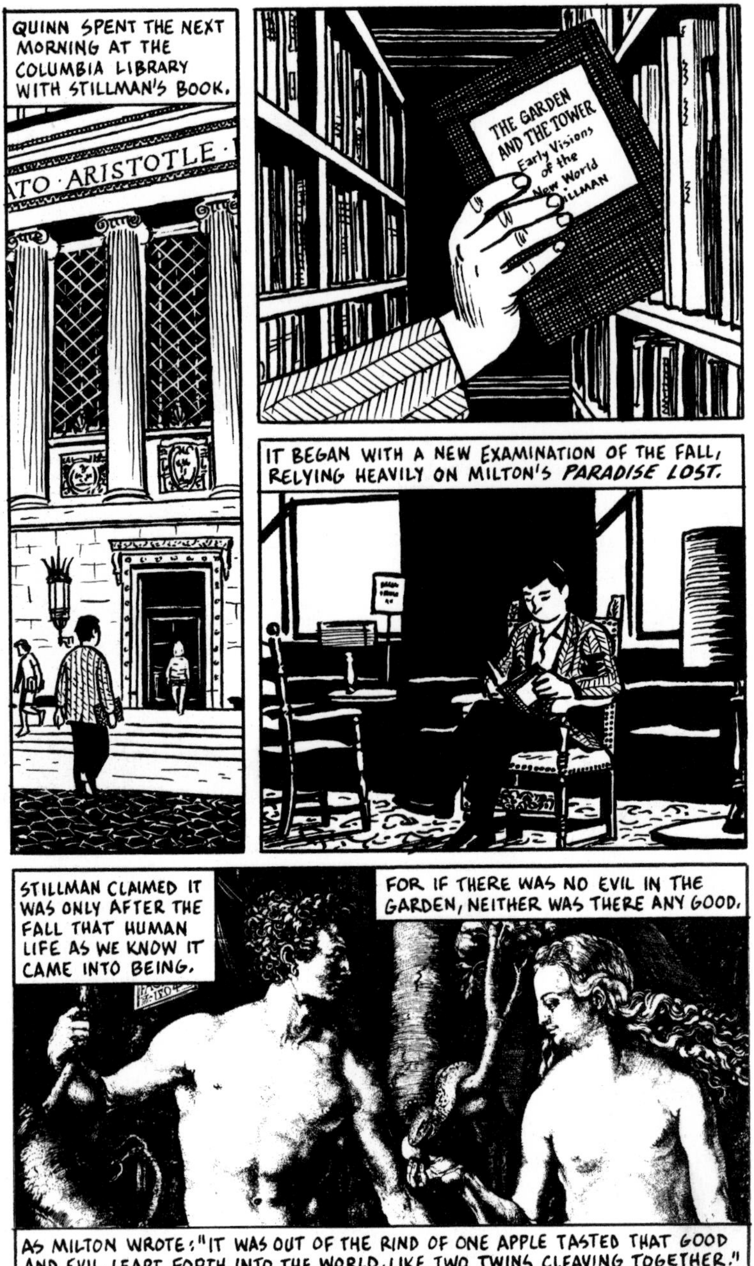
QUINN SPENT THE NEXT MORNING AT THE COLUMBIA LIBRARY WITH STILLMAN'S BOOK.
ATO · ARISTOTLE ·
THE GARDEN AND THE TOWER
Early Visions of the New World
IT BEGAN WITH A NEW EXAMINATION OF THE FALL, RELYING HEAVILY ON MILTON'S *PARADISE LOST.*
STILLMAN CLAIMED IT WAS ONLY AFTER THE FALL THAT HUMAN LIFE AS WE KNOW IT CAME INTO BEING.
FOR IF THERE WAS NO EVIL IN THE GARDEN, NEITHER WAS THERE ANY GOOD.
AS MILTON WROTE: "IT WAS OUT OF THE RIND OF ONE APPLE TASTED THAT GOOD AND EVIL LEAPT FORTH INTO THE WORLD, LIKE TWO TWINS CLEAVING TOGETHER."

STILLMAN DWELLED ON THE PARADOX OF THE WORD "CLEAVE", WHICH MEANS BOTH "TO JOIN TOGETHER",...

...AND "TO BREAK APART".

IN *PARADISE LOST*, EACH KEY WORD HAS TWO MEANINGS — ONE BEFORE THE FALL, FREE OF MORAL CONNOTATIONS, AND ONE AFTER, INFORMED BY A KNOWLEDGE OF EVIL.

"SINISTER"

"SERPENTINE"

"DELICIOUS"

ADAM'S TASK IN THE GARDEN HAD BEEN TO INVENT LANGUAGE.

Shadow

IN THAT STATE OF INNOCENCE, HIS WORDS HAD REVEALED THE ESSENCES OF THINGS.

shadow

A THING AND ITS NAME WERE INTERCHANGEABLE.

Shadow

AFTER THE FALL, THIS WAS NO LONGER TRUE.

Shadow

NAMES BECAME DETATCHED FROM THINGS.

LANGUAGE HAD BEEN SEVERED FROM GOD.

shadow

THE STORY, THEREFORE, RECORDS NOT ONLY THE FALL OF MAN, BUT THE FALL OF LANGUAGE.

shadow

39

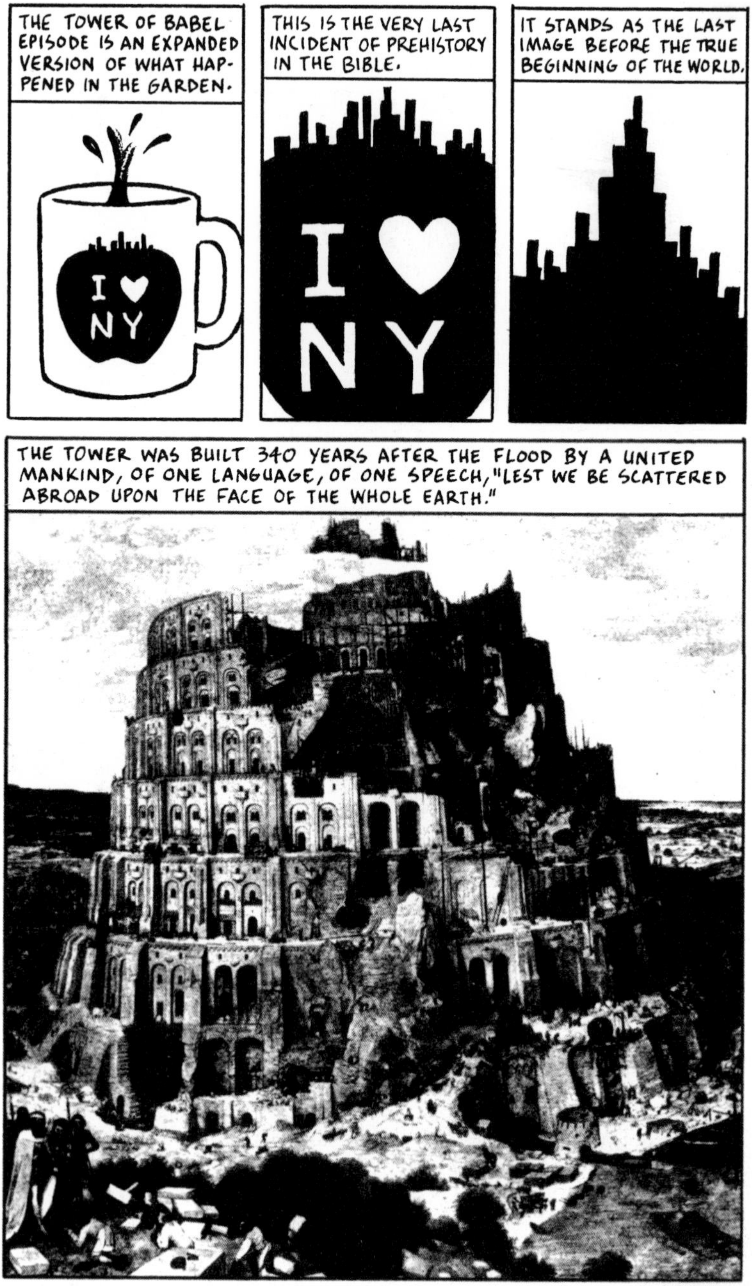
THE TOWER OF BABEL EPISODE IS AN EXPANDED VERSION OF WHAT HAPPENED IN THE GARDEN.
I ♥ NY
THIS IS THE VERY LAST INCIDENT OF PREHISTORY IN THE BIBLE.
I ♥ NY
IT STANDS AS THE LAST IMAGE BEFORE THE TRUE BEGINNING OF THE WORLD.
THE TOWER WAS BUILT 340 YEARS AFTER THE FLOOD BY A UNITED MANKIND, OF ONE LANGUAGE, OF ONE SPEECH, "LEST WE BE SCATTERED ABROAD UPON THE FACE OF THE WHOLE EARTH."

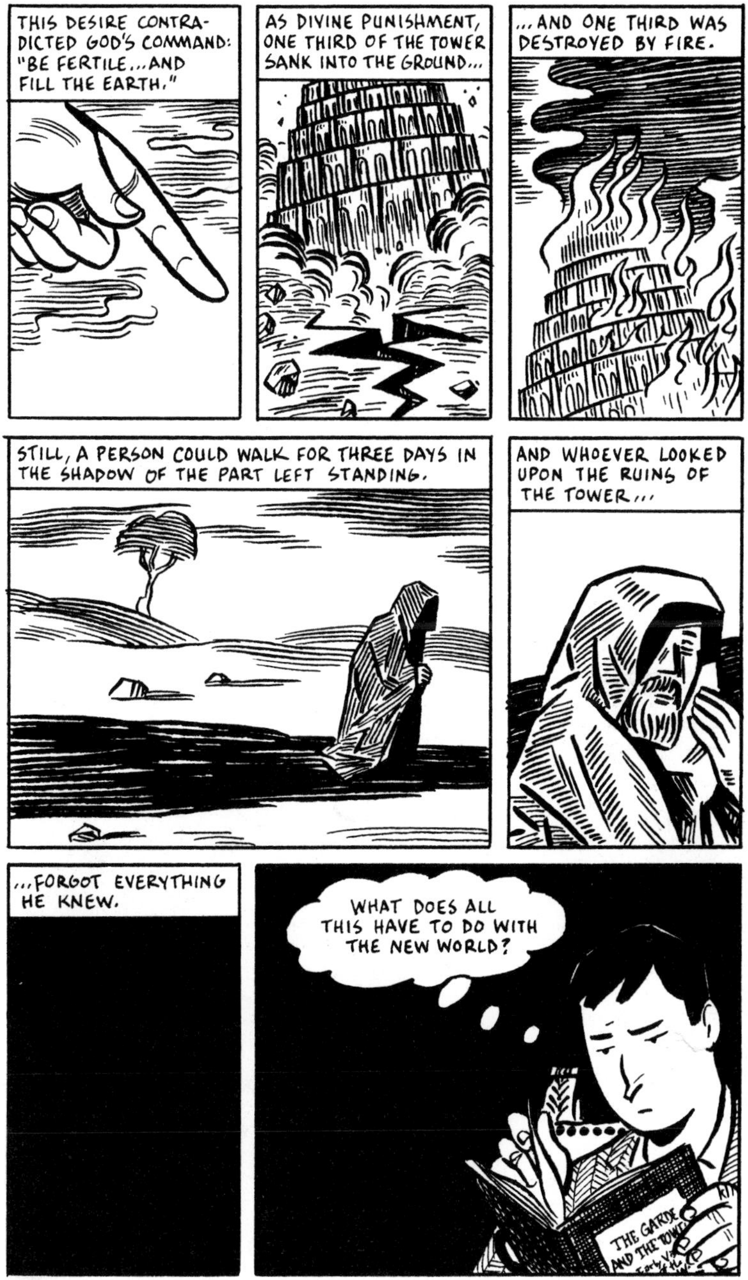
THIS DESIRE CONTRADICTED GOD'S COMMAND: "BE FERTILE...AND FILL THE EARTH."
AS DIVINE PUNISHMENT, ONE THIRD OF THE TOWER SANK INTO THE GROUND...
...AND ONE THIRD WAS DESTROYED BY FIRE.
STILL, A PERSON COULD WALK FOR THREE DAYS IN THE SHADOW OF THE PART LEFT STANDING.
AND WHOEVER LOOKED UPON THE RUINS OF THE TOWER...
...FORGOT EVERYTHING HE KNEW.
WHAT DOES ALL THIS HAVE TO DO WITH THE NEW WORLD?

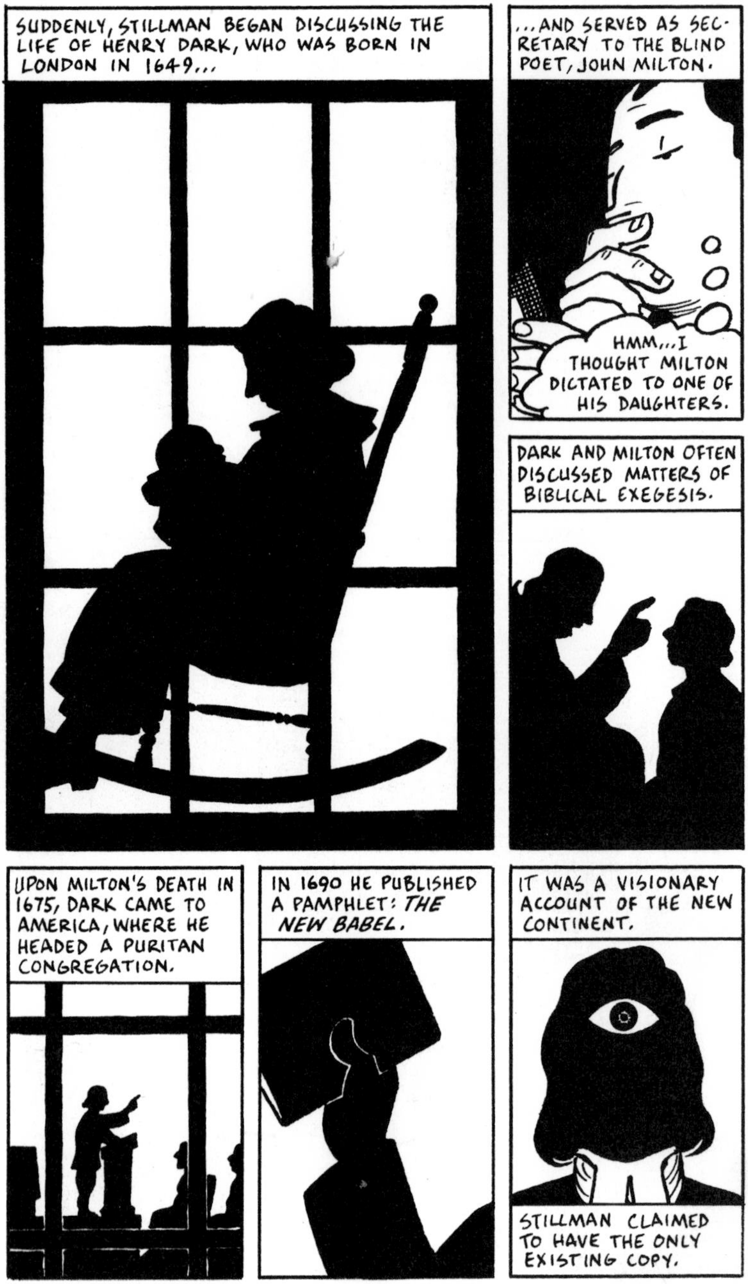
SUDDENLY, STILLMAN BEGAN DISCUSSING THE LIFE OF HENRY DARK, WHO WAS BORN IN LONDON IN 1649...
...AND SERVED AS SECRETARY TO THE BLIND POET, JOHN MILTON.
HMM,...I THOUGHT MILTON DICTATED TO ONE OF HIS DAUGHTERS.
DARK AND MILTON OFTEN DISCUSSED MATTERS OF BIBLICAL EXEGESIS.
UPON MILTON'S DEATH IN 1675, DARK CAME TO AMERICA, WHERE HE HEADED A PURITAN CONGREGATION.
IN 1690 HE PUBLISHED A PAMPHLET: *THE NEW BABEL*.
IT WAS A VISIONARY ACCOUNT OF THE NEW CONTINENT.
STILLMAN CLAIMED TO HAVE THE ONLY EXISTING COPY.

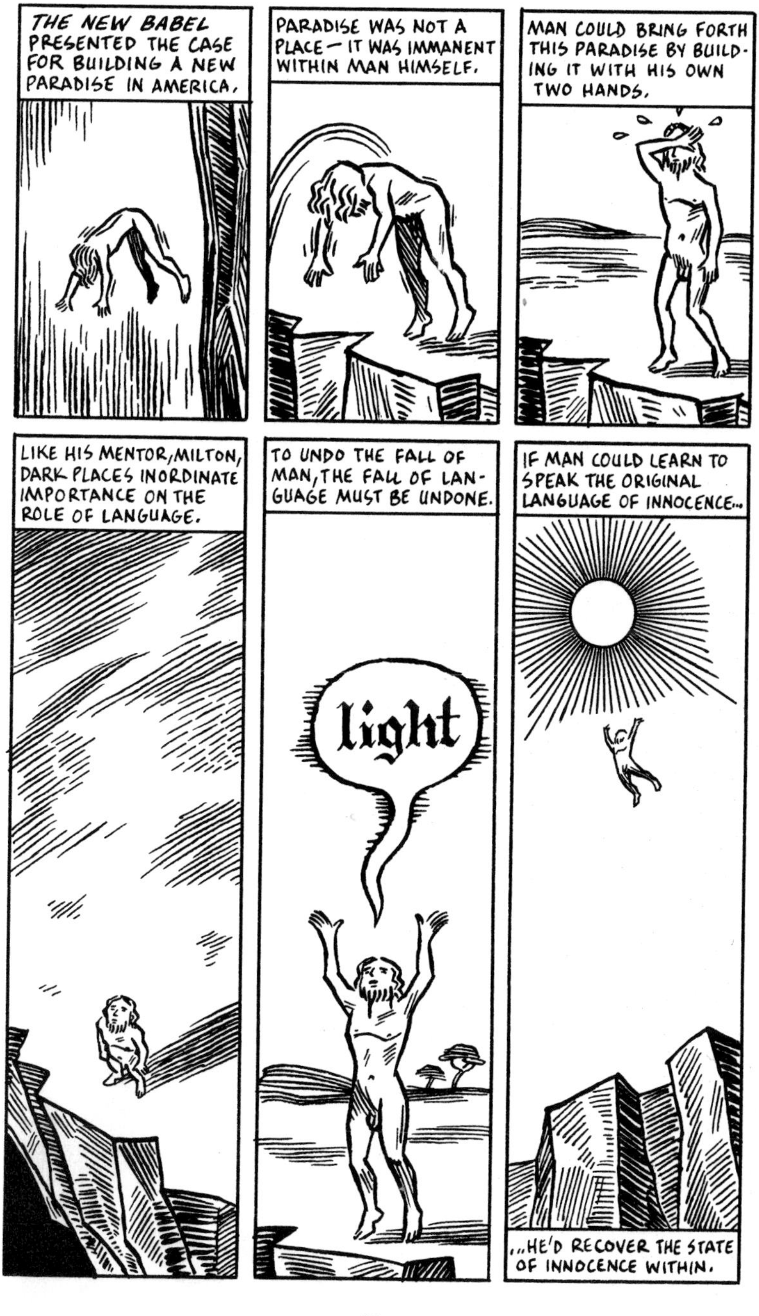
THE NEW BABEL PRESENTED THE CASE FOR BUILDING A NEW PARADISE IN AMERICA.
PARADISE WAS NOT A PLACE — IT WAS IMMANENT WITHIN MAN HIMSELF.
MAN COULD BRING FORTH THIS PARADISE BY BUILDING IT WITH HIS OWN TWO HANDS.
LIKE HIS MENTOR, MILTON, DARK PLACES INORDINATE IMPORTANCE ON THE ROLE OF LANGUAGE.
TO UNDO THE FALL OF MAN, THE FALL OF LANGUAGE MUST BE UNDONE.
light
IF MAN COULD LEARN TO SPEAK THE ORIGINAL LANGUAGE OF INNOCENCE...
...HE'D RECOVER THE STATE OF INNOCENCE WITHIN.

TURNING TO BABEL, DARK THEN ANNOUNCES HIS PROPHECY.

IN RESPONSE TO GOD'S COMMAND TO "BE FERTILE...AND FILL THE EARTH", MAN WOULD INEVITABLY MOVE WEST.

THE EARLY ENGLISH SETTLERS OF AMERICA FULFILLED THIS COMMANDMENT.

ONCE THAT CONTINENT WAS FILLED, THE IMPEDIMENT TO BUILDING A NEW BABEL WOULD BE REMOVED.

THEN IT WOULD BE POSSIBLE FOR THE WHOLE EARTH TO BE OF ONE LANGUAGE.

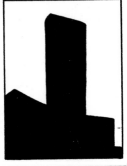

COULD PARADISE BE FAR BEHIND?

AS BABEL HAD BEEN BUILT 340 YEARS AFTER THE FLOOD, 340 YEARS AFTER THE MAYFLOWER THE COMMANDMENT WOULD BE CARRIED OUT.

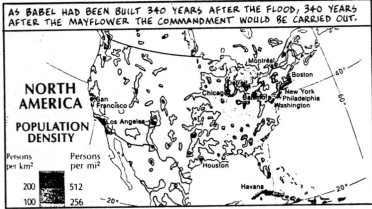

NORTH AMERICA

POPULATION DENSITY

Persons per km²		Persons per mi²
200		512
100		256

Montréal, Boston, Detroit, Chicago, Baltimore, New York, Philadelphia, Washington, San Francisco, Los Angeles, Houston, Havana

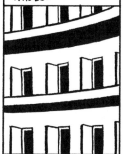

IN THE YEAR 1960, WHAT HAD FALLEN WOULD BE RAISED UP; WHAT HAD BEEN BROKEN, MADE WHOLE.

IN THE NEW TOWER, THERE WOULD BE A ROOM FOR EACH PERSON.

ONCE HE ENTERED THAT ROOM, HE WOULD FORGET EVERYTHING HE KNEW.

AFTER FORTY DAYS AND NIGHTS, HE WOULD EMERGE SPEAKING GOD'S LANGUAGE...

...PREPARED TO INHABIT EVERLASTING PARADISE.

1960.

...THE YEAR STILLMAN LOCKED UP PETER.

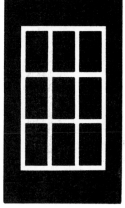

45

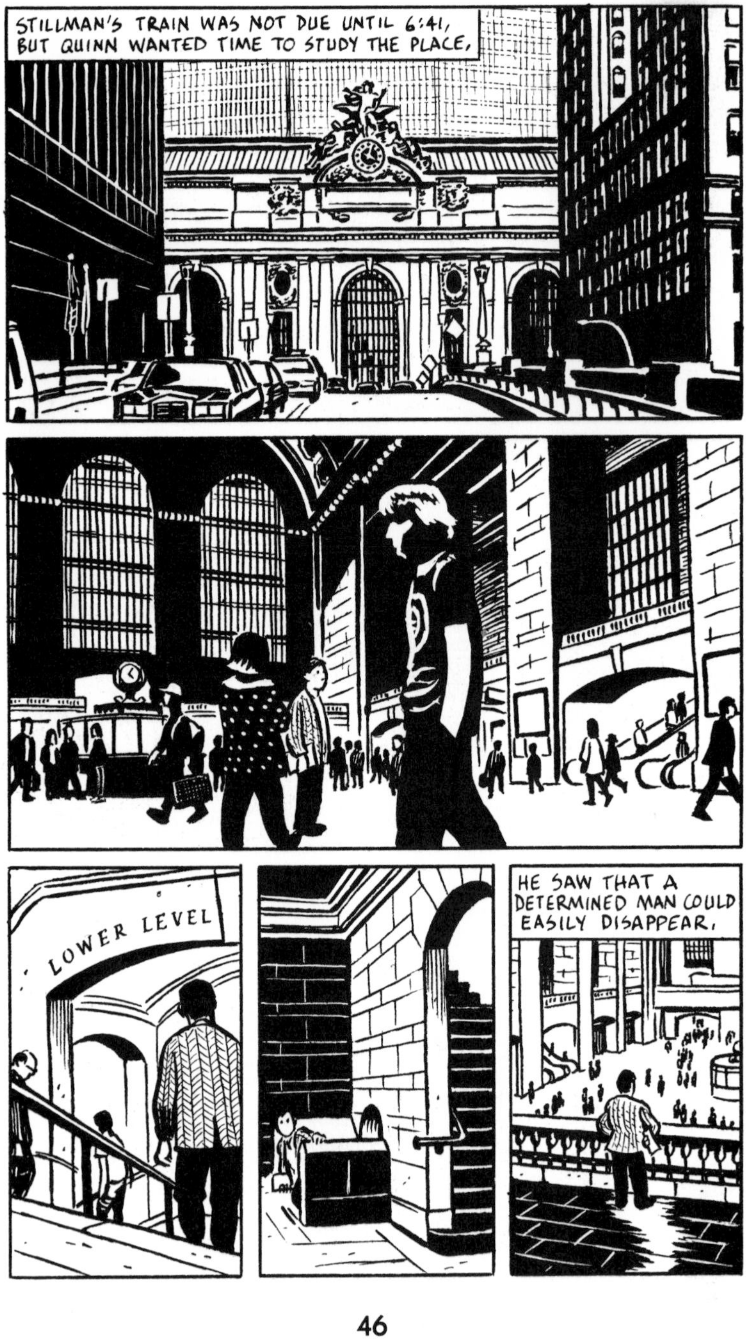
STILLMAN'S TRAIN WAS NOT DUE UNTIL 6:41, BUT QUINN WANTED TIME TO STUDY THE PLACE,
LOWER LEVEL
HE SAW THAT A DETERMINED MAN COULD EASILY DISAPPEAR.

I AM PAUL AUSTER.

QUINN FELT HE HAD BEEN TAKEN OUT OF HIMSELF, UNBURDENED OF HIS OWN CONSCIOUSNESS.

HE WAS NOT REALLY LOST; JUST PRETENDING.

AND THE PURPOSE TO HIS BEING PAUL AUSTER ABSOLVED HIM OF HAVING TO DEFEND HIS LIE.

HE WAS REMINDED OF VISITING NANTUCKET WITH HIS WIFE DURING HER FIRST MONTH OF PREGNANCY.

Kodak

LOOK AT IT THROUGH AUSTER'S EYES.

This good article is courtesy a DEAF MUTE. Pay any price

LEARN TO SPEAK TO YOUR FRIENDS

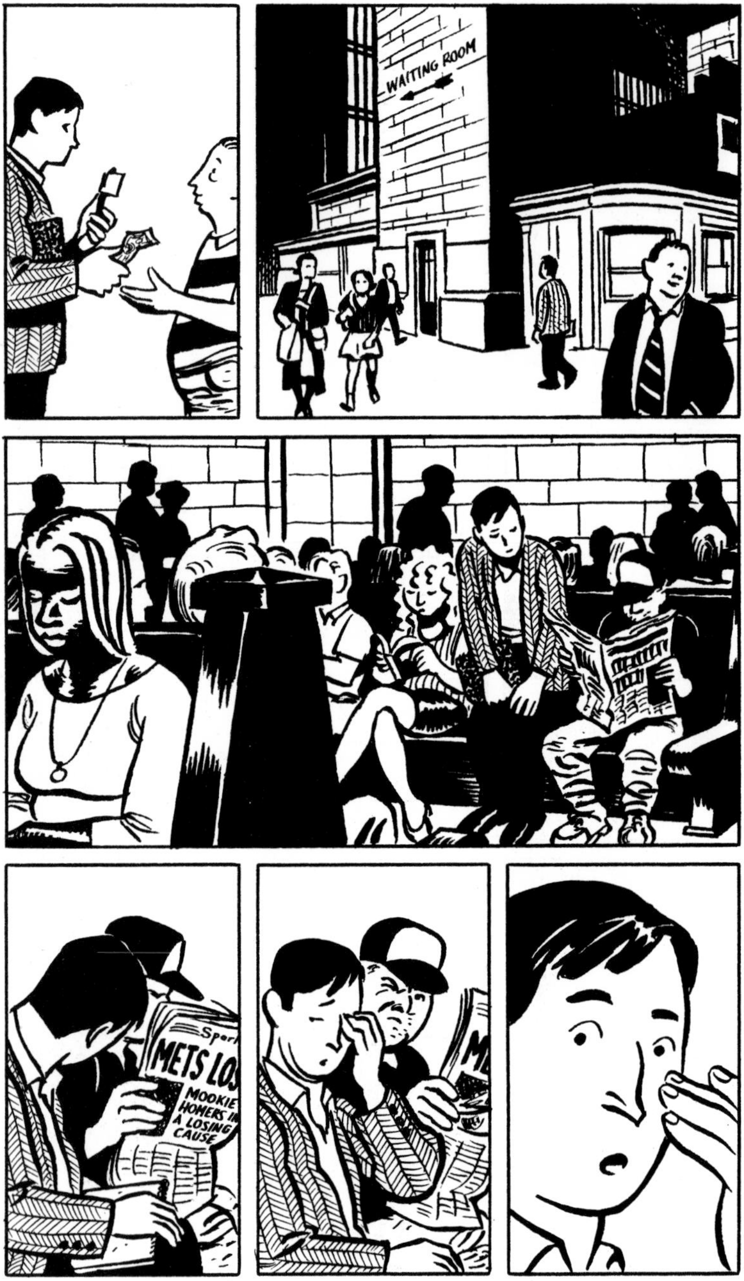
WAITING ROOM
Sports
METS LOS
MOOKIE HOMERS IN A LOSING CAUSE

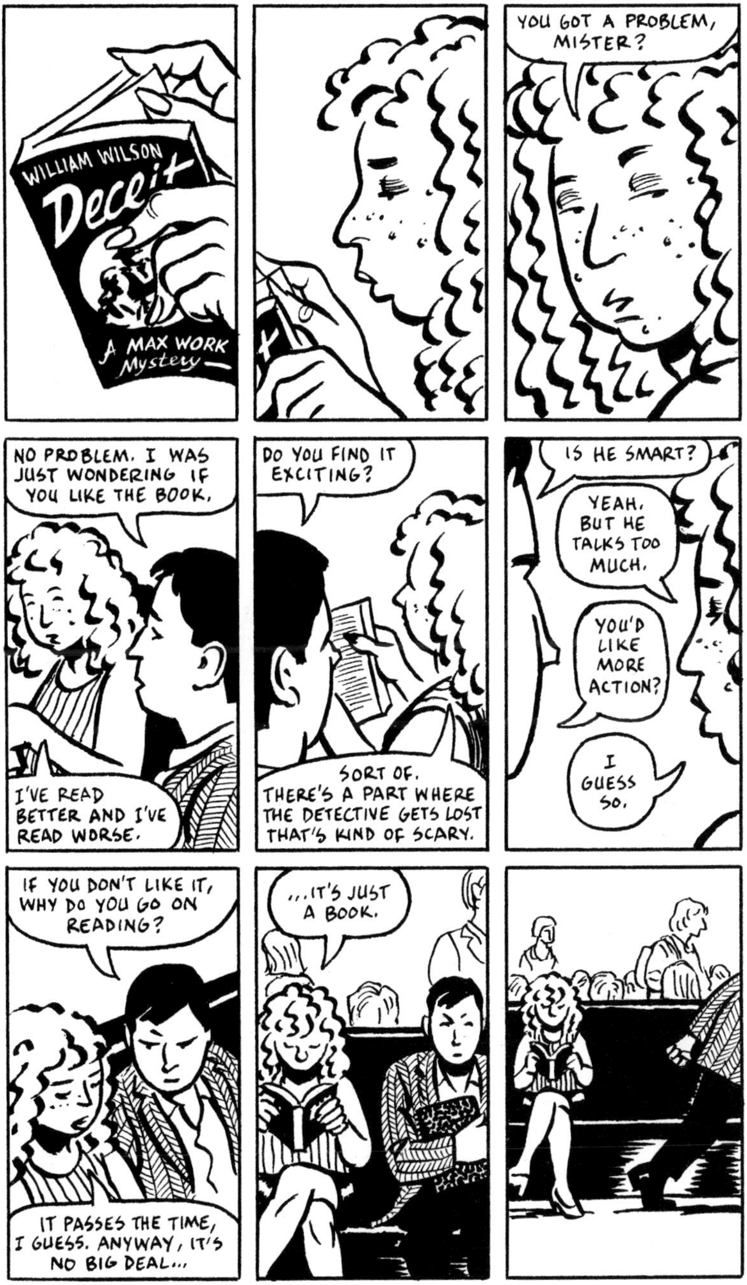
WILLIAM WILSON
Deceit
A MAX WORK Mystery
YOU GOT A PROBLEM, MISTER?
NO PROBLEM. I WAS JUST WONDERING IF YOU LIKE THE BOOK.
I'VE READ BETTER AND I'VE READ WORSE.
DO YOU FIND IT EXCITING?
SORT OF. THERE'S A PART WHERE THE DETECTIVE GETS LOST THAT'S KIND OF SCARY.
IS HE SMART?
YEAH. BUT HE TALKS TOO MUCH.
YOU'D LIKE MORE ACTION?
I GUESS SO.
IF YOU DON'T LIKE IT, WHY DO YOU GO ON READING?
IT PASSES THE TIME, I GUESS. ANYWAY, IT'S NO BIG DEAL...
...IT'S JUST A BOOK.

CLACK CLACK CLACK EL

CLACK BEDRACK FLACKLI YAYAYA

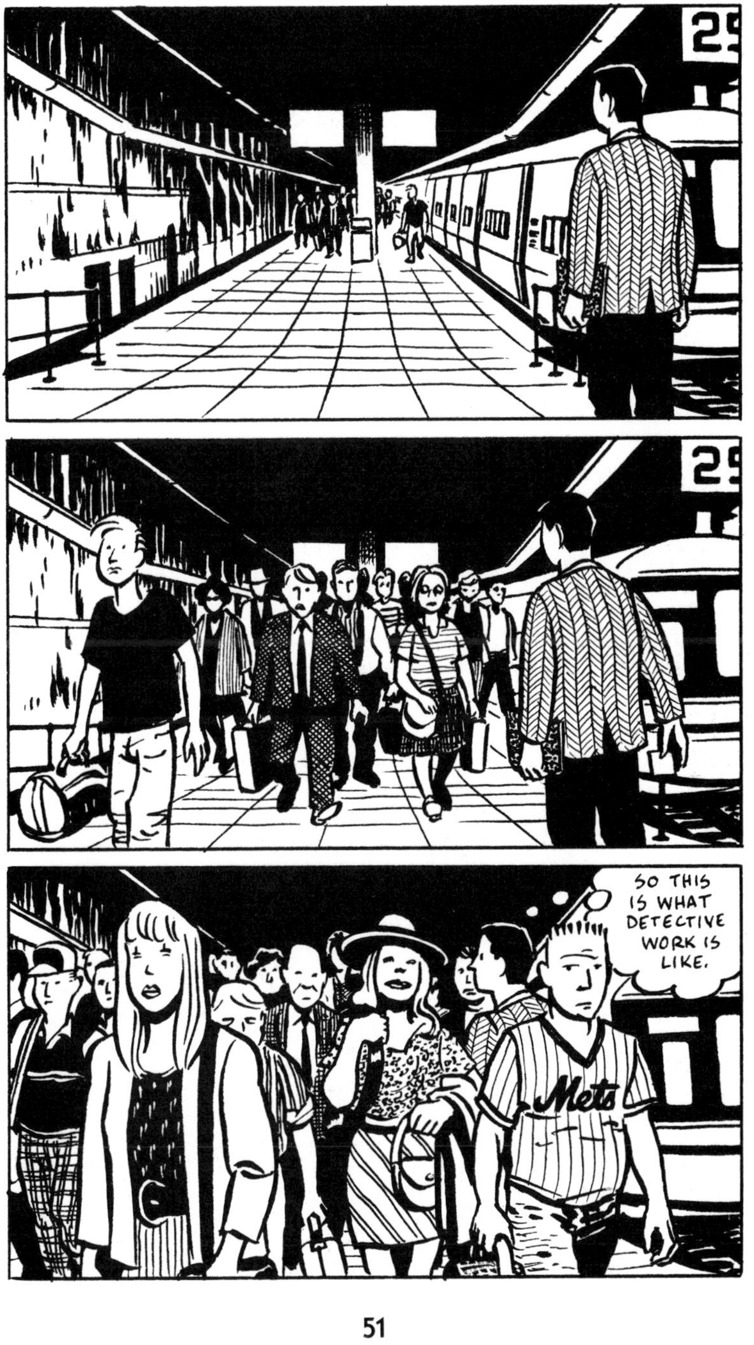
25
25
SO THIS IS WHAT DETECTIVE WORK IS LIKE.
Mets

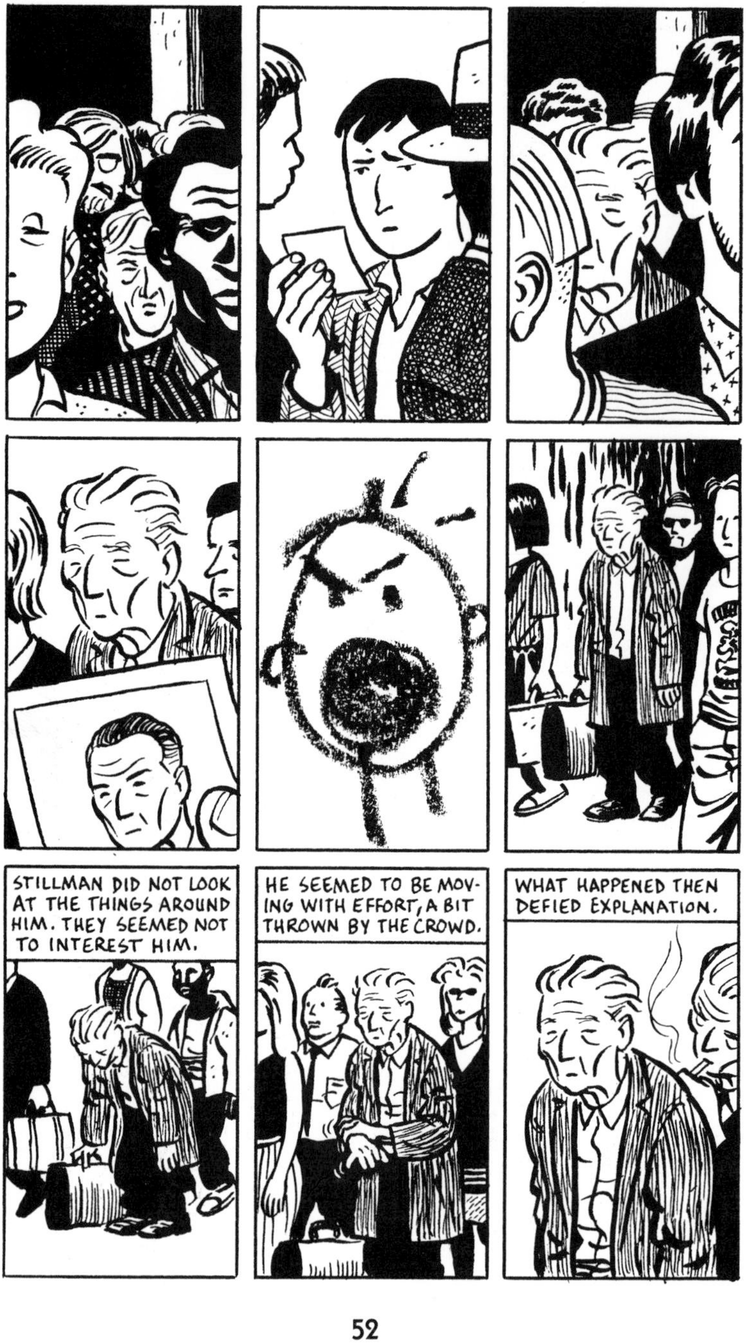
STILLMAN DID NOT LOOK AT THE THINGS AROUND HIM. THEY SEEMED NOT TO INTEREST HIM.
HE SEEMED TO BE MOVING WITH EFFORT, A BIT THROWN BY THE CROWD.
WHAT HAPPENED THEN DEFIED EXPLANATION.

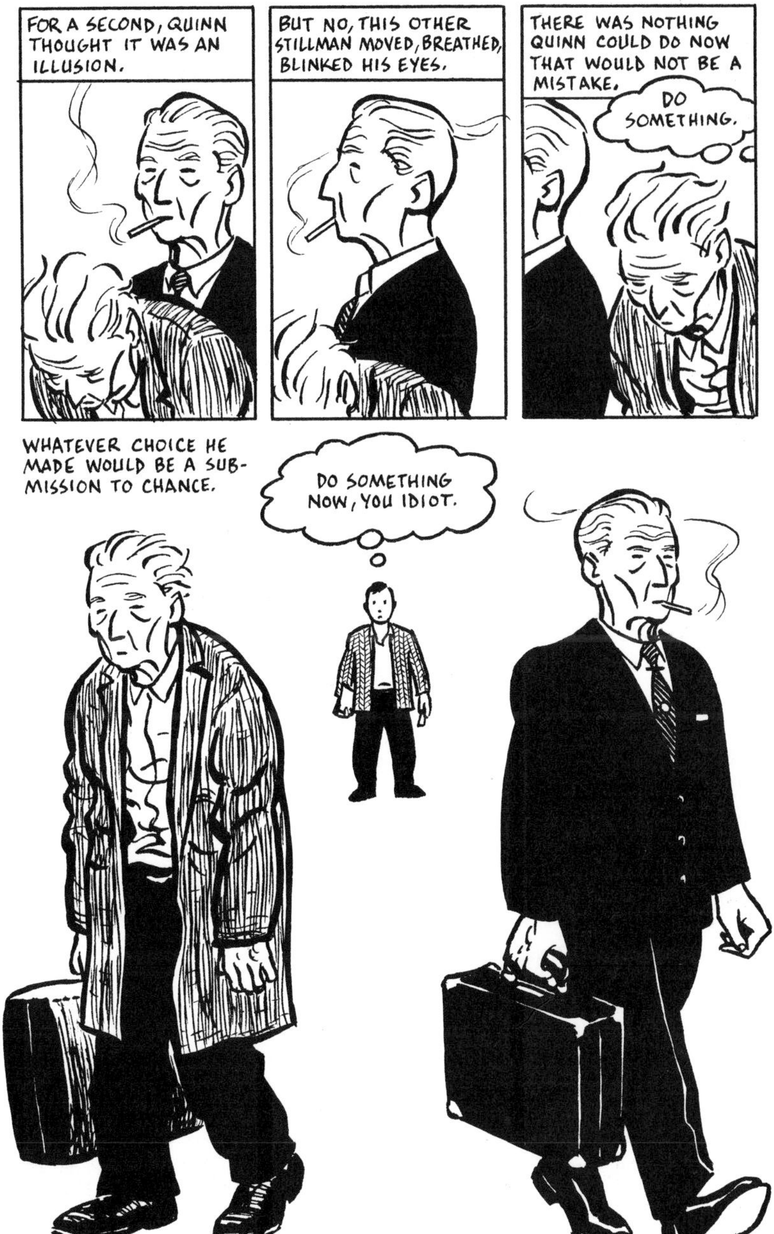
FOR A SECOND, QUINN THOUGHT IT WAS AN ILLUSION.
BUT NO, THIS OTHER STILLMAN MOVED, BREATHED, BLINKED HIS EYES.
THERE WAS NOTHING QUINN COULD DO NOW THAT WOULD NOT BE A MISTAKE.
DO SOMETHING.
WHATEVER CHOICE HE MADE WOULD BE A SUB-MISSION TO CHANCE.
DO SOMETHING NOW, YOU IDIOT.

Information
SHUTTLE 42 STREET
THERE WAS NO WAY TO KNOW: NOT THIS, NOT ANYTHING.

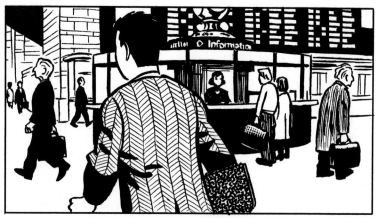

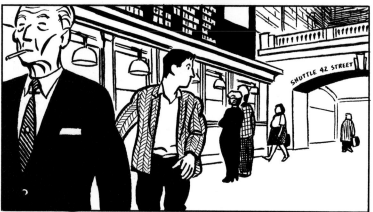

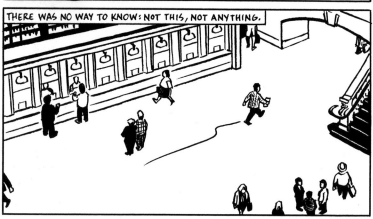

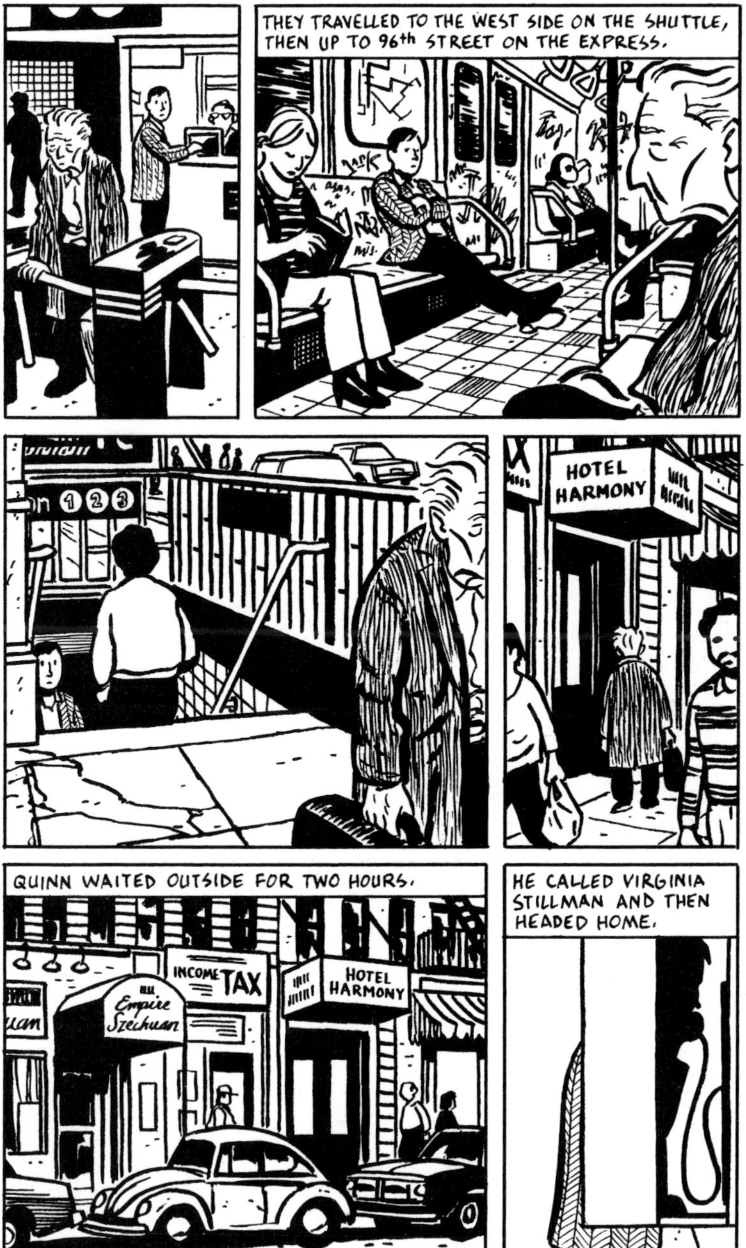
THEY TRAVELLED TO THE WEST SIDE ON THE SHUTTLE, THEN UP TO 96th STREET ON THE EXPRESS.
HOTEL HARMONY
QUINN WAITED OUTSIDE FOR TWO HOURS.
INCOME TAX
HOTEL HARMONY
Empire Szechuan
HE CALLED VIRGINIA STILLMAN AND THEN HEADED HOME.

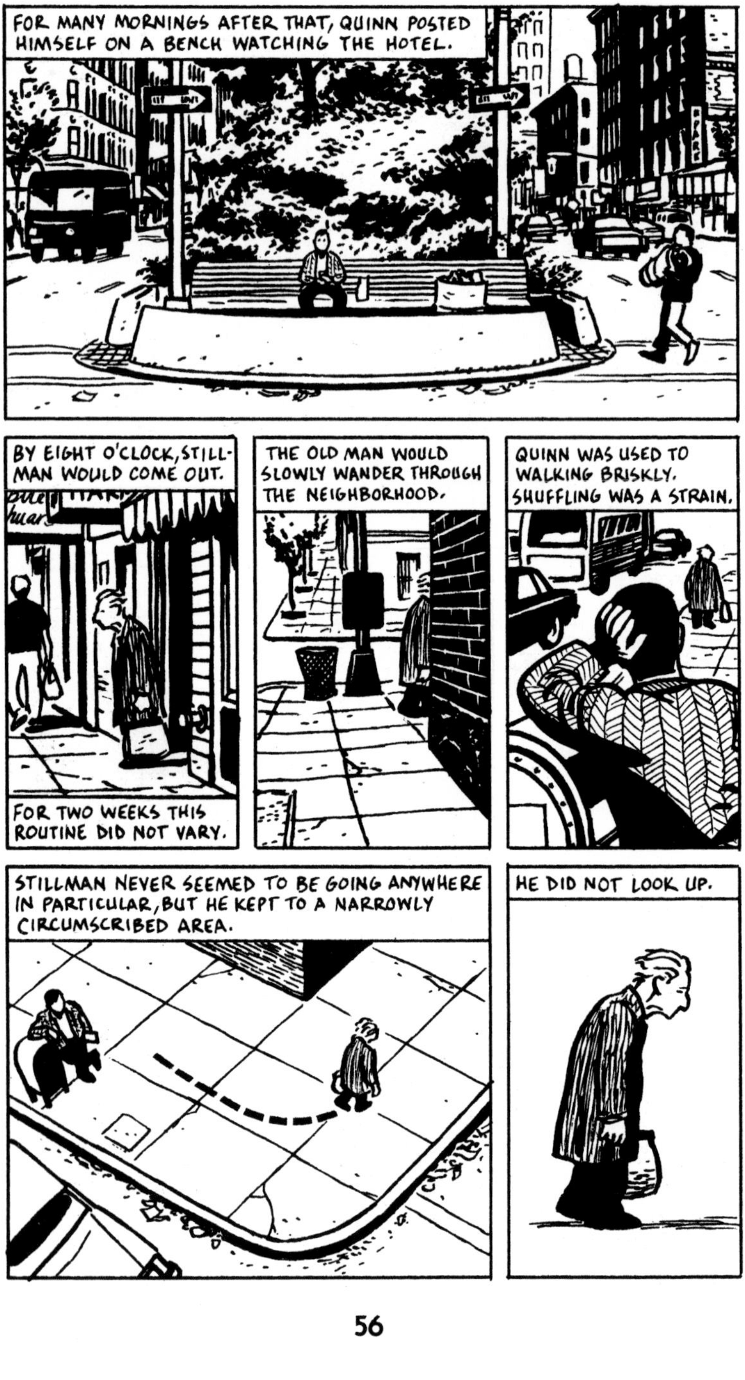
FOR MANY MORNINGS AFTER THAT, QUINN POSTED HIMSELF ON A BENCH WATCHING THE HOTEL.
BY EIGHT O'CLOCK, STILLMAN WOULD COME OUT.
FOR TWO WEEKS THIS ROUTINE DID NOT VARY.
THE OLD MAN WOULD SLOWLY WANDER THROUGH THE NEIGHBORHOOD.
QUINN WAS USED TO WALKING BRISKLY. SHUFFLING WAS A STRAIN.
STILLMAN NEVER SEEMED TO BE GOING ANYWHERE IN PARTICULAR, BUT HE KEPT TO A NARROWLY CIRCUMSCRIBED AREA.
HE DID NOT LOOK UP.

EVERY NOW AND THEN HE WOULD PICK SOME OBJECT OFF THE GROUND.

AS FAR AS QUINN COULD TELL THESE OBJECTS WERE VALUELESS.

THE FACT THAT STILLMAN TOOK THIS SCAVENGING SERIOUSLY INTRIGUED QUINN...

...BUT HE COULD DO NO MORE THAN OBSERVE,...

...WRITE DOWN WHAT HE SAW, HOVER STUPIDLY ON THE SURFACE OF THINGS.

OTHER THAN PICKING UP OBJECTS, STILLMAN SEEMED TO DO NOTHING.

HE DID NOT TALK TO ANYONE, GO INTO ANY STORE, OR SMILE.

HE SEEMED NEITHER HAPPY NOR SAD.

57

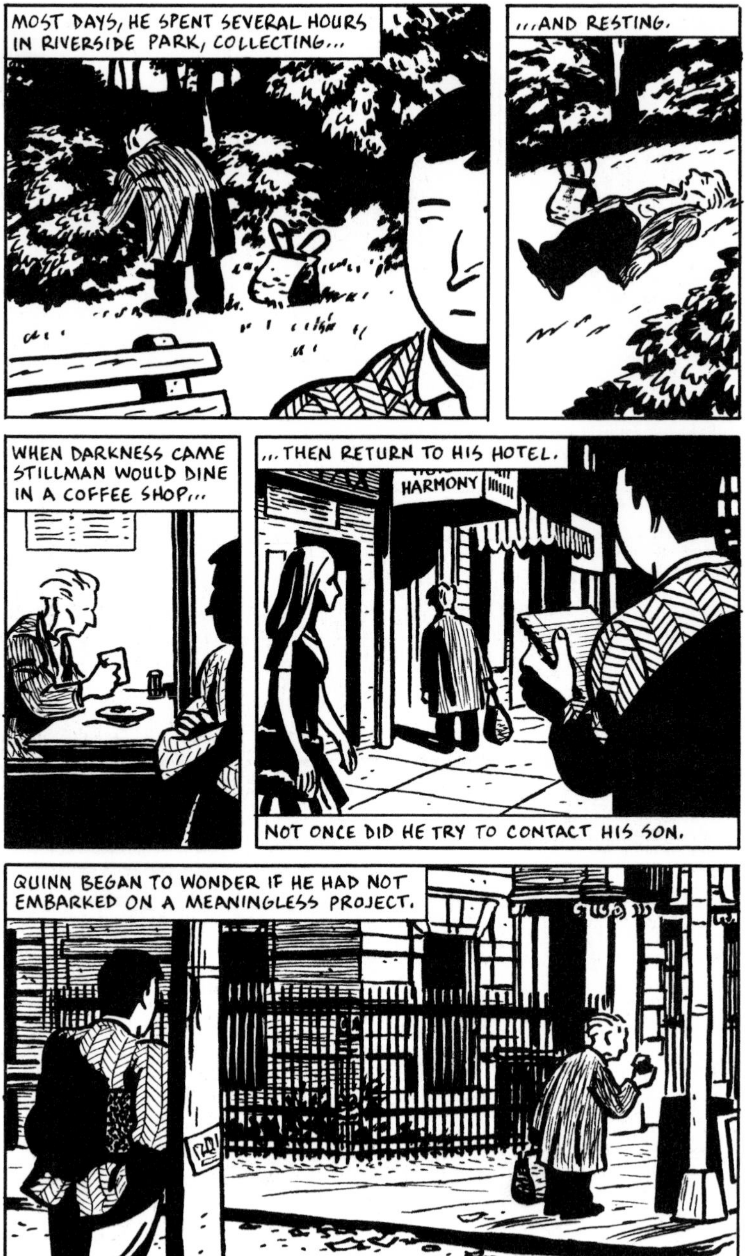
MOST DAYS, HE SPENT SEVERAL HOURS IN RIVERSIDE PARK, COLLECTING...
...AND RESTING.
WHEN DARKNESS CAME STILLMAN WOULD DINE IN A COFFEE SHOP...
...THEN RETURN TO HIS HOTEL.
HARMONY
NOT ONCE DID HE TRY TO CONTACT HIS SON.
QUINN BEGAN TO WONDER IF HE HAD NOT EMBARKED ON A MEANINGLESS PROJECT.

IT WAS POSSIBLE THAT STILLMAN WAS MERELY BIDING HIS TIME.
QUINN PREFERRED TO THINK THAT STILLMAN HAD A PLAN.
IT JUSTIFIED HIS TAILING HIM.
BUT TIME AND AGAIN HIS THOUGHTS WOULD BEGIN TO DRIFT.
THIS MEANT HE WAS CONSTANTLY IN DANGER OF OVERTAKING STILLMAN.
HE DECIDED TO RECORD EVERY DETAIL ABOUT STILLMAN HE POSSIBLY COULD.
turns right onto
Bdwy at 91 St.
Stops - picks up
scrap of paper.
THIS KEPT HIM OCCUPIED, AND SLOWED HIM DOWN.

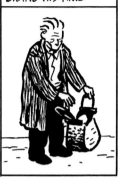

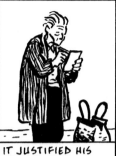

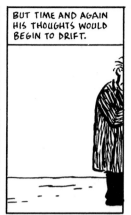

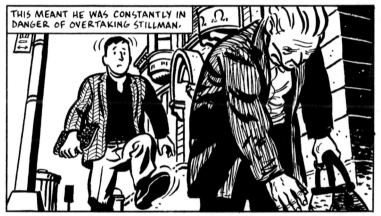

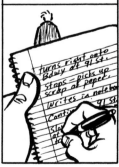

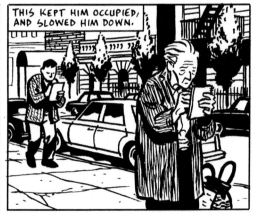

HIS NIGHTLY CONVERSATIONS WITH VIRGINIA STILLMAN WERE BRIEF.

FROM ALL I'VE SEEN, THERE'S NO THREAT.

YOU COULD BE RIGHT.

AT FIRST QUINN HAD EXPECTED HE WOULD EVENTUALLY FIND HER IN HIS ARMS.

BUT JUST TO REASSURE ME, GIVE IT A FEW MORE DAYS.

ON ONE CONDITION.

BUT THERE HAD BEEN NO FURTHER ROMANTIC DEVELOPMENTS.

NO MORE RESTRAINTS. I HAVE TO BE FREE TO TALK TO HIM.

WOULDN'T THAT BE RISKY?

PERHAPS HE HAD MOMENTARILY CONFUSED HIMSELF WITH MAX WORK.

HE WON'T GUESS WHAT I'M UP TO. TRUST ME.

ALL RIGHT. I DON'T SUPPOSE IT WILL HURT.

OR PERHAPS HE WAS JUST FEELING HIS LONELINESS MORE KEENLY.

GOOD. I'LL GIVE IT A FEW MORE DAYS.

MR. AUSTER?

MUCH LATER, LONG AFTER IT WAS TOO LATE, HE REALIZED HE HAD A SECRET HOPE.

YES?

I'M TERRIBLY GRATEFUL. PETER HAS BEEN IN SUCH GOOD SHAPE. YOU'RE LIKE— LIKE... A HERO TO HIM.

TO SOLVE THE CASE SO BRILLIANTLY THAT HE WOULD WIN VIRGINIA'S DESIRE.

AND HOW DOES MRS. STILLMAN FEEL?

MUCH THE SAME WAY.

THAT, OF COURSE, WAS A MISTAKE.

MAYBE SOMEDAY SHE'LL ALLOW ME TO FEEL GRATEFUL TO HER.

ANYTHING IS POSSIBLE. REMEMBER THAT.

BUT IT WAS NO WORSE THAN ANY OF THE OTHER MISTAKES HE MADE FROM BEGINNING TO END.

I WILL. I'D BE A FOOL NOT TO.

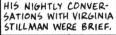

60

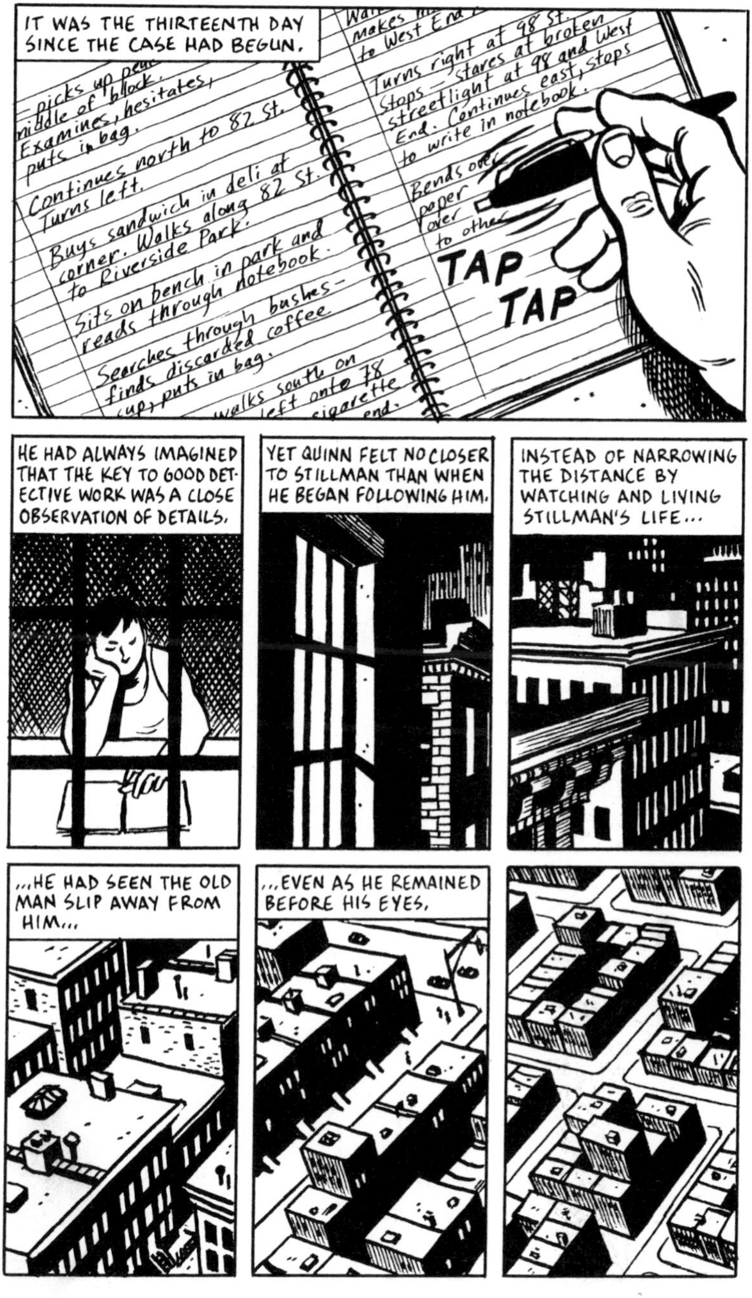

IT WAS THE THIRTEENTH DAY SINCE THE CASE HAD BEGUN.
middle of block.
Examines, hesitates,
puts in bag.
Continues north to 82 St.
Turns left.
Buys sandwich in deli at
corner. Walks along 82 St.
to Riverside Park.
Sits on bench in park and
reads through notebook.
Searches through bushes —
finds discarded coffee
cup, puts in bag.
to West End
Turns right at 98 St.
Stops — stares at broken
streetlight at 98 and West
End. Continues east, stops
to write in notebook.
TAP
TAP
HE HAD ALWAYS IMAGINED THAT THE KEY TO GOOD DETECTIVE WORK WAS A CLOSE OBSERVATION OF DETAILS.
YET QUINN FELT NO CLOSER TO STILLMAN THAN WHEN HE BEGAN FOLLOWING HIM.
INSTEAD OF NARROWING THE DISTANCE BY WATCHING AND LIVING STILLMAN'S LIFE...
...HE HAD SEEN THE OLD MAN SLIP AWAY FROM HIM...
...EVEN AS HE REMAINED BEFORE HIS EYES.

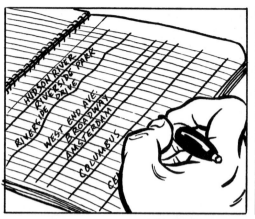

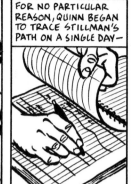

HUDSON RIVER
RIVERSIDE PARK
RIVERSIDE DRIVE
WEST END AVE.
BROADWAY
AMSTERDAM
COLUMBUS
FOR NO PARTICULAR REASON, QUINN BEGAN TO TRACE STILLMAN'S PATH ON A SINGLE DAY—
—THE FIRST DAY HE HAD KEPT A FULL RECORD OF THE OLD MAN'S WANDERINGS.
?
?
"O"?
QUINN WENT ON TO THE NEXT DAY TO SEE WHAT WOULD HAPPEN.
?
?
"W"?
AM I JUST KILLING TIME, OR WHAT?
HE TRACED OUT THE NEXT SEVEN DAYS.

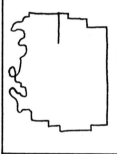

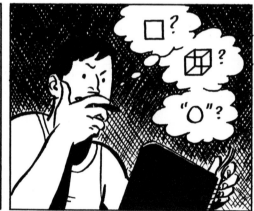

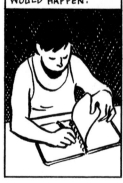

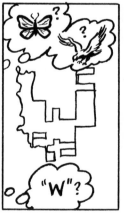

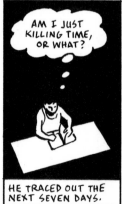

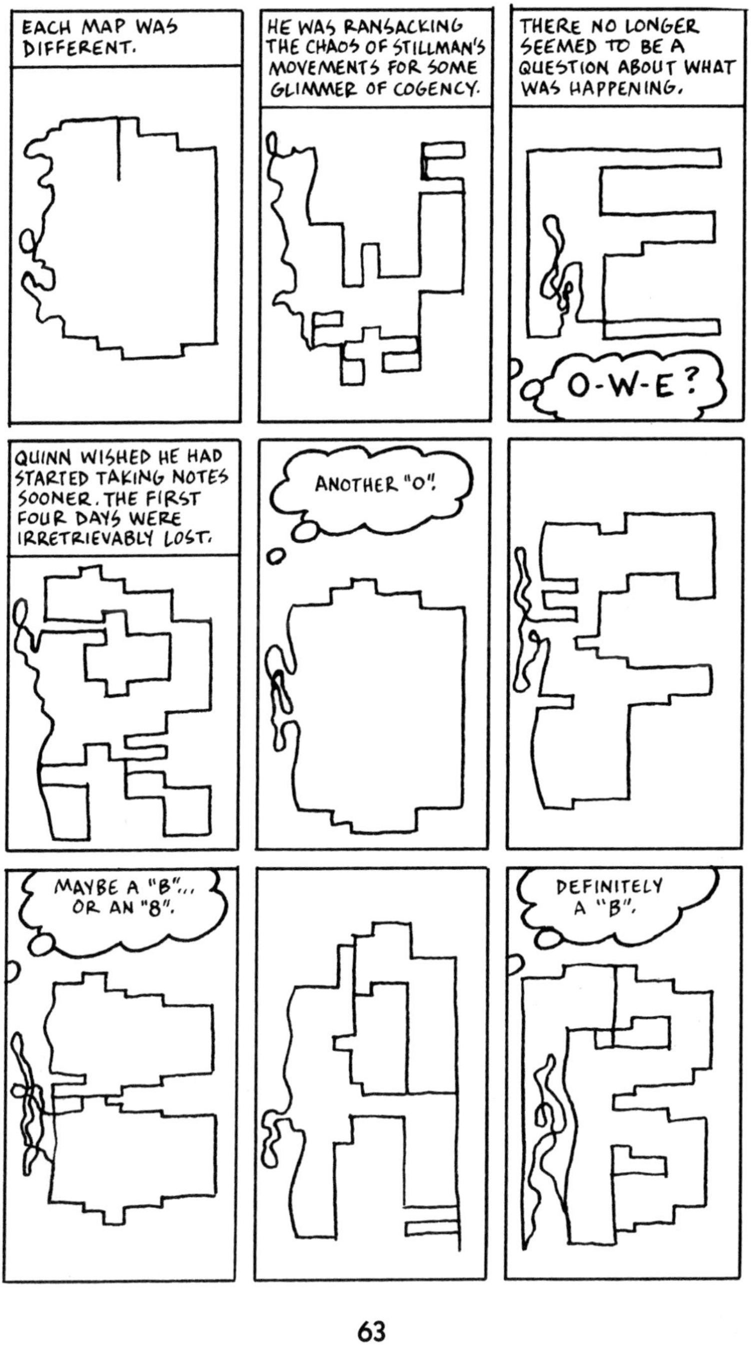
EACH MAP WAS DIFFERENT.
HE WAS RANSACKING THE CHAOS OF STILLMAN'S MOVEMENTS FOR SOME GLIMMER OF COGENCY.
THERE NO LONGER SEEMED TO BE A QUESTION ABOUT WHAT WAS HAPPENING.
O-W-E?
QUINN WISHED HE HAD STARTED TAKING NOTES SOONER. THE FIRST FOUR DAYS WERE IRRETRIEVABLY LOST.
ANOTHER "O".
MAYBE A "B"... OR AN "8".
DEFINITELY A "B".

OWEROFBAB

OWER
OF
B

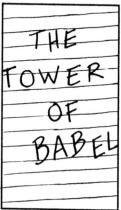

THE
TOWER
OF
BABEL

BUT, WHY? IT WAS LIKE DRAWING A PICTURE IN THE AIR WITH YOUR FINGER...

...THE IMAGE VANISHES AS YOU ARE MAKING IT.

AND YET...

...THE PICTURES DID EXIST...

...IN QUINN'S NOTEBOOK.

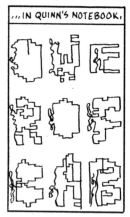

...A NOTE TO HIMSELF?

...A MESSAGE?

64

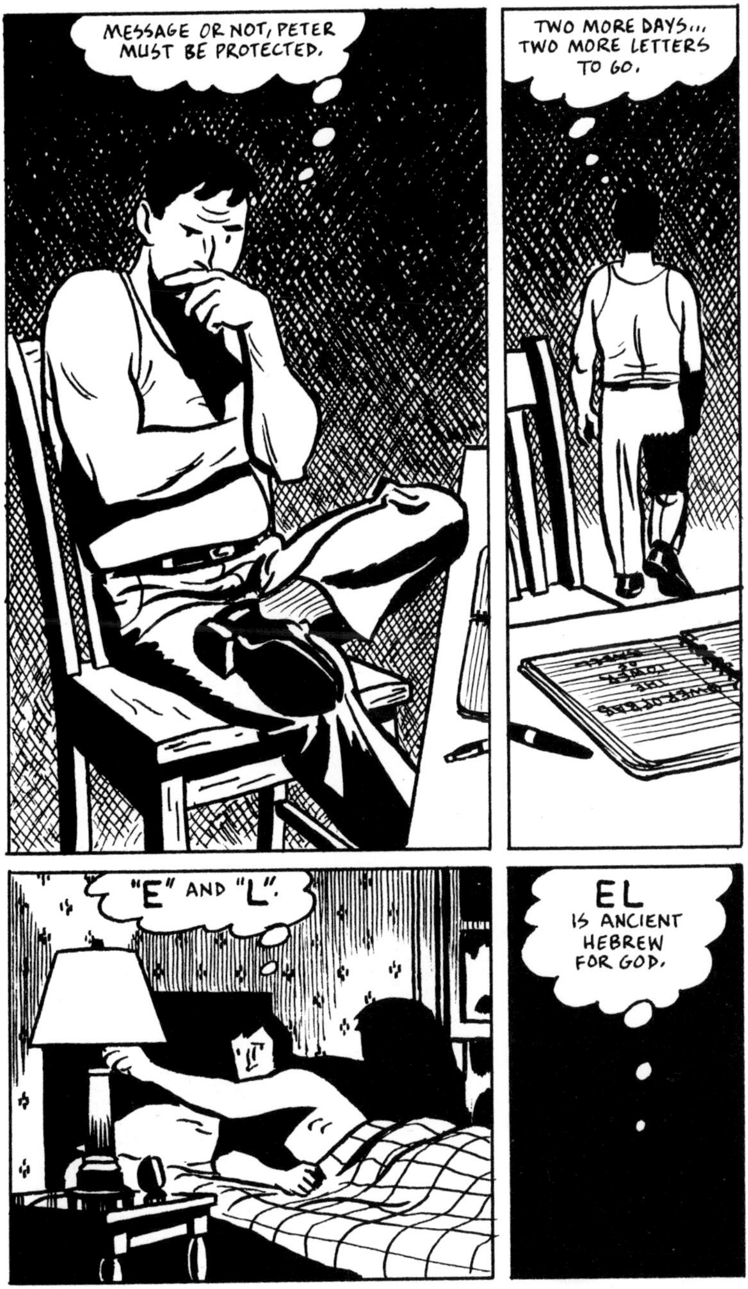
MESSAGE OR NOT, PETER MUST BE PROTECTED.
TWO MORE DAYS... TWO MORE LETTERS TO GO.
"E" AND "L".
EL IS ANCIENT HEBREW FOR GOD.

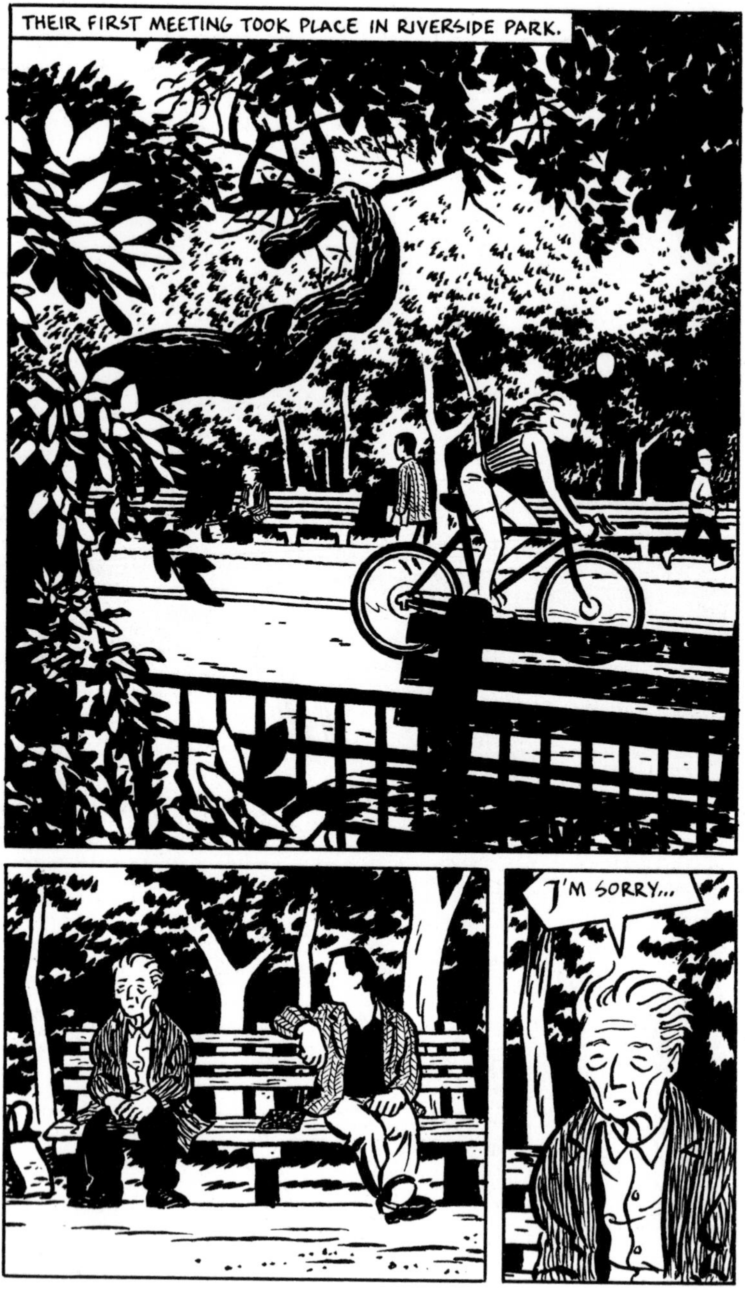
THEIR FIRST MEETING TOOK PLACE IN RIVERSIDE PARK.
I'M SORRY...

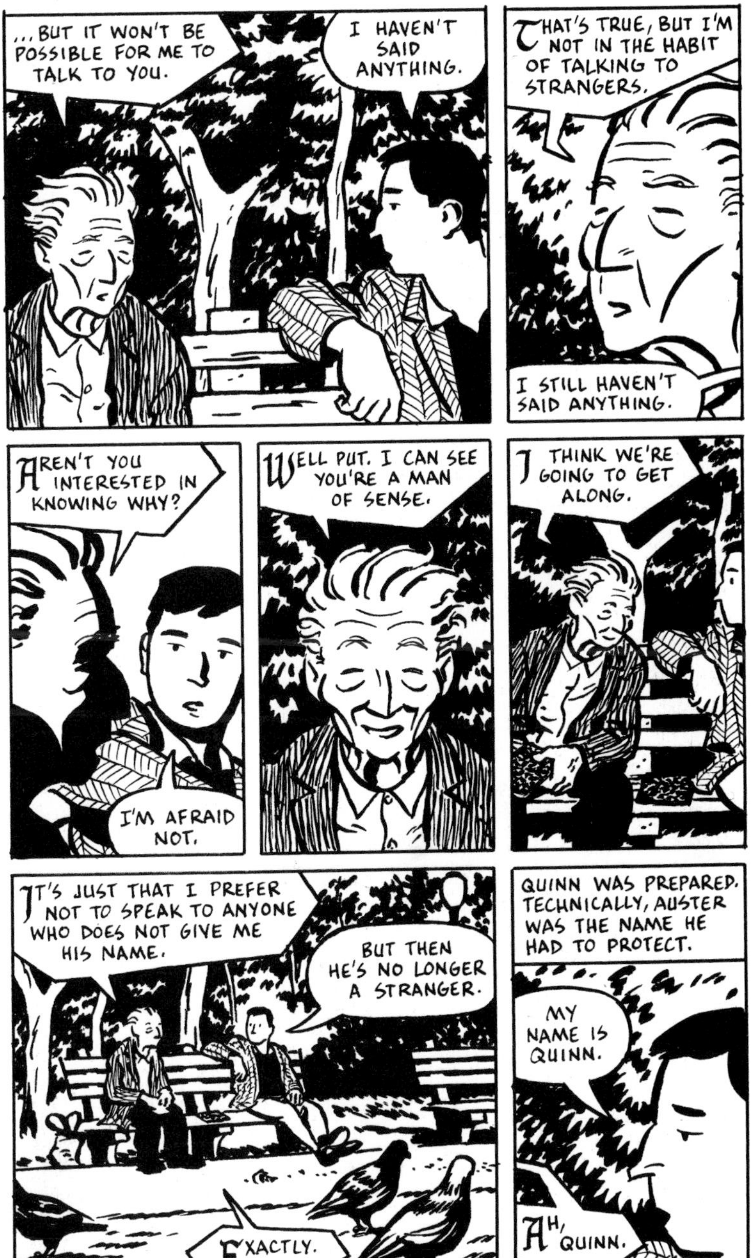
...BUT IT WON'T BE POSSIBLE FOR ME TO TALK TO YOU.
I HAVEN'T SAID ANYTHING.
THAT'S TRUE, BUT I'M NOT IN THE HABIT OF TALKING TO STRANGERS.
I STILL HAVEN'T SAID ANYTHING.
AREN'T YOU INTERESTED IN KNOWING WHY?
I'M AFRAID NOT.
WELL PUT. I CAN SEE YOU'RE A MAN OF SENSE.
I THINK WE'RE GOING TO GET ALONG.
IT'S JUST THAT I PREFER NOT TO SPEAK TO ANYONE WHO DOES NOT GIVE ME HIS NAME.
BUT THEN HE'S NO LONGER A STRANGER.
EXACTLY.
QUINN WAS PREPARED. TECHNICALLY, AUSTER WAS THE NAME HE HAD TO PROTECT.
MY NAME IS QUINN.
AH, QUINN.

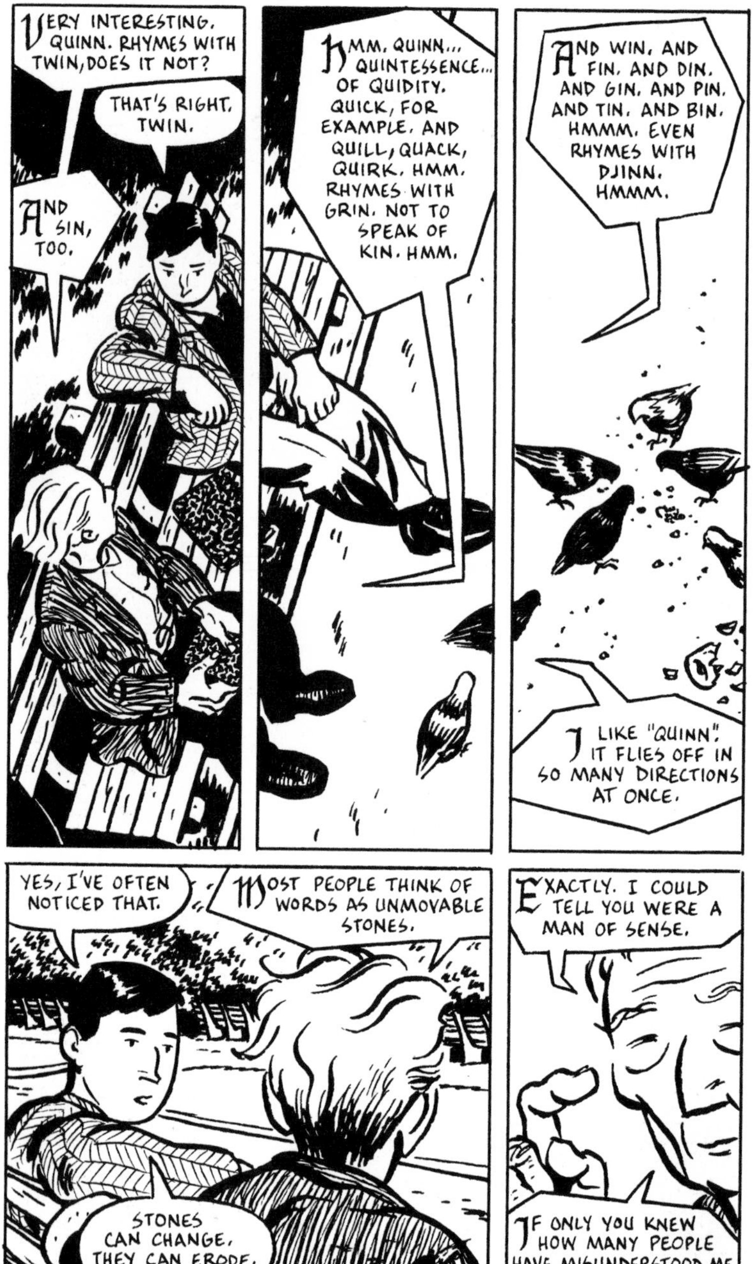
VERY INTERESTING. QUINN. RHYMES WITH TWIN, DOES IT NOT?
THAT'S RIGHT. TWIN.
AND SIN, TOO.
HMM. QUINN... QUINTESSENCE... OF QUIDITY. QUICK, FOR EXAMPLE. AND QUILL, QUACK, QUIRK. HMM. RHYMES WITH GRIN. NOT TO SPEAK OF KIN. HMM.
AND WIN. AND FIN. AND DIN. AND GIN. AND PIN. AND TIN. AND BIN. HMMM. EVEN RHYMES WITH DJINN. HMMM.
I LIKE "QUINN". IT FLIES OFF IN SO MANY DIRECTIONS AT ONCE.
YES, I'VE OFTEN NOTICED THAT.
MOST PEOPLE THINK OF WORDS AS UNMOVABLE STONES.
STONES CAN CHANGE. THEY CAN ERODE.
EXACTLY. I COULD TELL YOU WERE A MAN OF SENSE.
IF ONLY YOU KNEW HOW MANY PEOPLE HAVE MISUNDERSTOOD ME.

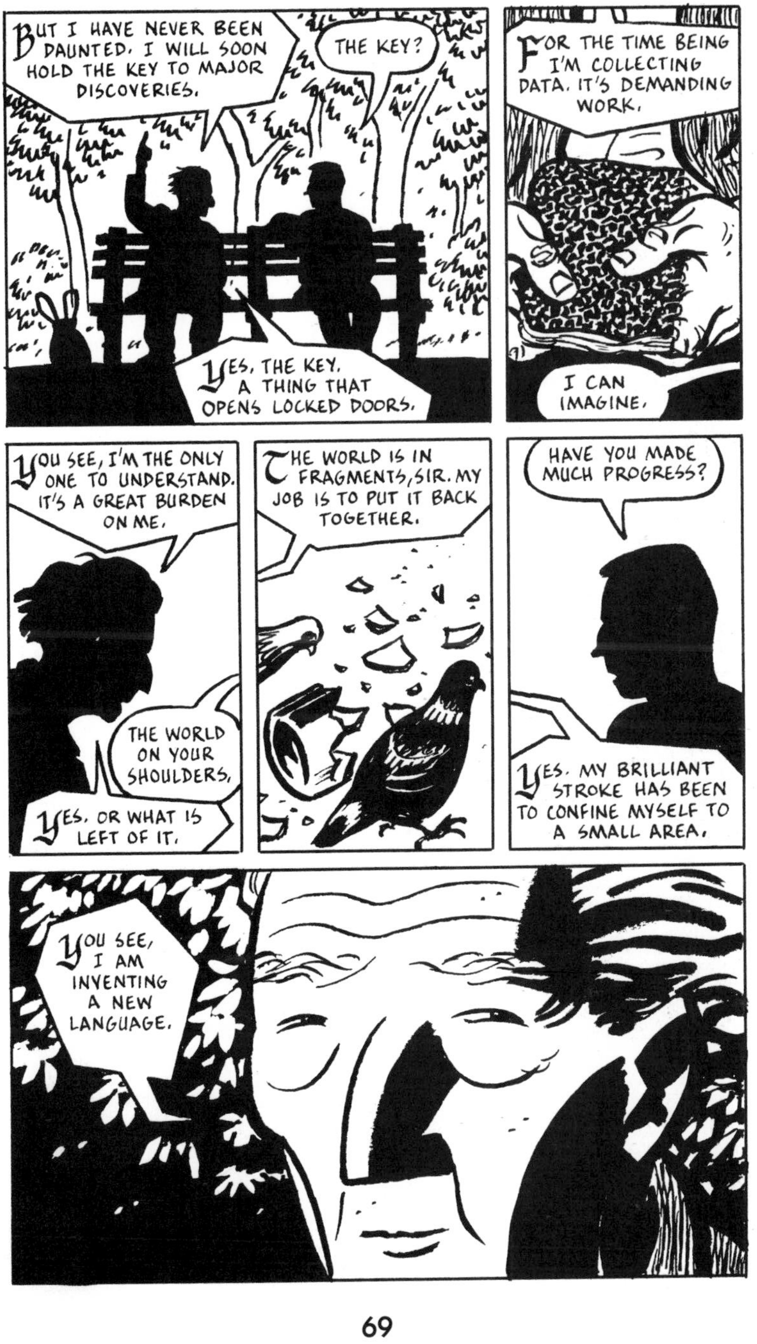

BUT I HAVE NEVER BEEN DAUNTED. I WILL SOON HOLD THE KEY TO MAJOR DISCOVERIES.
THE KEY?
YES, THE KEY. A THING THAT OPENS LOCKED DOORS.
FOR THE TIME BEING I'M COLLECTING DATA. IT'S DEMANDING WORK.
I CAN IMAGINE.
YOU SEE, I'M THE ONLY ONE TO UNDERSTAND. IT'S A GREAT BURDEN ON ME.
THE WORLD ON YOUR SHOULDERS.
YES. OR WHAT IS LEFT OF IT.
THE WORLD IS IN FRAGMENTS, SIR. MY JOB IS TO PUT IT BACK TOGETHER.
HAVE YOU MADE MUCH PROGRESS?
YES. MY BRILLIANT STROKE HAS BEEN TO CONFINE MYSELF TO A SMALL AREA.
YOU SEE, I AM INVENTING A NEW LANGUAGE.

A NEW LANGUAGE?

YES, WHEN THINGS WERE WHOLE OUR WORDS COULD EXPRESS THEM.

BUT THINGS HAVE BROKEN APART, AND OUR WORDS HAVE NOT ADAPTED.

"WHEN AN UMBRELLA BREAKS AND YOU GET WET, IS IT STILL AN UMBRELLA?"

"IT HAS CHANGED, BUT THE WORD IS THE SAME. IT IS IMPRECISE, FALSE."

AND IF WE CAN'T NAME A COMMON OBJECT, HOW CAN WE SPEAK OF THINGS THAT TRULY CONCERN US?

AND YOUR WORK?

MY WORK IS SIMPLE. IN NEW YORK BROKEN-NESS IS EVERYWHERE.

BROKEN PEOPLE, BROKEN THINGS, BROKEN THOUGHTS.

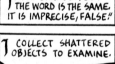

I COLLECT SHATTERED OBJECTS TO EXAMINE.

MY SAMPLES NOW NUMBER IN THE HUNDREDS.

WHAT DO YOU DO WITH THESE THINGS?

I GIVE THEM NAMES.

NAMES?

70

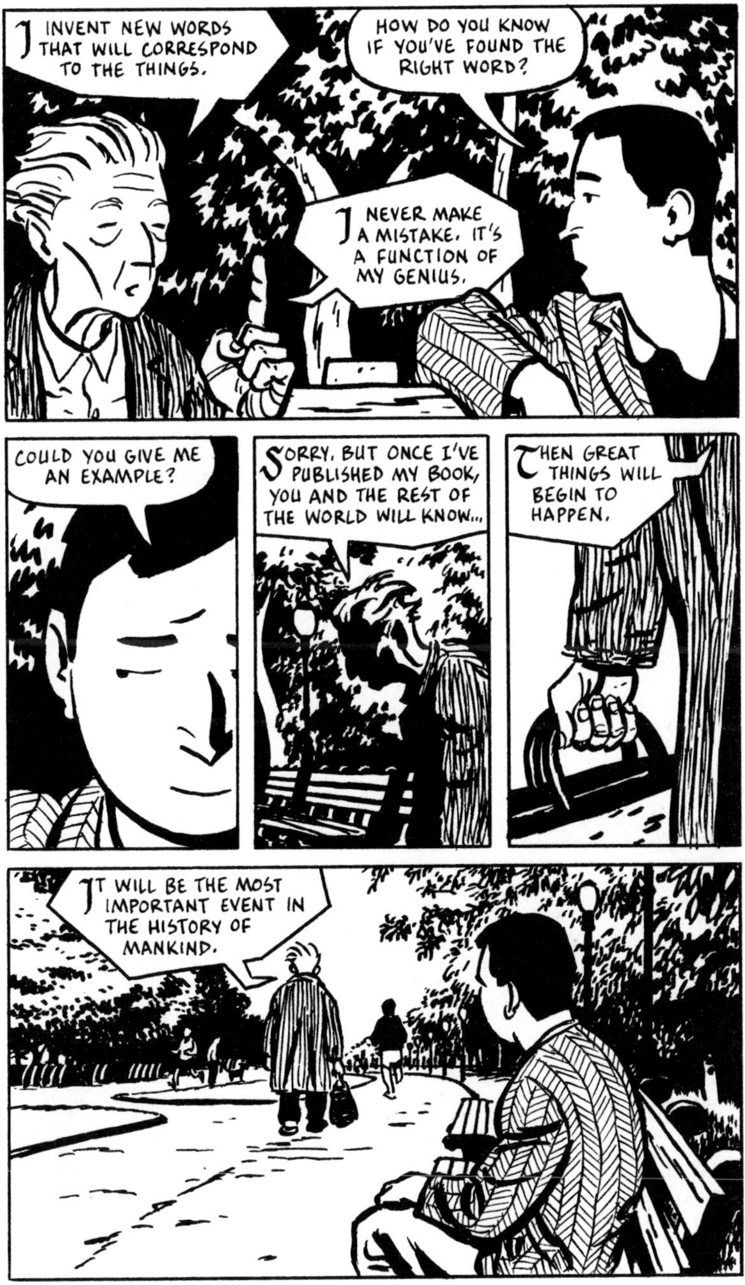
I INVENT NEW WORDS THAT WILL CORRESPOND TO THE THINGS.
HOW DO YOU KNOW IF YOU'VE FOUND THE RIGHT WORD?
I NEVER MAKE A MISTAKE. IT'S A FUNCTION OF MY GENIUS.
COULD YOU GIVE ME AN EXAMPLE?
SORRY. BUT ONCE I'VE PUBLISHED MY BOOK, YOU AND THE REST OF THE WORLD WILL KNOW...
THEN GREAT THINGS WILL BEGIN TO HAPPEN.
IT WILL BE THE MOST IMPORTANT EVENT IN THE HISTORY OF MANKIND.

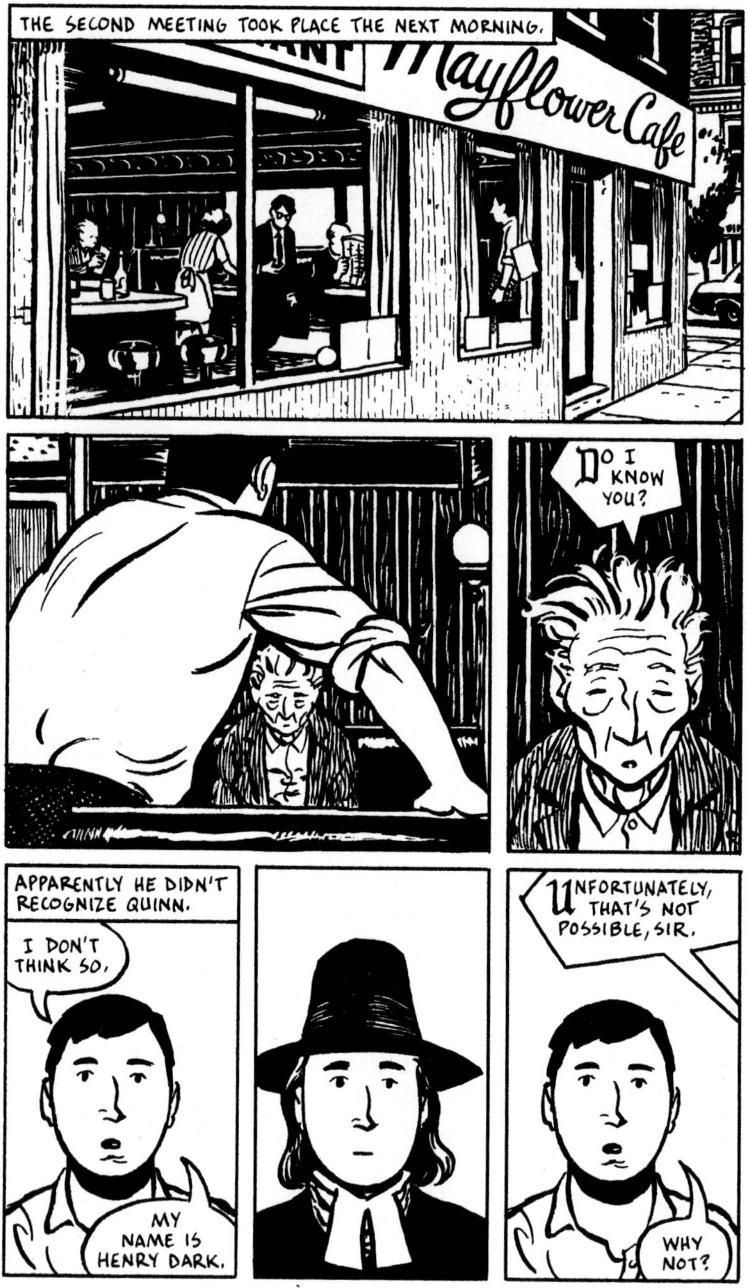
THE SECOND MEETING TOOK PLACE THE NEXT MORNING.
Mayflower Cafe
DO I KNOW YOU?
APPARENTLY HE DIDN'T RECOGNIZE QUINN.
I DON'T THINK SO.
MY NAME IS HENRY DARK.
UNFORTUNATELY, THAT'S NOT POSSIBLE, SIR.
WHY NOT?

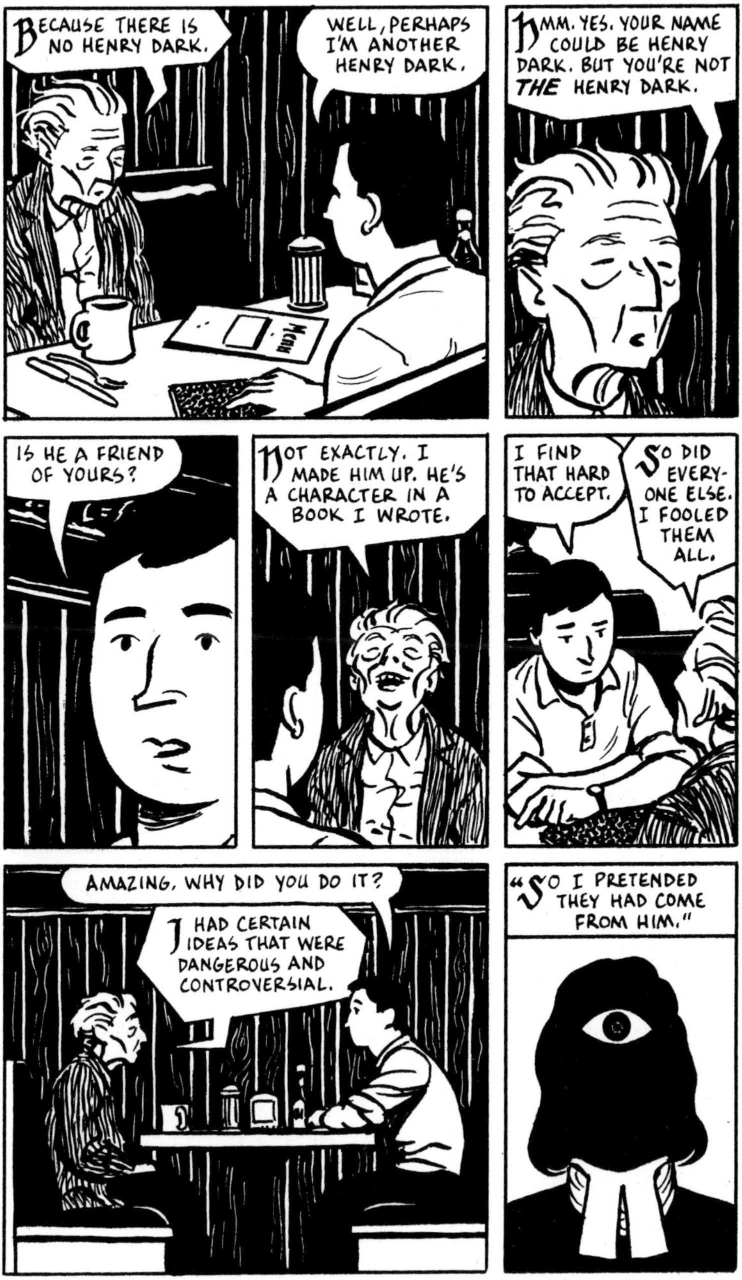
BECAUSE THERE IS NO HENRY DARK.
WELL, PERHAPS I'M ANOTHER HENRY DARK.
HMM. YES. YOUR NAME COULD BE HENRY DARK. BUT YOU'RE NOT THE HENRY DARK.
IS HE A FRIEND OF YOURS?
NOT EXACTLY. I MADE HIM UP. HE'S A CHARACTER IN A BOOK I WROTE.
I FIND THAT HARD TO ACCEPT.
SO DID EVERYONE ELSE. I FOOLED THEM ALL.
AMAZING. WHY DID YOU DO IT?
I HAD CERTAIN IDEAS THAT WERE DANGEROUS AND CONTROVERSIAL.
"SO I PRETENDED THEY HAD COME FROM HIM."

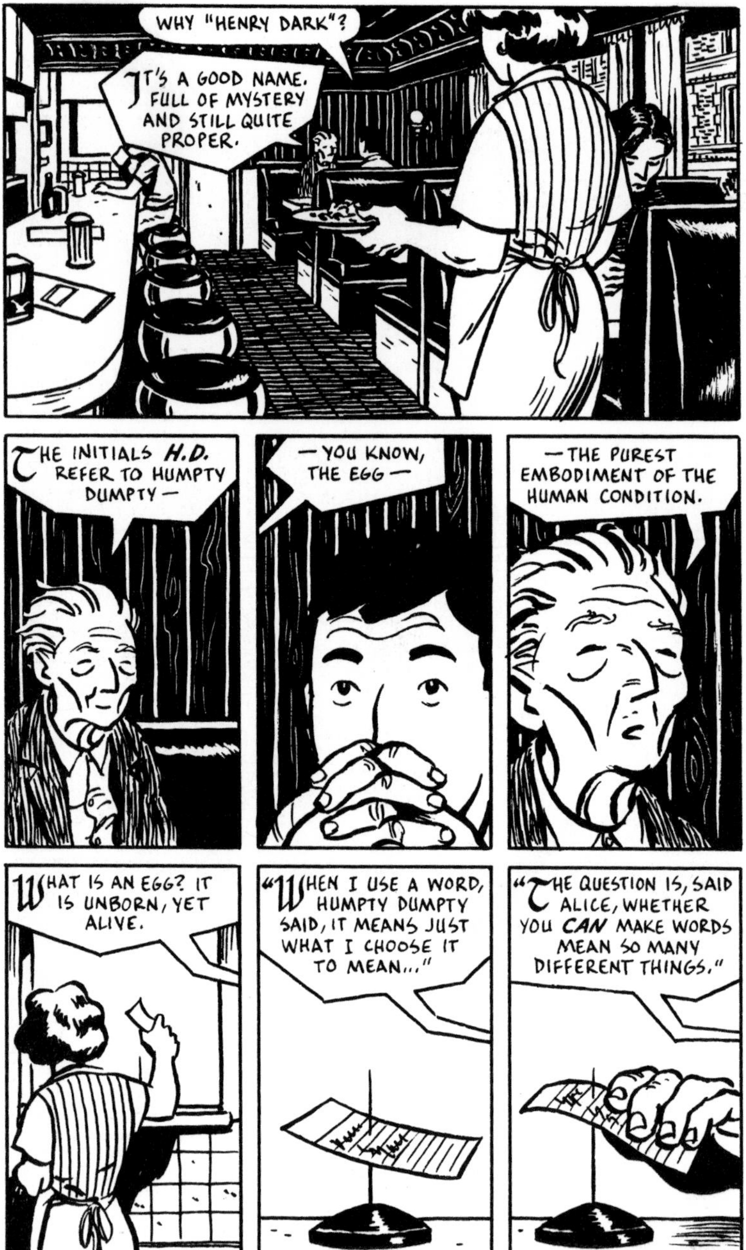
WHY "HENRY DARK"?
IT'S A GOOD NAME. FULL OF MYSTERY AND STILL QUITE PROPER.
THE INITIALS H.D. REFER TO HUMPTY DUMPTY —
— YOU KNOW, THE EGG —
— THE PUREST EMBODIMENT OF THE HUMAN CONDITION.
WHAT IS AN EGG? IT IS UNBORN, YET ALIVE.
"WHEN I USE A WORD, HUMPTY DUMPTY SAID, IT MEANS JUST WHAT I CHOOSE IT TO MEAN..."
"THE QUESTION IS, SAID ALICE, WHETHER YOU CAN MAKE WORDS MEAN SO MANY DIFFERENT THINGS."

"THE QUESTION IS, SAID HUMPTY DUMPTY, WHICH IS TO BE THE MASTER—THAT'S ALL."

THUS WE SEE THE FUTURE OF HUMAN SALVATION:

TO BECOME MASTERS OF THE WORDS WE SPEAK.

HUMPTY DUMPTY WAS A MAN WHO SPOKE TRUTHS THE WORLD WAS NOT READY FOR.

A MAN?

A SLIP OF THE TONGUE. I MEAN EGG...

...BUT ALL MEN ARE EGGS. WE HAVE NOT YET ACHIEVED THE FORM THAT IS OUR DESTINY.

"MAN IS A FALLEN CREATURE, AS IS HUMPTY DUMPTY."

"HE FALLS FROM HIS WALL AND NO ONE CAN PUT HIM TOGETHER AGAIN."

BUT THAT IS OUR DUTY AS HUMAN BEINGS: TO PUT THE EGG BACK TOGETHER AGAIN.

AND TO HELP HUMPTY DUMPTY IS TO HELP OURSELVES.

75

A CONVINCING ARGUMENT, NO CRACKS IN THAT EGG.

EXACTLY.

BUT THERE IS ANOTHER FAMOUS EGG AS WELL.

ANOTHER?

COLUMBUS'S EGG.

AH, YES.

GIVEN THE PROBLEM OF HOW TO STAND AN EGG ON ITS END, HE TAPPED THE SHELL'S BOTTOM...

...TO CREATE A FLATNESS THAT WOULD SUPPORT THE EGG.

COLUMBUS WAS A GENIUS, HE SOUGHT PARADISE AND DISCOVERED THE NEW WORLD.

IT IS STILL NOT TOO LATE FOR IT TO BECOME PARADISE.

INDEED.

TAP TAP

AS YOU CAN SEE, SIR, I LEAVE NO STONE UNTURNED.

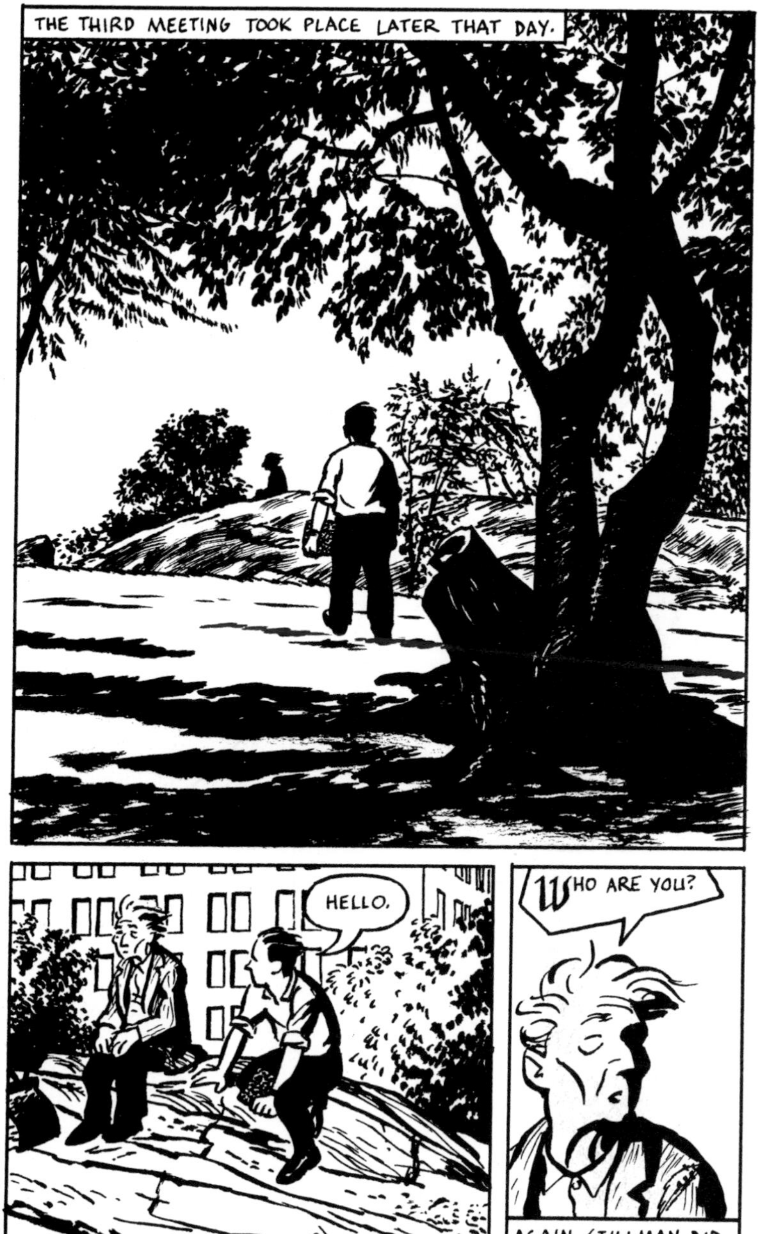
THE THIRD MEETING TOOK PLACE LATER THAT DAY.
HELLO.
WHO ARE YOU?
AGAIN, STILLMAN DID NOT RECOGNIZE HIM.

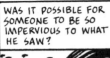

WAS IT POSSIBLE FOR SOMEONE TO BE SO IMPERVIOUS TO WHAT HE SAW?

MY NAME IS PETER STILLMAN.

THAT'S MY NAME.

I'M PETER STILLMAN.

I'M THE OTHER PETER STILLMAN.

OH, YOU MEAN MY SON. YES, THAT'S POSSIBLE.

OF COURSE, HE IS BLOND, BUT PEOPLE CHANGE.

ONE MINUTE WE'RE ONE THING, AND ANOTHER ANOTHER.

EXACTLY.

I'VE OFTEN THOUGHT: "I WONDER HOW PETER IS GETTING ALONG."

I'M MUCH BETTER NOW, THANK YOU.

I CAN SEE THAT. AND YOU SPEAK SO WELL, TOO.

ALL WORDS ARE AVAILABLE TO ME NOW.

I'M PROUD OF YOU, PETER.

I OWE IT ALL TO YOU.

78

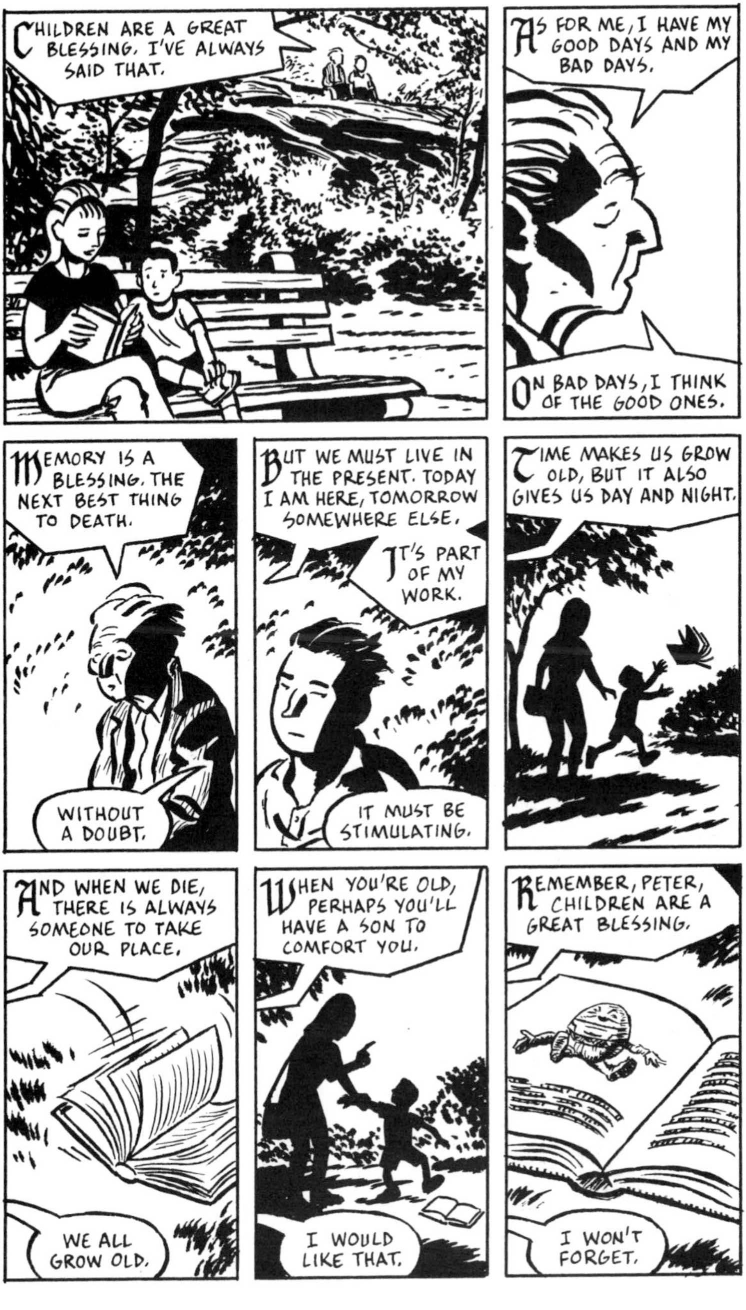
CHILDREN ARE A GREAT BLESSING. I'VE ALWAYS SAID THAT.
AS FOR ME, I HAVE MY GOOD DAYS AND MY BAD DAYS.
ON BAD DAYS, I THINK OF THE GOOD ONES.
MEMORY IS A BLESSING. THE NEXT BEST THING TO DEATH.
WITHOUT A DOUBT.
BUT WE MUST LIVE IN THE PRESENT. TODAY I AM HERE, TOMORROW SOMEWHERE ELSE.
IT'S PART OF MY WORK.
IT MUST BE STIMULATING.
TIME MAKES US GROW OLD, BUT IT ALSO GIVES US DAY AND NIGHT.
AND WHEN WE DIE, THERE IS ALWAYS SOMEONE TO TAKE OUR PLACE.
WE ALL GROW OLD.
WHEN YOU'RE OLD, PERHAPS YOU'LL HAVE A SON TO COMFORT YOU.
I WOULD LIKE THAT.
REMEMBER, PETER, CHILDREN ARE A GREAT BLESSING.
I WON'T FORGET.

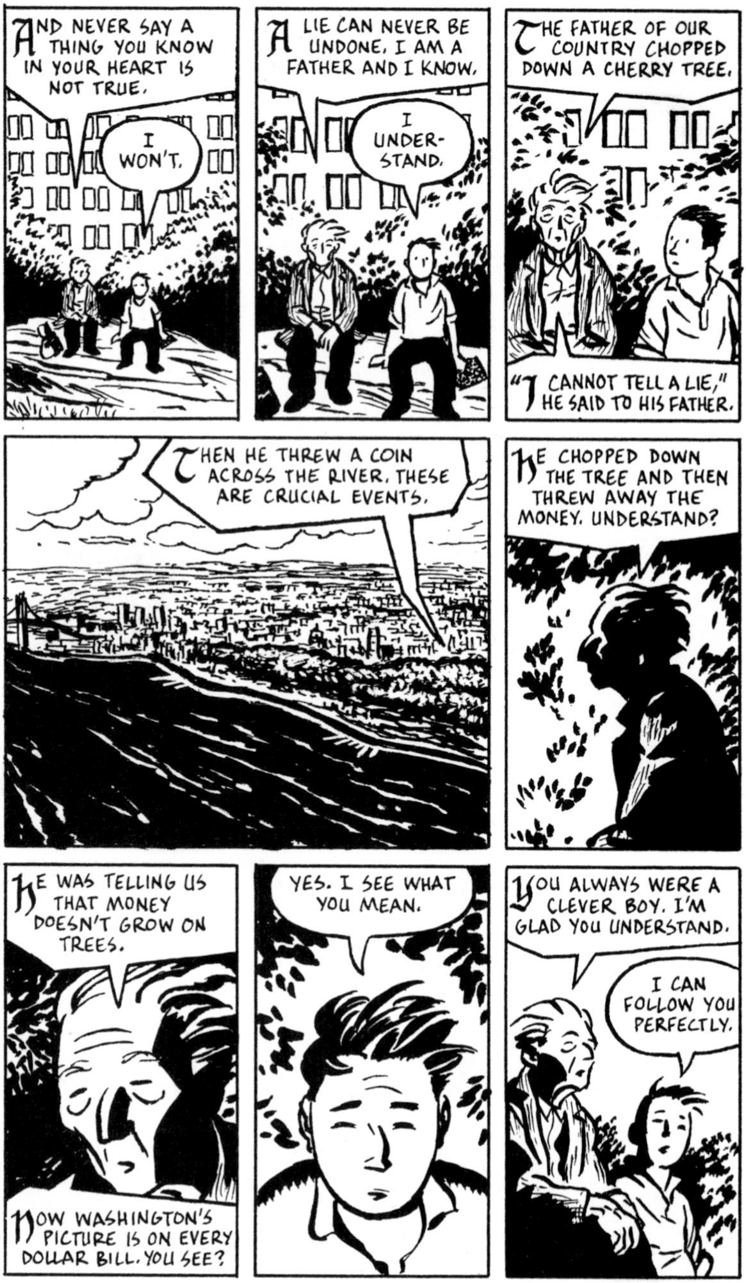
AND NEVER SAY A THING YOU KNOW IN YOUR HEART IS NOT TRUE.
I WON'T.
A LIE CAN NEVER BE UNDONE. I AM A FATHER AND I KNOW.
I UNDERSTAND.
THE FATHER OF OUR COUNTRY CHOPPED DOWN A CHERRY TREE.
"I CANNOT TELL A LIE," HE SAID TO HIS FATHER.
THEN HE THREW A COIN ACROSS THE RIVER. THESE ARE CRUCIAL EVENTS.
HE CHOPPED DOWN THE TREE AND THEN THREW AWAY THE MONEY. UNDERSTAND?
HE WAS TELLING US THAT MONEY DOESN'T GROW ON TREES.
HOW WASHINGTON'S PICTURE IS ON EVERY DOLLAR BILL. YOU SEE?
YES. I SEE WHAT YOU MEAN.
YOU ALWAYS WERE A CLEVER BOY. I'M GLAD YOU UNDERSTAND.
I CAN FOLLOW YOU PERFECTLY.

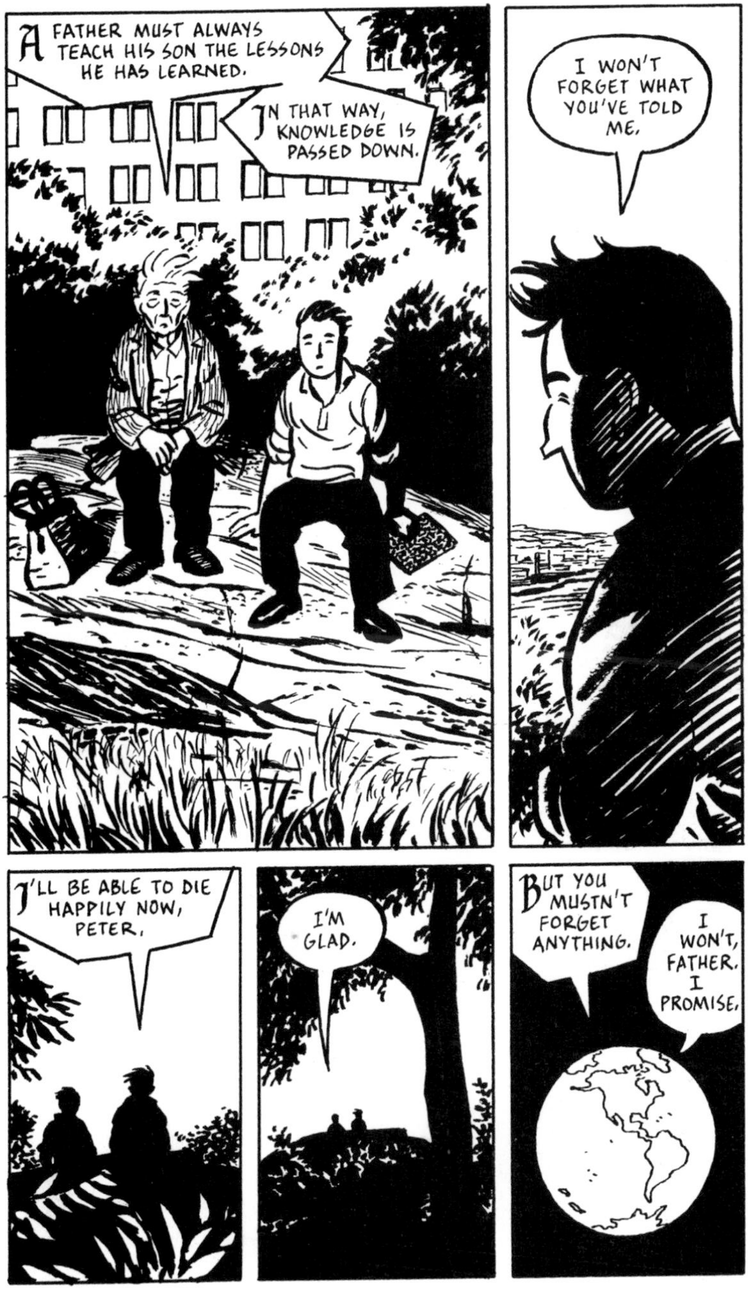
A FATHER MUST ALWAYS TEACH HIS SON THE LESSONS HE HAS LEARNED.
IN THAT WAY, KNOWLEDGE IS PASSED DOWN.
I WON'T FORGET WHAT YOU'VE TOLD ME.
I'LL BE ABLE TO DIE HAPPILY NOW, PETER.
I'M GLAD.
BUT YOU MUSTN'T FORGET ANYTHING.
I WON'T, FATHER. I PROMISE.

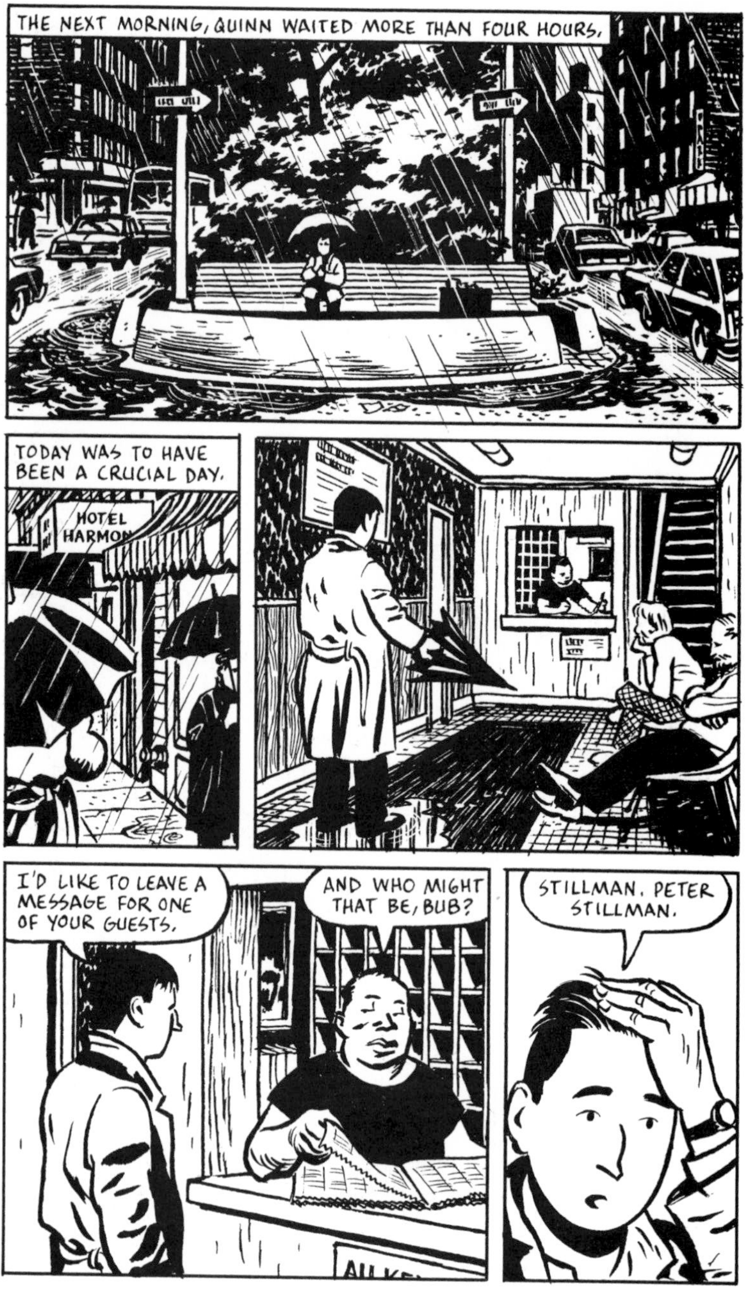

THE NEXT MORNING, QUINN WAITED MORE THAN FOUR HOURS.
TODAY WAS TO HAVE BEEN A CRUCIAL DAY.
HOTEL HARMON
I'D LIKE TO LEAVE A MESSAGE FOR ONE OF YOUR GUESTS.
AND WHO MIGHT THAT BE, BUB?
STILLMAN. PETER STILLMAN.

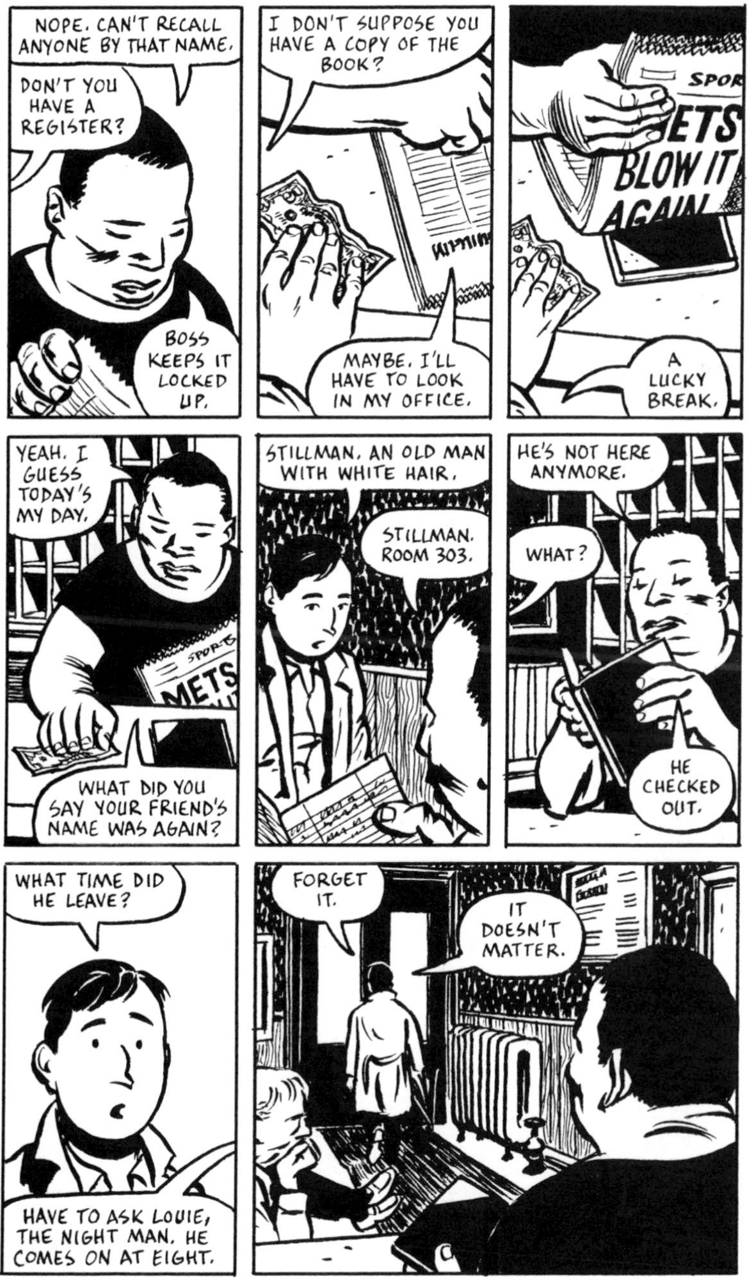
NOPE. CAN'T RECALL ANYONE BY THAT NAME.
DON'T YOU HAVE A REGISTER?
BOSS KEEPS IT LOCKED UP.
I DON'T SUPPOSE YOU HAVE A COPY OF THE BOOK?
MAYBE. I'LL HAVE TO LOOK IN MY OFFICE.
SPOR
METS BLOW IT AGAIN
A LUCKY BREAK.
YEAH. I GUESS TODAY'S MY DAY.
WHAT DID YOU SAY YOUR FRIEND'S NAME WAS AGAIN?
STILLMAN. AN OLD MAN WITH WHITE HAIR.
STILLMAN. ROOM 303.
HE'S NOT HERE ANYMORE.
WHAT?
HE CHECKED OUT.
WHAT TIME DID HE LEAVE?
HAVE TO ASK LOUIE, THE NIGHT MAN. HE COMES ON AT EIGHT.
FORGET IT.
IT DOESN'T MATTER.

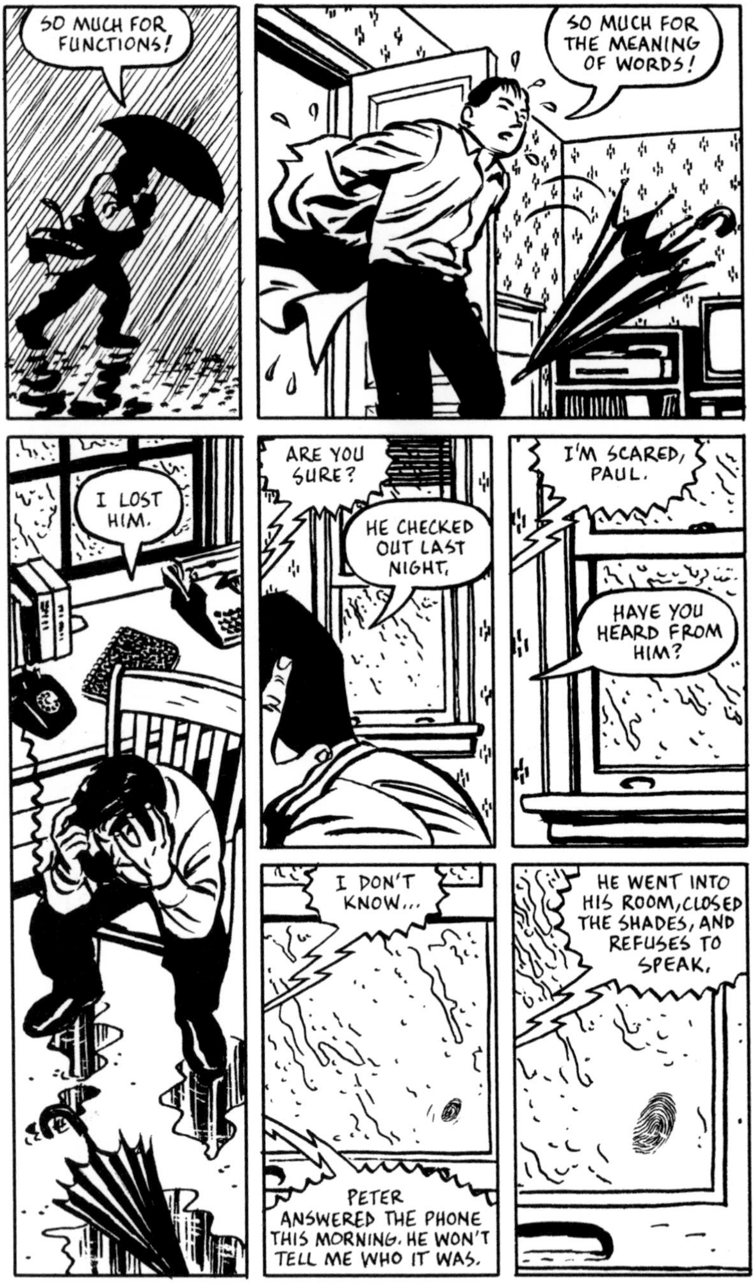
SO MUCH FOR FUNCTIONS!
SO MUCH FOR THE MEANING OF WORDS!
I LOST HIM.
ARE YOU SURE?
HE CHECKED OUT LAST NIGHT.
I'M SCARED, PAUL.
HAVE YOU HEARD FROM HIM?
I DON'T KNOW...
PETER ANSWERED THE PHONE THIS MORNING. HE WON'T TELL ME WHO IT WAS.
HE WENT INTO HIS ROOM, CLOSED THE SHADES, AND REFUSES TO SPEAK.

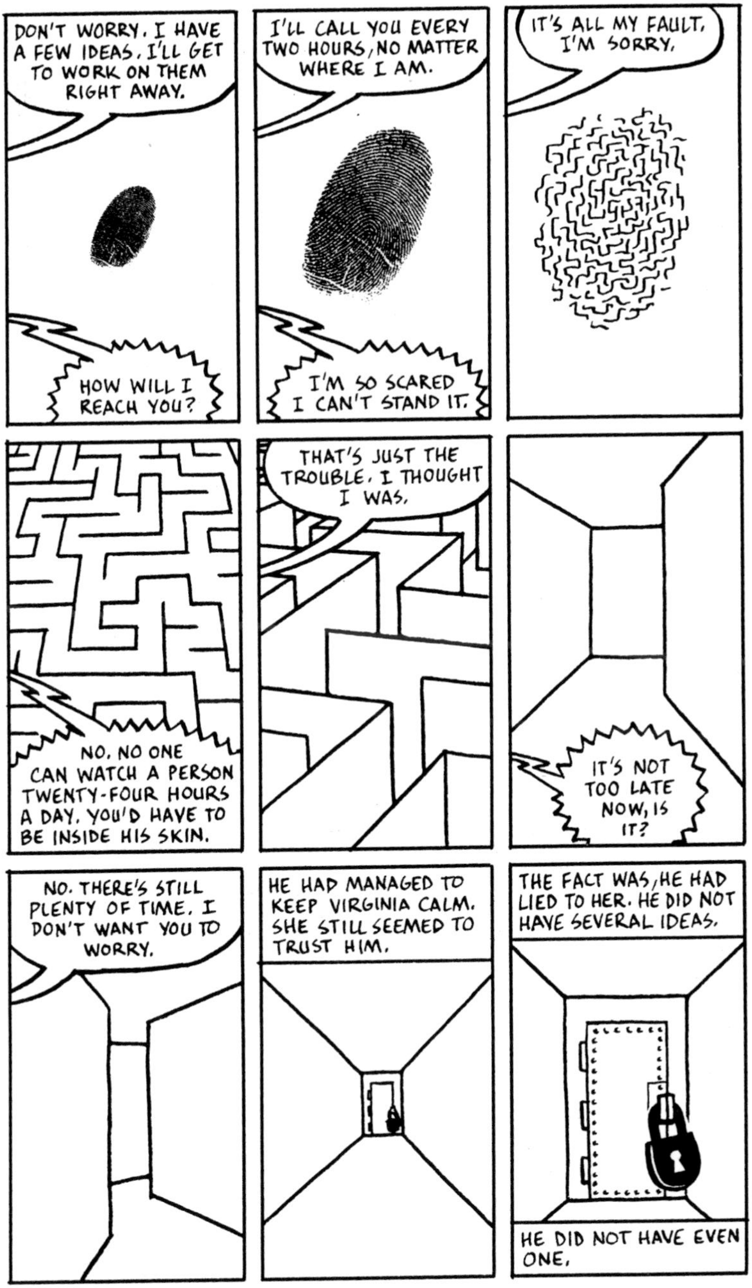
DON'T WORRY. I HAVE A FEW IDEAS. I'LL GET TO WORK ON THEM RIGHT AWAY.
HOW WILL I REACH YOU?
I'LL CALL YOU EVERY TWO HOURS, NO MATTER WHERE I AM.
I'M SO SCARED I CAN'T STAND IT.
IT'S ALL MY FAULT, I'M SORRY.
NO. NO ONE CAN WATCH A PERSON TWENTY-FOUR HOURS A DAY. YOU'D HAVE TO BE INSIDE HIS SKIN.
THAT'S JUST THE TROUBLE. I THOUGHT I WAS.
IT'S NOT TOO LATE NOW, IS IT?
NO. THERE'S STILL PLENTY OF TIME. I DON'T WANT YOU TO WORRY.
HE HAD MANAGED TO KEEP VIRGINIA CALM. SHE STILL SEEMED TO TRUST HIM.
THE FACT WAS, HE HAD LIED TO HER. HE DID NOT HAVE SEVERAL IDEAS.
HE DID NOT HAVE EVEN ONE.

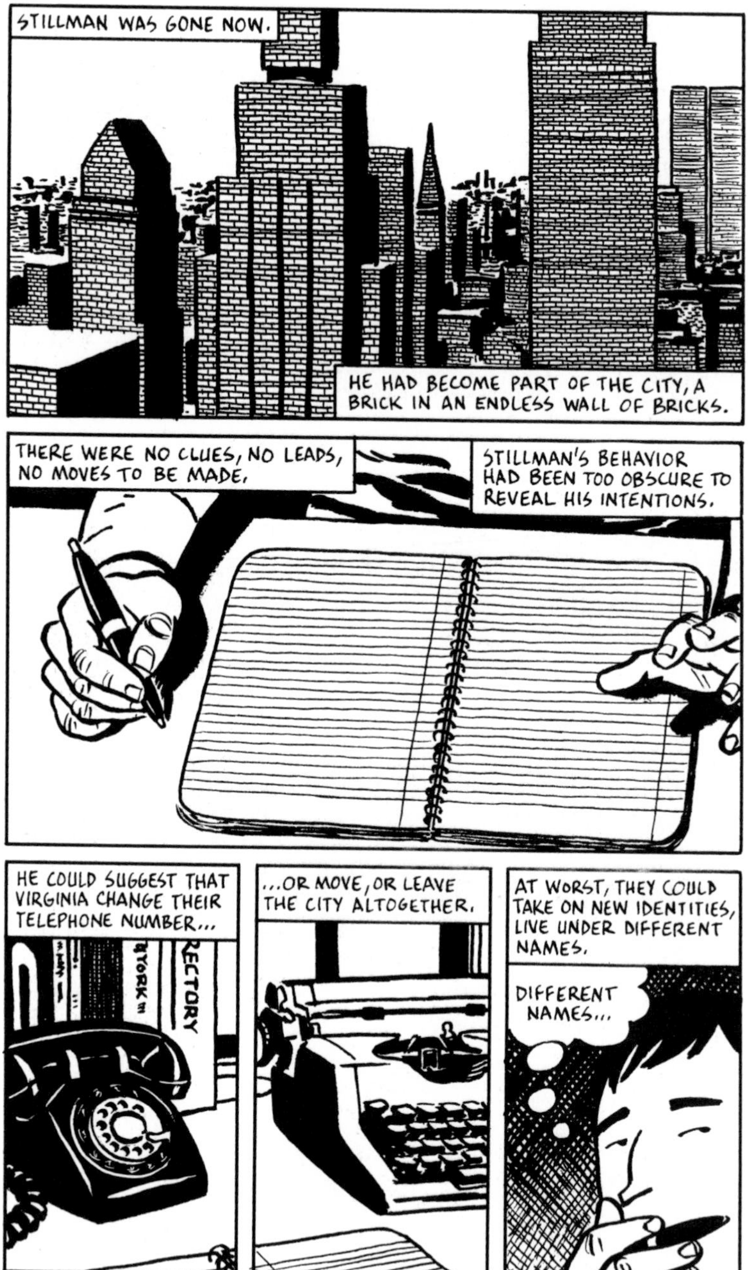
STILLMAN WAS GONE NOW.
HE HAD BECOME PART OF THE CITY, A BRICK IN AN ENDLESS WALL OF BRICKS.
THERE WERE NO CLUES, NO LEADS, NO MOVES TO BE MADE.
STILLMAN'S BEHAVIOR HAD BEEN TOO OBSCURE TO REVEAL HIS INTENTIONS.
HE COULD SUGGEST THAT VIRGINIA CHANGE THEIR TELEPHONE NUMBER...
...OR MOVE, OR LEAVE THE CITY ALTOGETHER.
AT WORST, THEY COULD TAKE ON NEW IDENTITIES, LIVE UNDER DIFFERENT NAMES.
DIFFERENT NAMES...

IF AUSTER IS AS GOOD AS THE STILLMANS THOUGHT, MAYBE HE CAN HELP.

QUINN WOULD MAKE A CLEAN BREAST OF IT, AUSTER WOULD FORGIVE HIM...

ONLY ONE AUSTER, ON RIVERSIDE DRIVE...

...AND TOGETHER THEY WOULD WORK TO SAVE PETER STILLMAN.

FOR A FEW BLOCKS HE WALKED AT THE OLD SHUFFLING PACE OF STILLMAN'S,

THE SPELL WAS OVER, AND YET HIS BODY DID NOT KNOW IT.

K. POLO

H. IRIS

P. AUSTER

MENARD

Hauser

BRRRRT

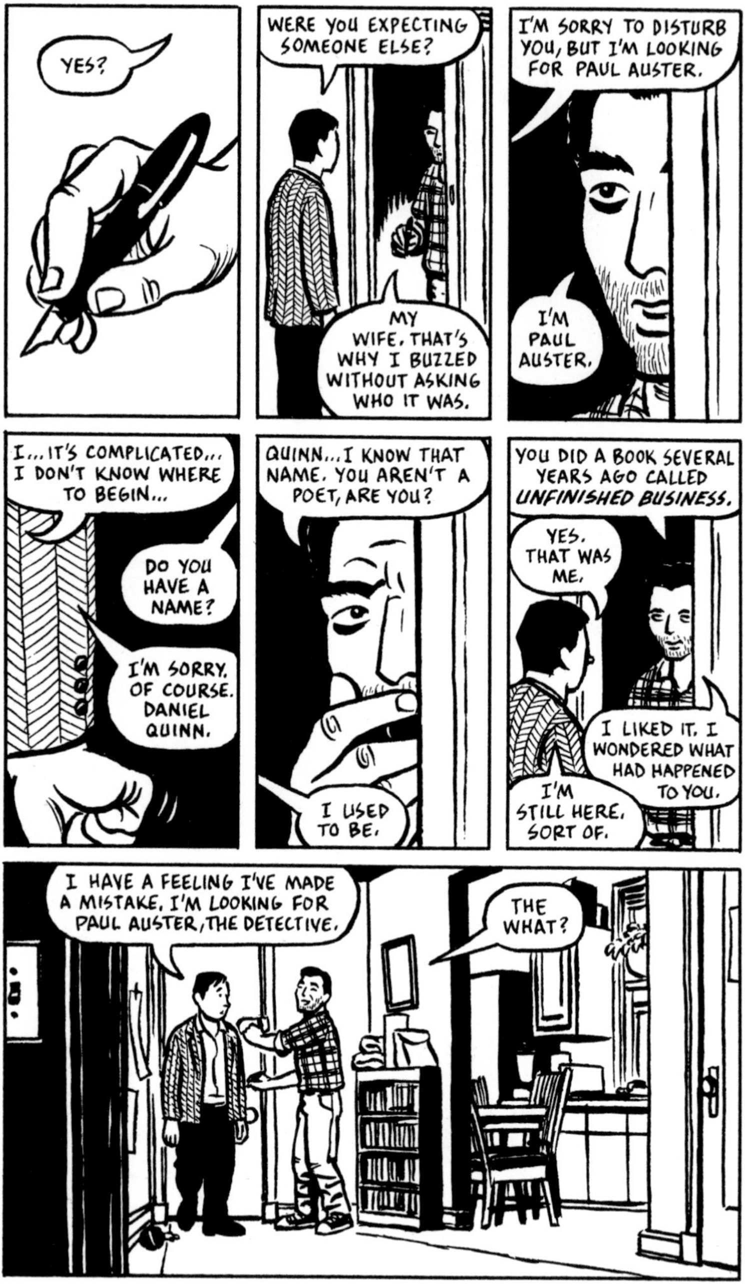
YES?
WERE YOU EXPECTING SOMEONE ELSE?
MY WIFE. THAT'S WHY I BUZZED WITHOUT ASKING WHO IT WAS.
I'M SORRY TO DISTURB YOU, BUT I'M LOOKING FOR PAUL AUSTER.
I'M PAUL AUSTER.
I... IT'S COMPLICATED... I DON'T KNOW WHERE TO BEGIN...
DO YOU HAVE A NAME?
I'M SORRY. OF COURSE. DANIEL QUINN.
QUINN... I KNOW THAT NAME. YOU AREN'T A POET, ARE YOU?
I USED TO BE.
YOU DID A BOOK SEVERAL YEARS AGO CALLED *UNFINISHED BUSINESS.*
YES. THAT WAS ME.
I LIKED IT. I WONDERED WHAT HAD HAPPENED TO YOU.
I'M STILL HERE. SORT OF.
I HAVE A FEELING I'VE MADE A MISTAKE. I'M LOOKING FOR PAUL AUSTER, THE DETECTIVE.
THE WHAT?

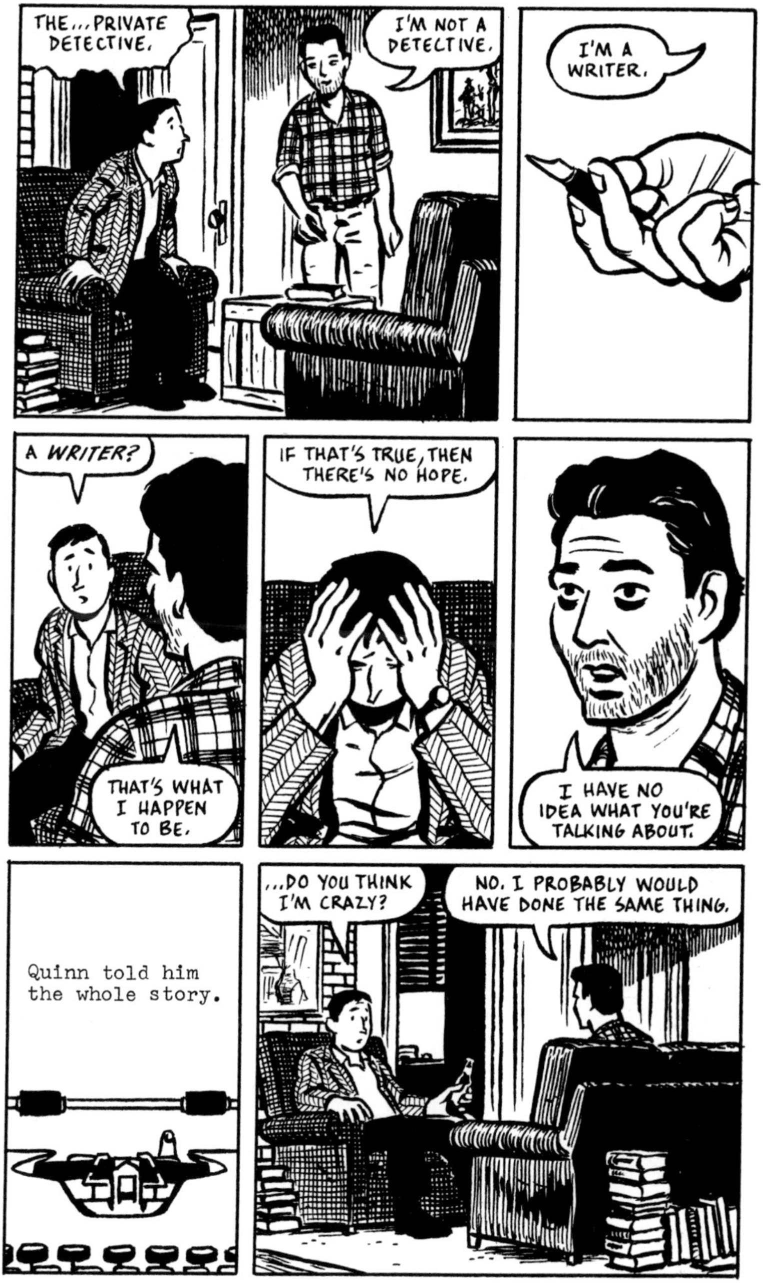
THE...PRIVATE DETECTIVE.
I'M NOT A DETECTIVE.
I'M A WRITER.
A WRITER?
THAT'S WHAT I HAPPEN TO BE.
IF THAT'S TRUE, THEN THERE'S NO HOPE.
I HAVE NO IDEA WHAT YOU'RE TALKING ABOUT.
Quinn told him the whole story.
...DO YOU THINK I'M CRAZY?
NO. I PROBABLY WOULD HAVE DONE THE SAME THING.

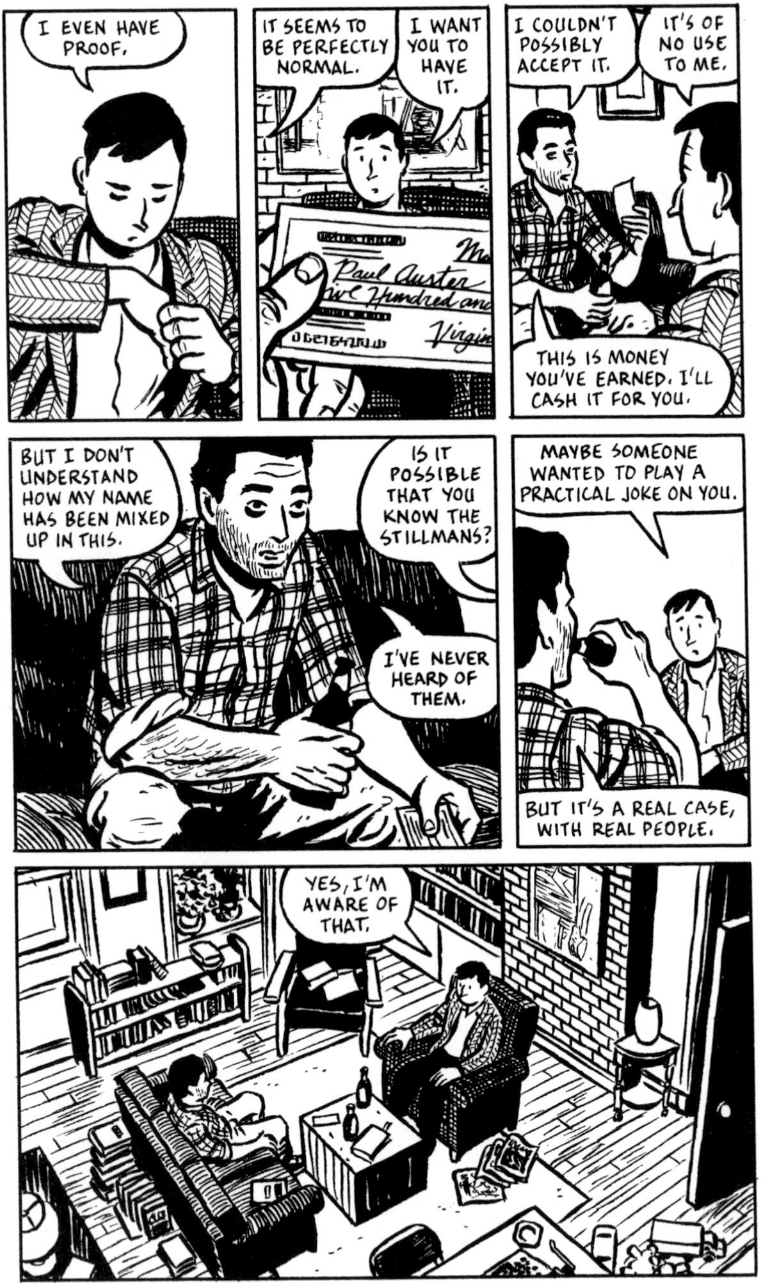
I EVEN HAVE PROOF.
IT SEEMS TO BE PERFECTLY NORMAL.
I WANT YOU TO HAVE IT.
Paul Auster
I COULDN'T POSSIBLY ACCEPT IT.
IT'S OF NO USE TO ME.
THIS IS MONEY YOU'VE EARNED. I'LL CASH IT FOR YOU.
BUT I DON'T UNDERSTAND HOW MY NAME HAS BEEN MIXED UP IN THIS.
IS IT POSSIBLE THAT YOU KNOW THE STILLMANS?
I'VE NEVER HEARD OF THEM.
MAYBE SOMEONE WANTED TO PLAY A PRACTICAL JOKE ON YOU.
BUT IT'S A REAL CASE, WITH REAL PEOPLE.
YES, I'M AWARE OF THAT.

HOW DOES A HAM OMELETTE SOUND?
I REALLY SHOULD BE GOING...
BUT YES, THANK YOU.
...BREAKING EGGS."
"YOU CAN'T MAKE AN OMELETTE WITHOUT BREAKING EGGS"
"YOU CAN'T MAKE AN OMELETTE WITHOU—"
BUSH MILLER
BUSH MILLER
QUINN TRIED TO REMAIN CALM...
...BUT TEARS LURKED MYSTERIOUSLY BEHIND HIS EYES.
SO...
...WHAT ARE YOU WORKING ON NOW?

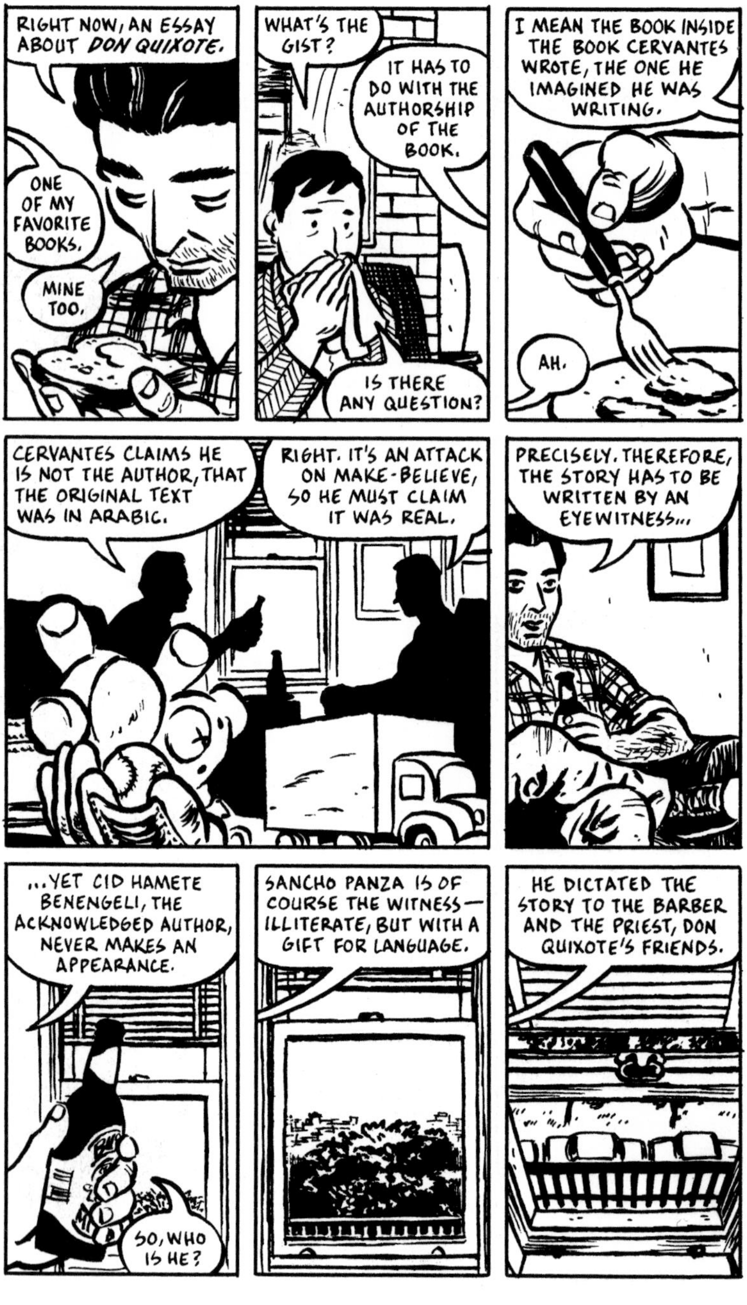
RIGHT NOW, AN ESSAY ABOUT *DON QUIXOTE*.
ONE OF MY FAVORITE BOOKS.
MINE TOO.
WHAT'S THE GIST?
IT HAS TO DO WITH THE AUTHORSHIP OF THE BOOK.
IS THERE ANY QUESTION?
I MEAN THE BOOK INSIDE THE BOOK CERVANTES WROTE, THE ONE HE IMAGINED HE WAS WRITING.
AH.
CERVANTES CLAIMS HE IS NOT THE AUTHOR, THAT THE ORIGINAL TEXT WAS IN ARABIC.
RIGHT. IT'S AN ATTACK ON MAKE-BELIEVE, SO HE MUST CLAIM IT WAS REAL.
PRECISELY. THEREFORE, THE STORY HAS TO BE WRITTEN BY AN EYEWITNESS...
...YET CID HAMETE BENENGELI, THE ACKNOWLEDGED AUTHOR, NEVER MAKES AN APPEARANCE.
SO, WHO IS HE?
SANCHO PANZA IS OF COURSE THE WITNESS— ILLITERATE, BUT WITH A GIFT FOR LANGUAGE.
HE DICTATED THE STORY TO THE BARBER AND THE PRIEST, DON QUIXOTE'S FRIENDS.

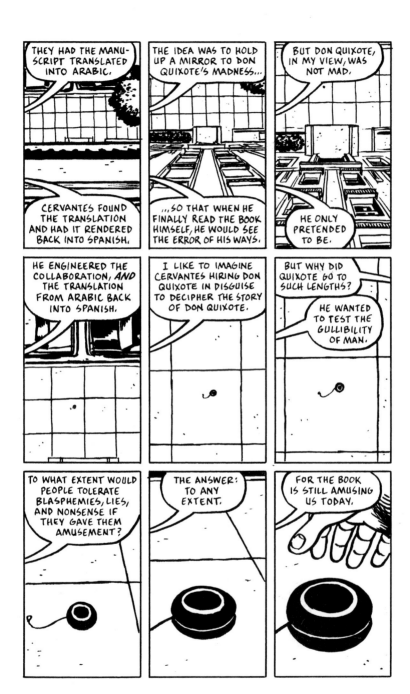

THEY HAD THE MANU-SCRIPT TRANSLATED INTO ARABIC.

THE IDEA WAS TO HOLD UP A MIRROR TO DON QUIXOTE'S MADNESS...

BUT DON QUIXOTE, IN MY VIEW, WAS NOT MAD.

CERVANTES FOUND THE TRANSLATION AND HAD IT RENDERED BACK INTO SPANISH.

...SO THAT WHEN HE FINALLY READ THE BOOK HIMSELF, HE WOULD SEE THE ERROR OF HIS WAYS.

HE ONLY PRETENDED TO BE.

HE ENGINEERED THE COLLABORATION, *AND* THE TRANSLATION FROM ARABIC BACK INTO SPANISH.

I LIKE TO IMAGINE CERVANTES HIRING DON QUIXOTE IN DISGUISE TO DECIPHER THE STORY OF DON QUIXOTE.

BUT WHY DID QUIXOTE GO TO SUCH LENGTHS?

HE WANTED TO TEST THE GULLIBILITY OF MAN.

TO WHAT EXTENT WOULD PEOPLE TOLERATE BLASPHEMIES, LIES, AND NONSENSE IF THEY GAVE THEM AMUSEMENT?

THE ANSWER: TO ANY EXTENT.

FOR THE BOOK IS STILL AMUSING US TODAY.

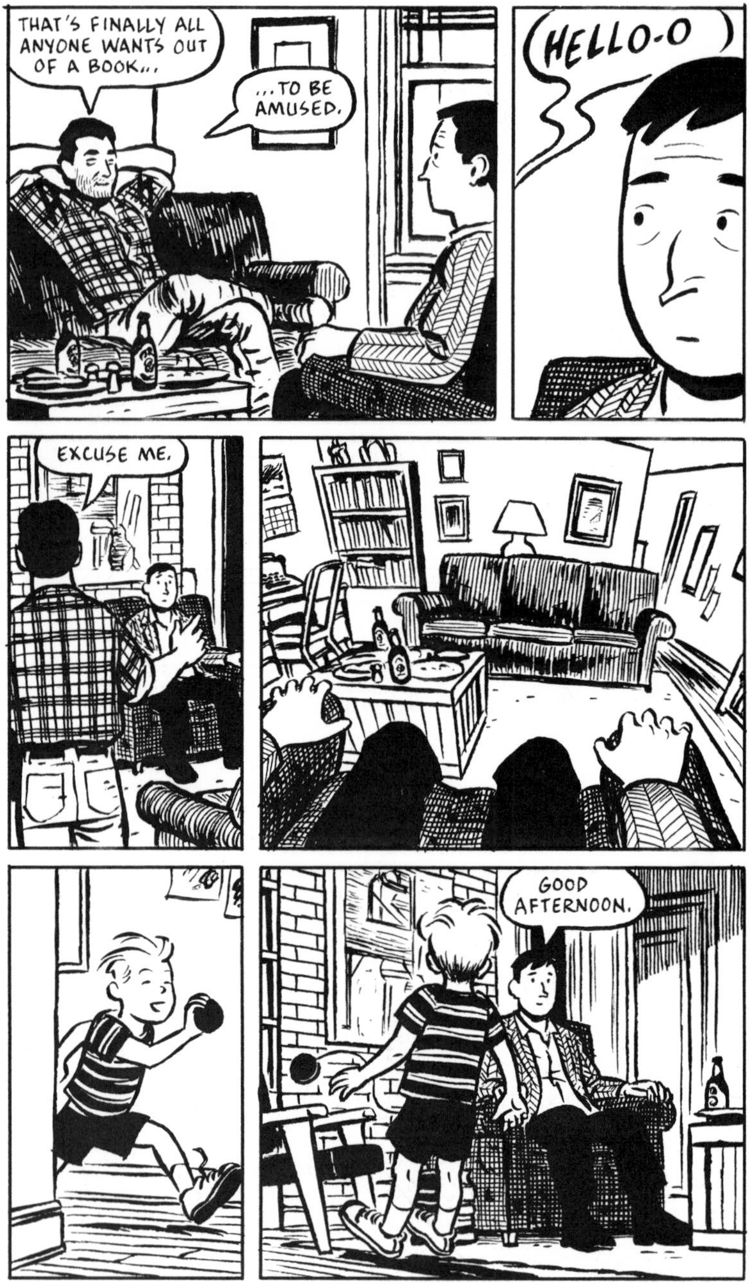
THAT'S FINALLY ALL ANYONE WANTS OUT OF A BOOK...
...TO BE AMUSED.
HELLO-O
EXCUSE ME.
GOOD AFTERNOON.

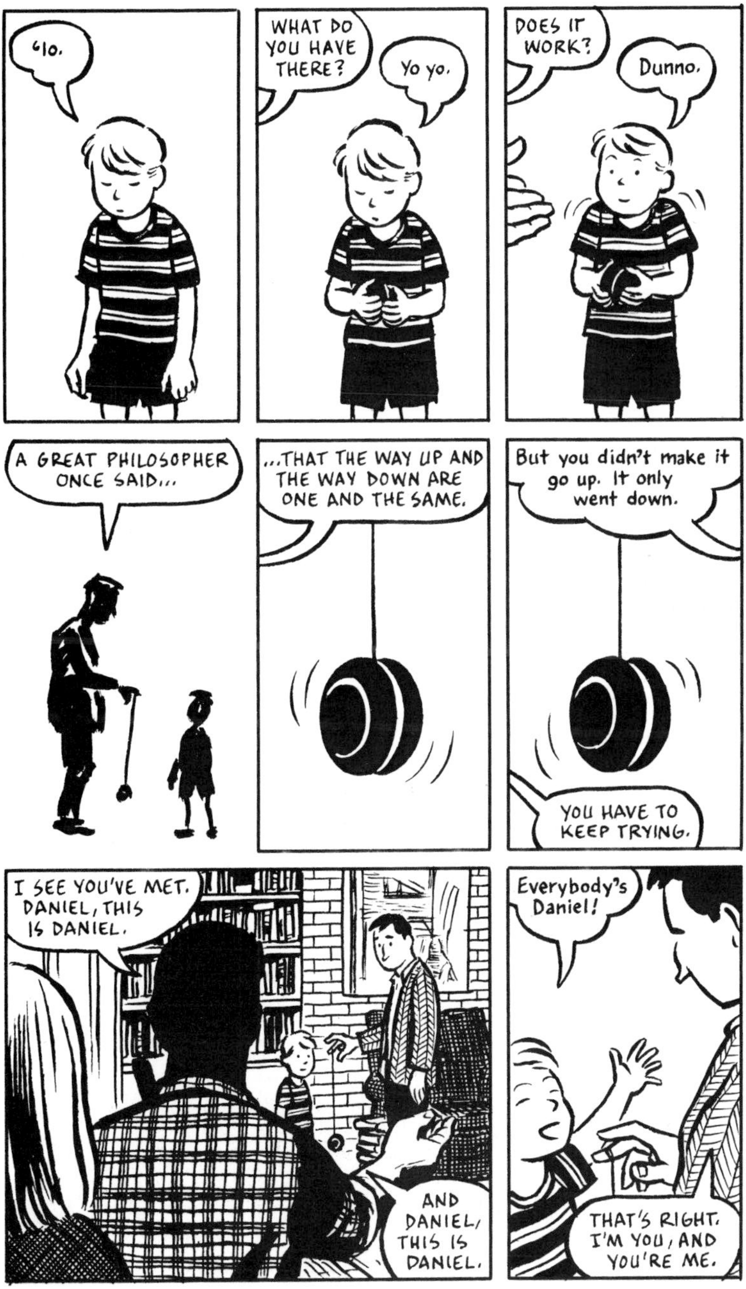
'lo.
WHAT DO YOU HAVE THERE?
Yo yo.
DOES IT WORK?
Dunno.
A GREAT PHILOSOPHER ONCE SAID...
...THAT THE WAY UP AND THE WAY DOWN ARE ONE AND THE SAME.
But you didn't make it go up. It only went down.
YOU HAVE TO KEEP TRYING.
I SEE YOU'VE MET. DANIEL, THIS IS DANIEL.
AND DANIEL, THIS IS DANIEL.
Everybody's Daniel!
THAT'S RIGHT. I'M YOU, AND YOU'RE ME.

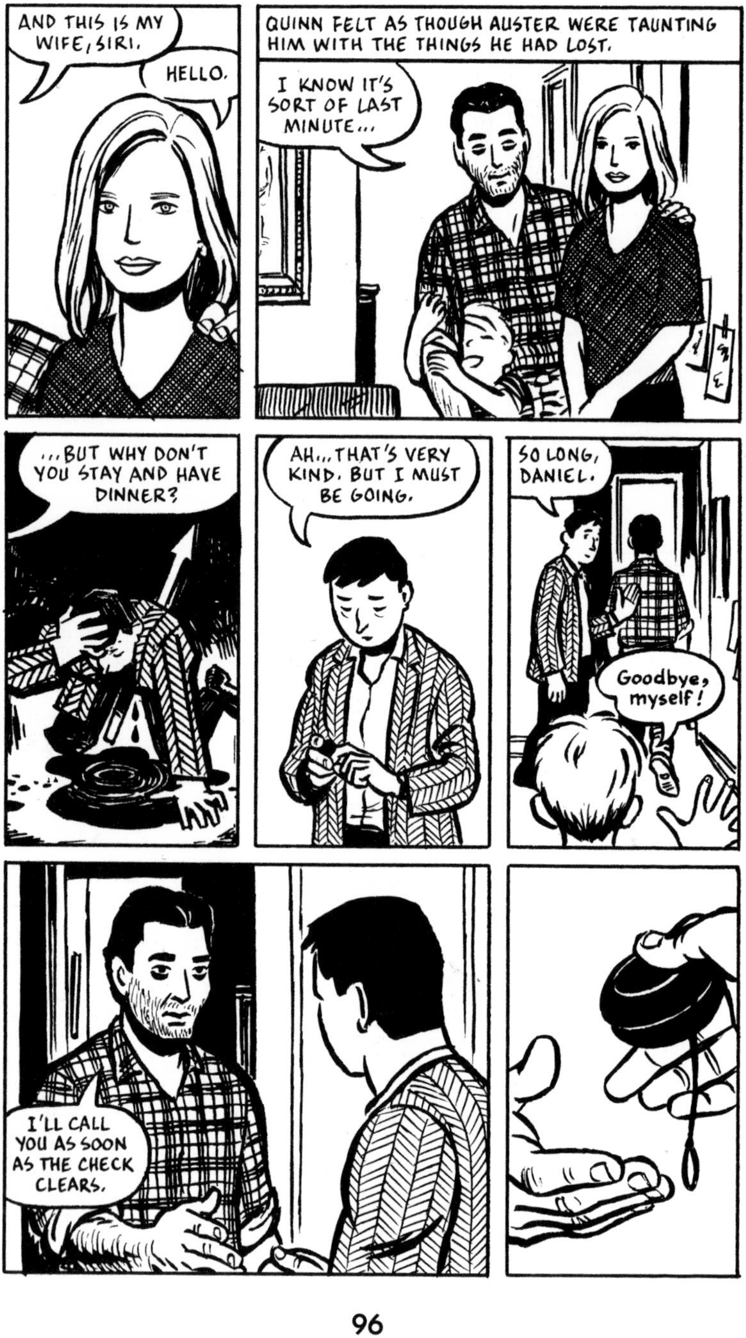
AND THIS IS MY WIFE, SIRI.
HELLO.
QUINN FELT AS THOUGH AUSTER WERE TAUNTING HIM WITH THE THINGS HE HAD LOST.
I KNOW IT'S SORT OF LAST MINUTE...
...BUT WHY DON'T YOU STAY AND HAVE DINNER?
AH...THAT'S VERY KIND. BUT I MUST BE GOING.
SO LONG, DANIEL.
Goodbye, myself!
I'LL CALL YOU AS SOON AS THE CHECK CLEARS.

QUINN WAS NOWHERE NOW.

IT'S JUNE SECOND.

HE HAD NOTHING, HE KNEW NOTHING.

THIS IS NEW YORK.

HE KNEW THAT HE KNEW NOTHING.

TOMORROW WILL BE JUNE THIRD.

BUT NOTHING IS CERTAIN.

HE HAD BEEN SENT BACK SO FAR BEFORE THE BEGINNING THAT IT WAS WORSE THAN ANY END HE COULD IMAGINE.

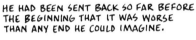

I COULD FORGET ABOUT THE CASE...

...GET BACK TO MY ROUTINE...

...WRITE ANOTHER BOOK...

...TAKE A TRIP.

THE HOUR HAD PASSED FOR HIS CALL TO VIRGINIA.

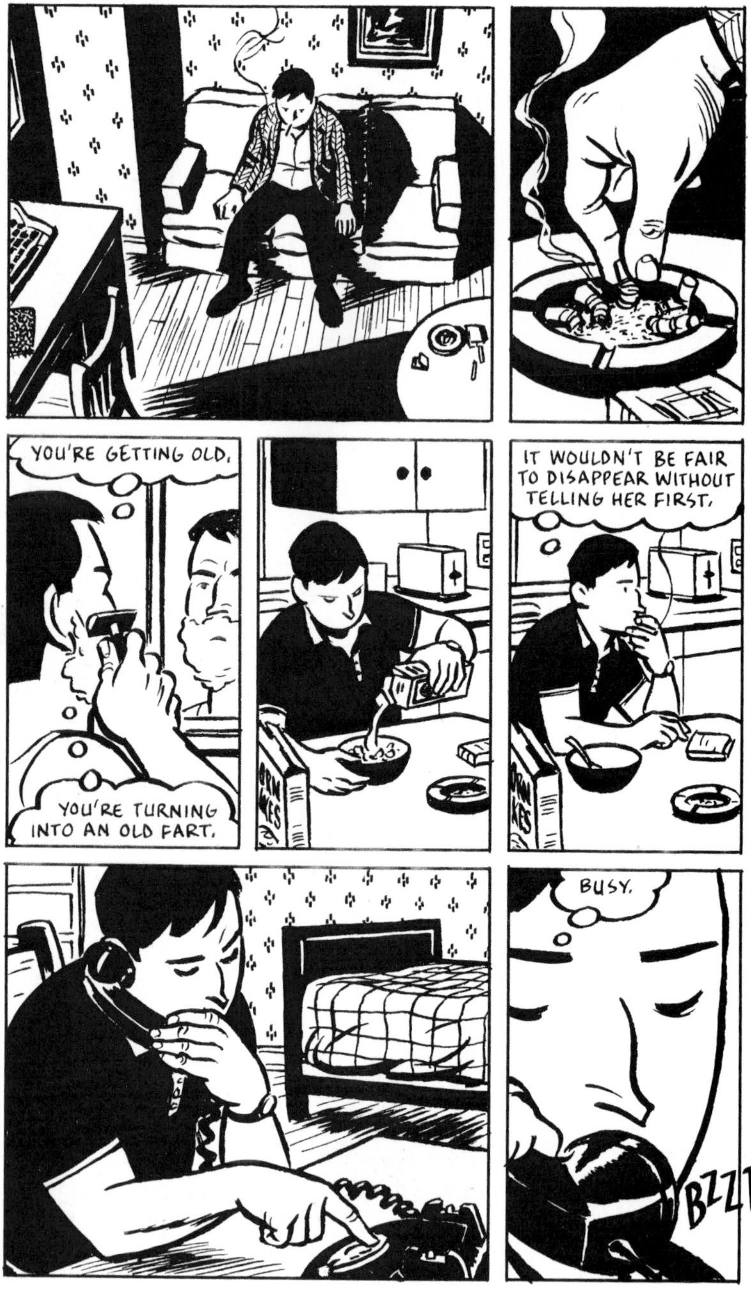
YOU'RE GETTING OLD.
YOU'RE TURNING INTO AN OLD FART.
IT WOULDN'T BE FAIR TO DISAPPEAR WITHOUT TELLING HER FIRST.
BUSY.
BZZT

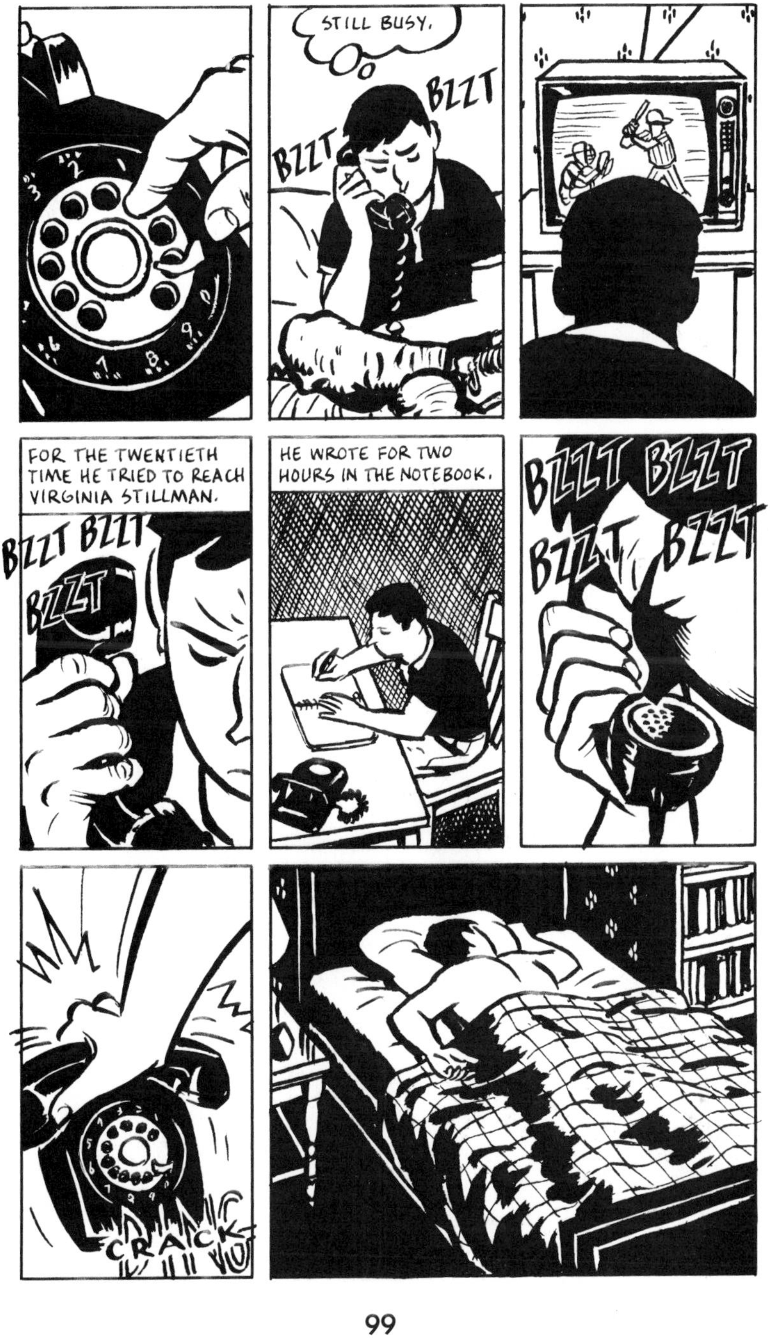
STILL BUSY.
BZZT
BZZT
FOR THE TWENTIETH TIME HE TRIED TO REACH VIRGINIA STILLMAN.
BZZT BZZT
BZZT
HE WROTE FOR TWO HOURS IN THE NOTEBOOK.
BZZT BZZT
BZZT BZZT
CRACK

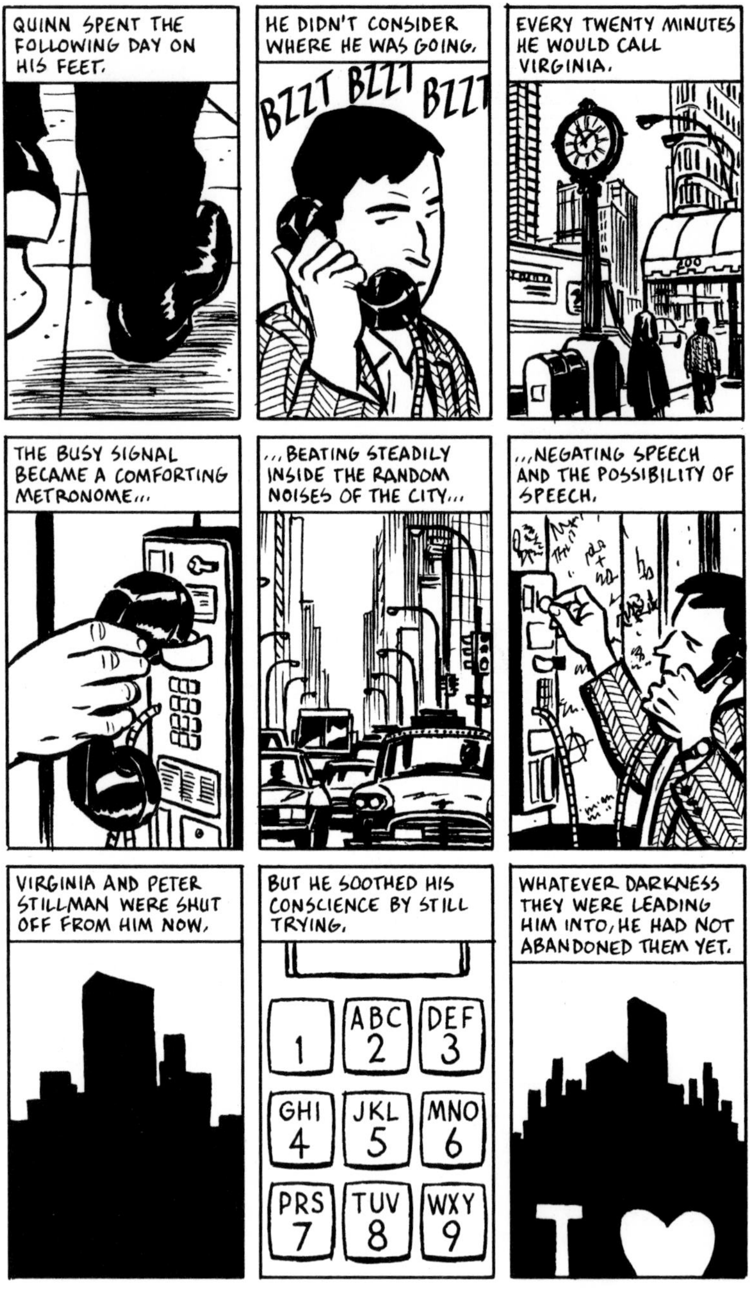
QUINN SPENT THE FOLLOWING DAY ON HIS FEET.
HE DIDN'T CONSIDER WHERE HE WAS GOING.
BZZT BZZT BZZT
EVERY TWENTY MINUTES HE WOULD CALL VIRGINIA.
THE BUSY SIGNAL BECAME A COMFORTING METRONOME...
...BEATING STEADILY INSIDE THE RANDOM NOISES OF THE CITY...
...NEGATING SPEECH AND THE POSSIBILITY OF SPEECH.
VIRGINIA AND PETER STILLMAN WERE SHUT OFF FROM HIM NOW.
BUT HE SOOTHED HIS CONSCIENCE BY STILL TRYING.
ABC DEF
1 2 3
GHI JKL MNO
4 5 6
PRS TUV WXY
7 8 9
WHATEVER DARKNESS THEY WERE LEADING HIM INTO, HE HAD NOT ABANDONED THEM YET.

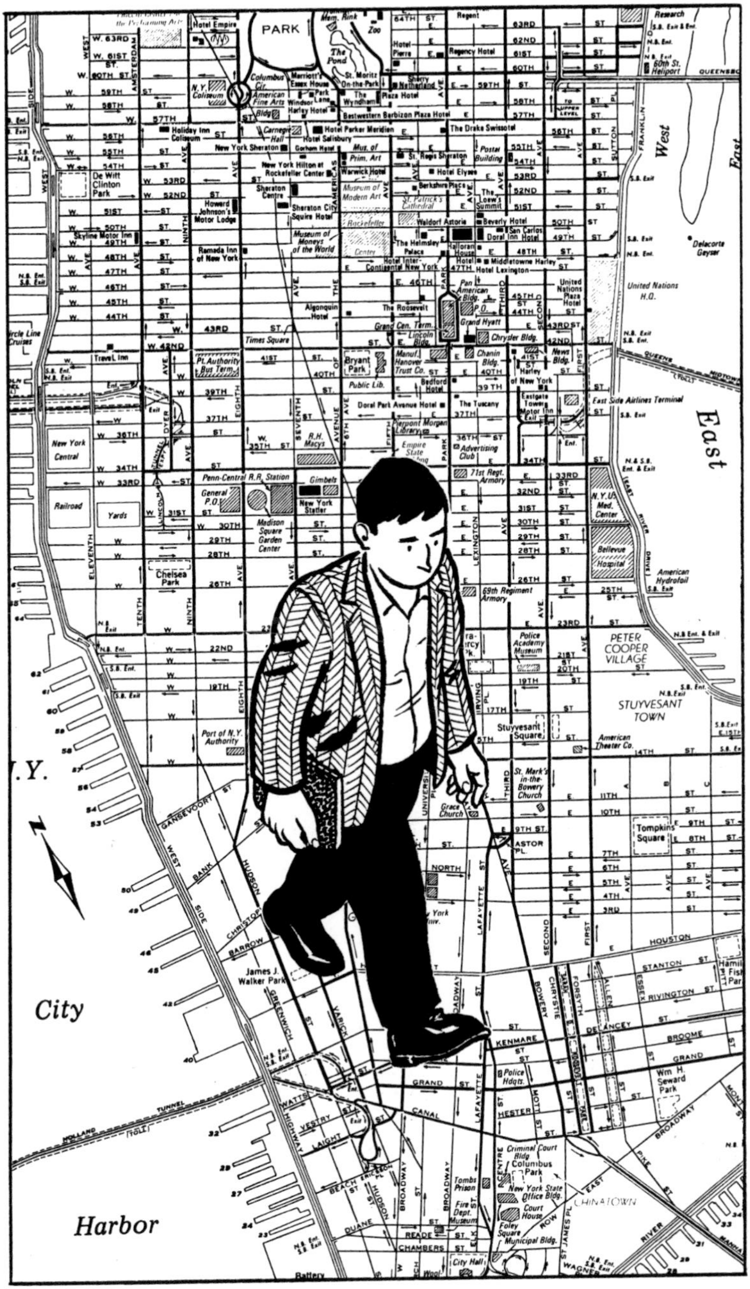
PARK
Hotel Empire
Columbus Cir.
N.Y. Coliseum
American Fine Arts Bldg.
Marriott's Essex House
St. Moritz On-the-Park
The Pond
Zoo
Hotel Pierre
Regency Hotel
Sherry Netherland
Plaza Hotel
The Wyndham
Windsor Harley Hotel
Bestwestern Barbizon Plaza Hotel
Research
60th St. Heliport
QUEENSBORO
Hotel Parker Meridien
The Drake Swissotel
Holiday Inn Coliseum
Carnegie Hall
Hotel Salisbury
New York Sheraton
Gorham Hotel
Mus. of Prim. Art
St. Regis Sheraton
Postal Building
New York Hilton at Rockefeller Center
Warwick Hotel
Hotel Elysee
De Witt Clinton Park
Sheraton Centre
Museum of Modern Art
Berkshire Place
The Loew's Summit
Howard Johnson's Motor Lodge
Sheraton City Squire Hotel
St. Patrick's Cathedral
Waldorf Astoria
Beverly Hotel
San Carlos Doral Inn Hotel
Skyline Motor Inn
Museum of Moneys of the World
Rockefeller Center
The Helmsley Palace
Halloran House
Delacorte Geyser
Ramada Inn of New York
Hotel Inter-Continental New York
Middletowne Harley
Hotel Lexington
United Nations Plaza Hotel
United Nations H.Q.
Pan American Bldg.
P.O.
Algonquin Hotel
The Roosevelt
Grand Hyatt
Circle Line Cruises
Times Square
Grand Cen. Term.
Lincoln Bldg.
Chrysler Bldg.
TravL Inn
Pt. Authority Bus Term.
Bryant Park
Manuf. Hanover Trust Co.
Chanin Bldg.
Harley of New York
News Bldg.
Public Lib.
Bedford Hotel
Doral Park Avenue Hotel
The Tuscany
Eastgate Tower Motor Inn
East Side Airlines Terminal
East
R.H. Macys
Pierpont Morgan Library
Empire State
Advertising Club
New York Central
Railroad
Yards
Penn-Central R.R. Station
Gimbels
General P.O.
New York Statler
71st Regt. Armory
Madison Square Garden Center
N.Y.U. Med. Center
Bellevue Hospital
American Hydrofoil
Chelsea Park
69th Regiment Armory
Police Academy Museum
PETER COOPER VILLAGE
STUYVESANT TOWN
Stuyvesant Square
Port of N.Y. Authority
American Theater Co.
N.Y.
St. Mark's in-the-Bowery Church
Grace Church
Tompkins Square
ASTOR PL.
GANSEVOORT
BANK
HUDSON
CHRISTOPHER
BARROW
James J. Walker Park
HOUSTON
STANTON
RIVINGTON
DELANCEY
KENMARE
BROOME
GRAND
Wm H. Seward Park
City
Police Hdqts.
CANAL
HESTER
HOLLAND TUNNEL
Criminal Court Bldg.
Columbus Park
New York State Office Bldg.
Court House
CHINATOWN
Tombs Prison
Fire Dept. Museum
Foley Square
Municipal Bldg.
Harbor
DUANE
READE
CHAMBERS
City Hall
Battery
EAST RIVER
BROADWAY
BOWERY

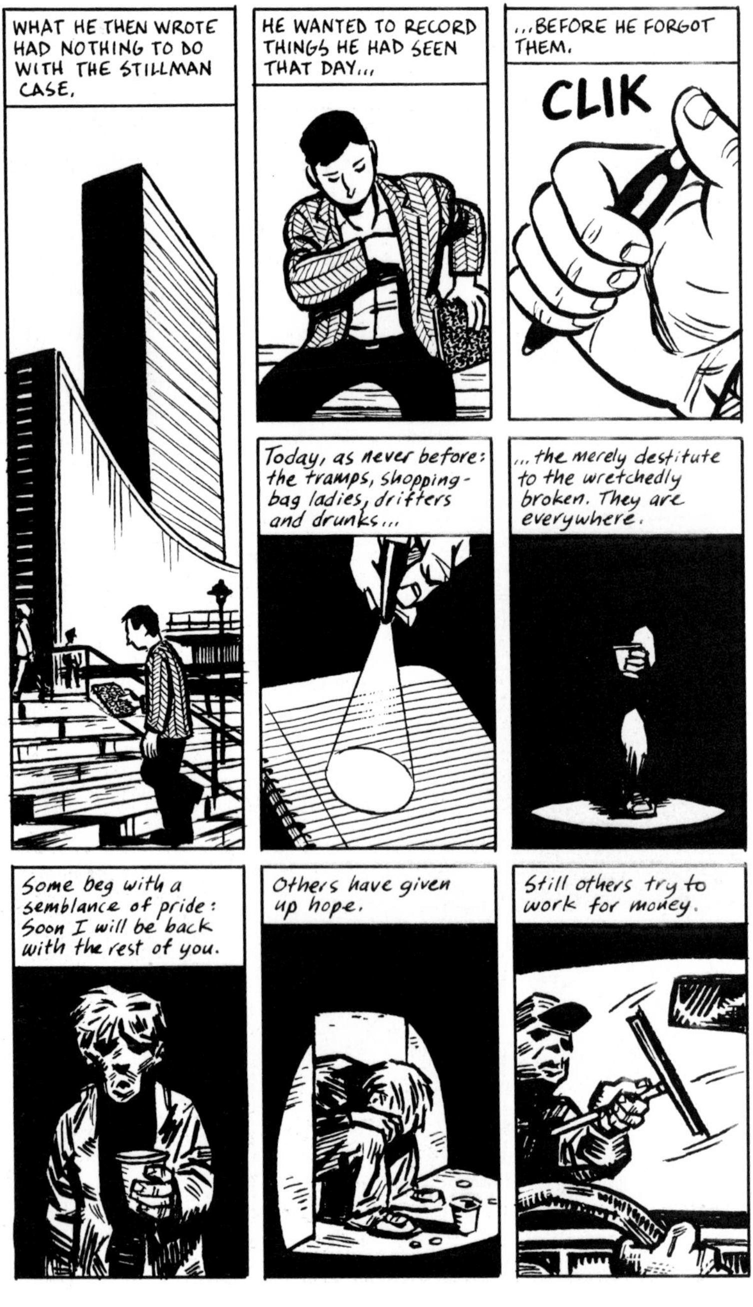
WHAT HE THEN WROTE HAD NOTHING TO DO WITH THE STILLMAN CASE.
HE WANTED TO RECORD THINGS HE HAD SEEN THAT DAY...
...BEFORE HE FORGOT THEM.
CLIK
Today, as never before: the tramps, shopping-bag ladies, drifters and drunks...
...the merely destitute to the wretchedly broken. They are everywhere.
Some beg with a semblance of pride: Soon I will be back with the rest of you.
Others have given up hope.
Still others try to work for money.

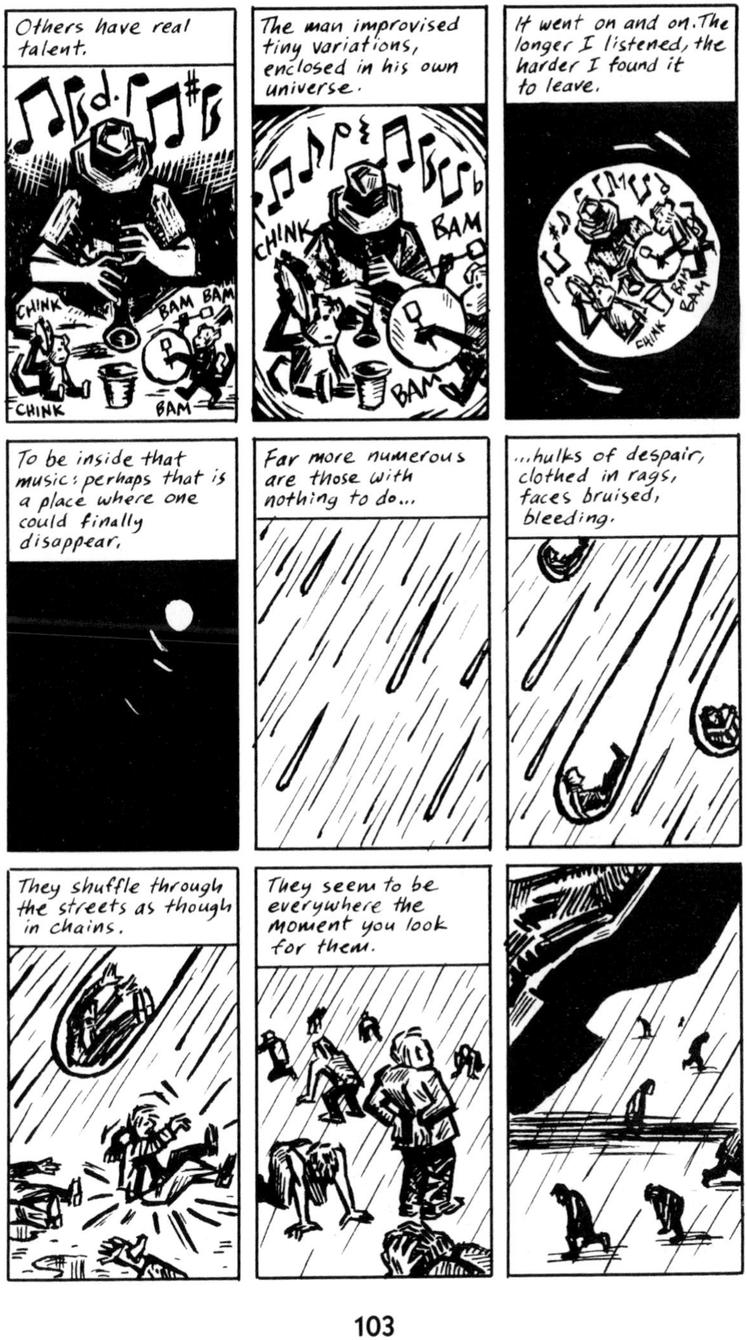
Others have real talent.
CHINK
BAM BAM
CHINK
BAM
The man improvised tiny variations, enclosed in his own universe.
CHINK
BAM
BAM
It went on and on. The longer I listened, the harder I found it to leave.
BAM
BAM
CHINK
To be inside that music: perhaps that is a place where one could finally disappear.
Far more numerous are those with nothing to do...
...hulks of despair, clothed in rags, faces bruised, bleeding.
They shuffle through the streets as though in chains.
They seem to be everywhere the moment you look for them.

There are others locked inside madness—

TAKA TAKA TAKA T

—unable to exit the world that stands at the threshold of their bodies.

TUNG TU

KA TAK TAKA TAK

Perhaps if he stopped drumming, the city would fall apart.

TAK
TANG

TAK TAKA TAKA

There are those forever on the move, as if it mattered where they were.

AND WHAT IF I DON'T WANT TO? WHAT IF I JUST DON'T WANT

Baudelaire: Il me semble que je serais toujours bien là où je ne suis pas.

"It seems to me that I will always be happy in the place where I am not."

Or, more bluntly: Wherever I am not is the place where I am myself.

104

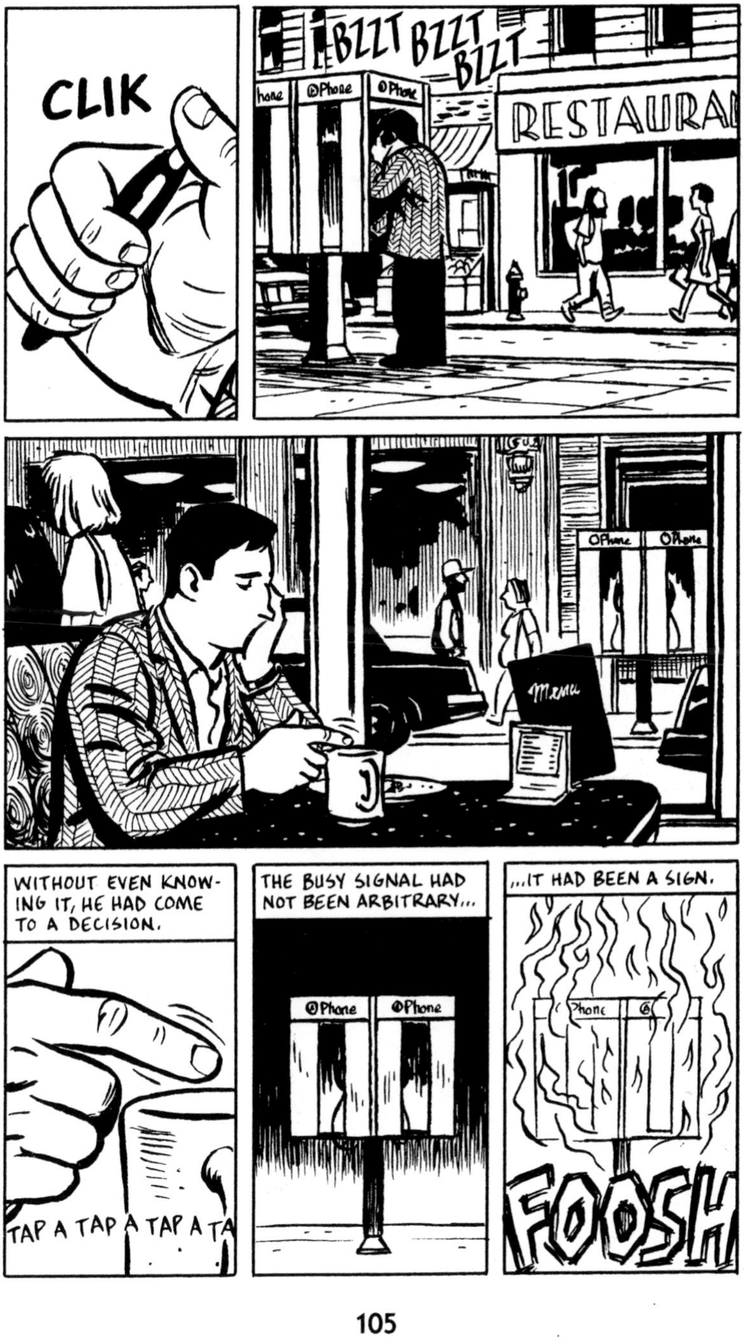
CLIK
BZZT BZZT BZZT
Phone
Phone
Phone
RESTAURA
Phone
Phone
Menu
WITHOUT EVEN KNOWING IT, HE HAD COME TO A DECISION.
TAP A TAP A TAP A TA
THE BUSY SIGNAL HAD NOT BEEN ARBITRARY...
Phone
Phone
...IT HAD BEEN A SIGN.
Phone
FOOSH

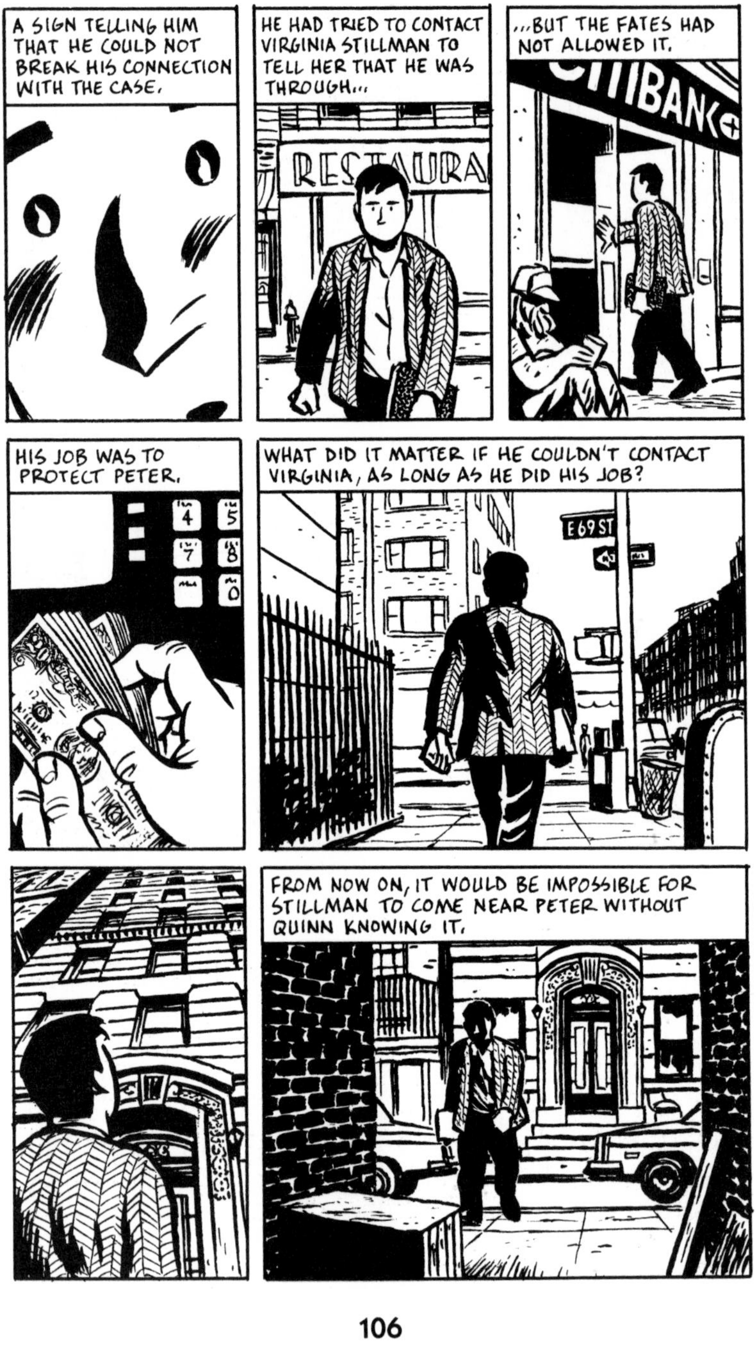
A SIGN TELLING HIM THAT HE COULD NOT BREAK HIS CONNECTION WITH THE CASE.
HE HAD TRIED TO CONTACT VIRGINIA STILLMAN TO TELL HER THAT HE WAS THROUGH...
RESTAURA
...BUT THE FATES HAD NOT ALLOWED IT.
ITIBANK
HIS JOB WAS TO PROTECT PETER.
WHAT DID IT MATTER IF HE COULDN'T CONTACT VIRGINIA, AS LONG AS HE DID HIS JOB?
E 69 ST
FROM NOW ON, IT WOULD BE IMPOSSIBLE FOR STILLMAN TO COME NEAR PETER WITHOUT QUINN KNOWING IT.

A LONG TIME PASSED. WEEKS, PERHAPS MONTHS.

The account of this period is less full than the author would have liked.

Facts are scarce, and even the notebook, which has provided much information, is suspect.

We cannot say for certain what happened to Quinn during this period.

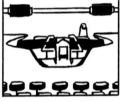

For it is at this point in the story that he began to lose his grip.

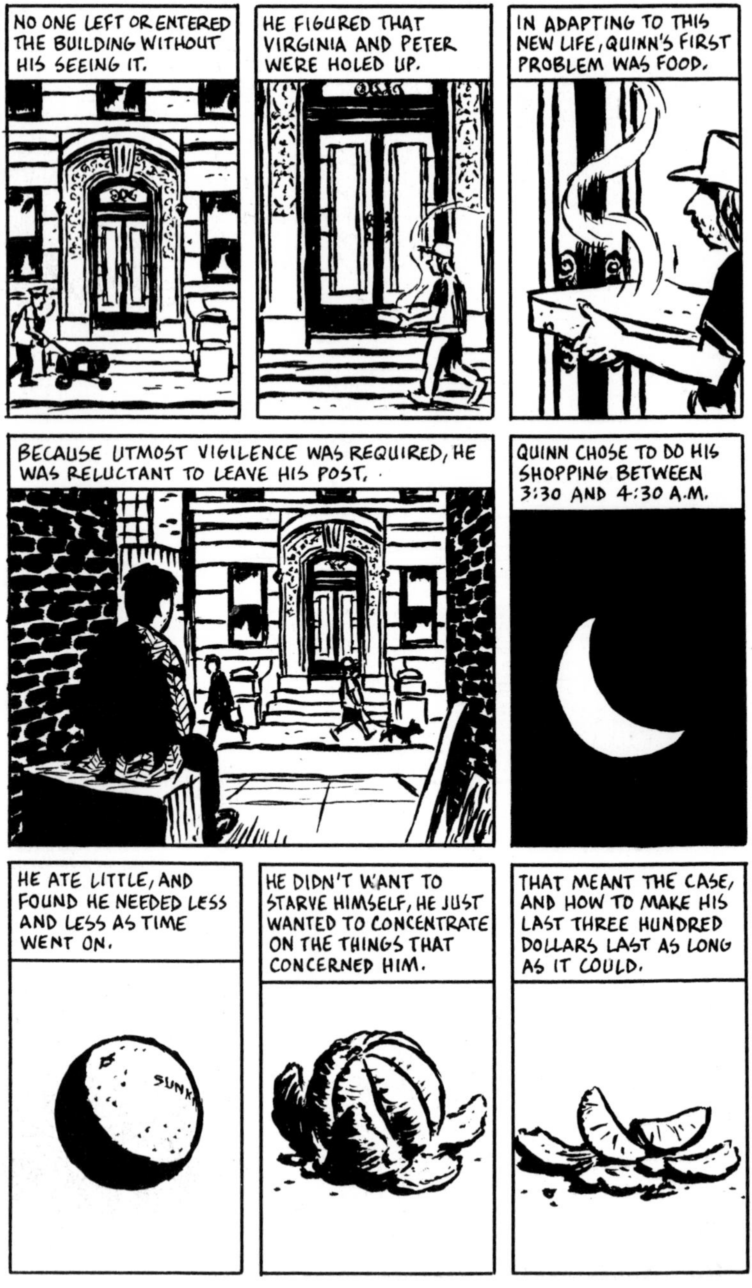
NO ONE LEFT OR ENTERED THE BUILDING WITHOUT HIS SEEING IT.
HE FIGURED THAT VIRGINIA AND PETER WERE HOLED UP.
IN ADAPTING TO THIS NEW LIFE, QUINN'S FIRST PROBLEM WAS FOOD.
BECAUSE UTMOST VIGILENCE WAS REQUIRED, HE WAS RELUCTANT TO LEAVE HIS POST.
QUINN CHOSE TO DO HIS SHOPPING BETWEEN 3:30 AND 4:30 A.M.
HE ATE LITTLE, AND FOUND HE NEEDED LESS AND LESS AS TIME WENT ON.
HE DIDN'T WANT TO STARVE HIMSELF, HE JUST WANTED TO CONCENTRATE ON THE THINGS THAT CONCERNED HIM.
THAT MEANT THE CASE, AND HOW TO MAKE HIS LAST THREE HUNDRED DOLLARS LAST AS LONG AS IT COULD.

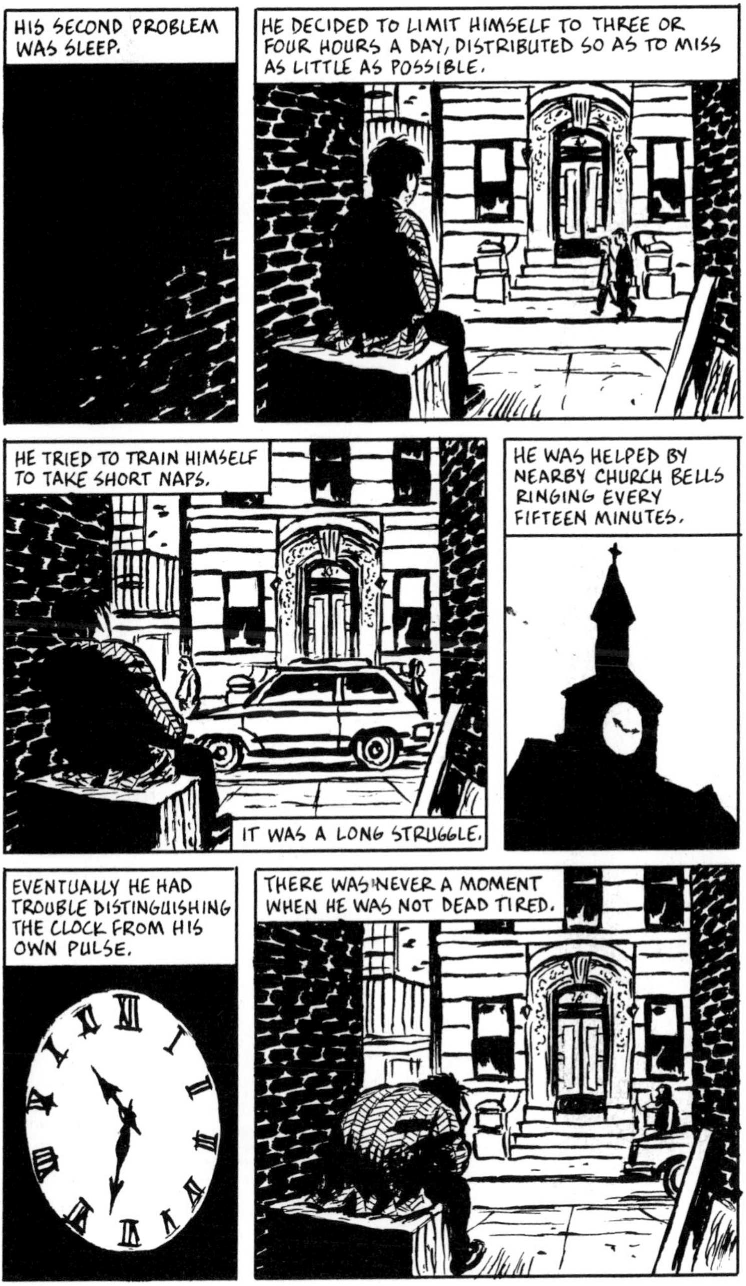
HIS SECOND PROBLEM WAS SLEEP.
HE DECIDED TO LIMIT HIMSELF TO THREE OR FOUR HOURS A DAY, DISTRIBUTED SO AS TO MISS AS LITTLE AS POSSIBLE.
HE TRIED TO TRAIN HIMSELF TO TAKE SHORT NAPS.
IT WAS A LONG STRUGGLE.
HE WAS HELPED BY NEARBY CHURCH BELLS RINGING EVERY FIFTEEN MINUTES.
EVENTUALLY HE HAD TROUBLE DISTINGUISHING THE CLOCK FROM HIS OWN PULSE.
THERE WAS NEVER A MOMENT WHEN HE WAS NOT DEAD TIRED.

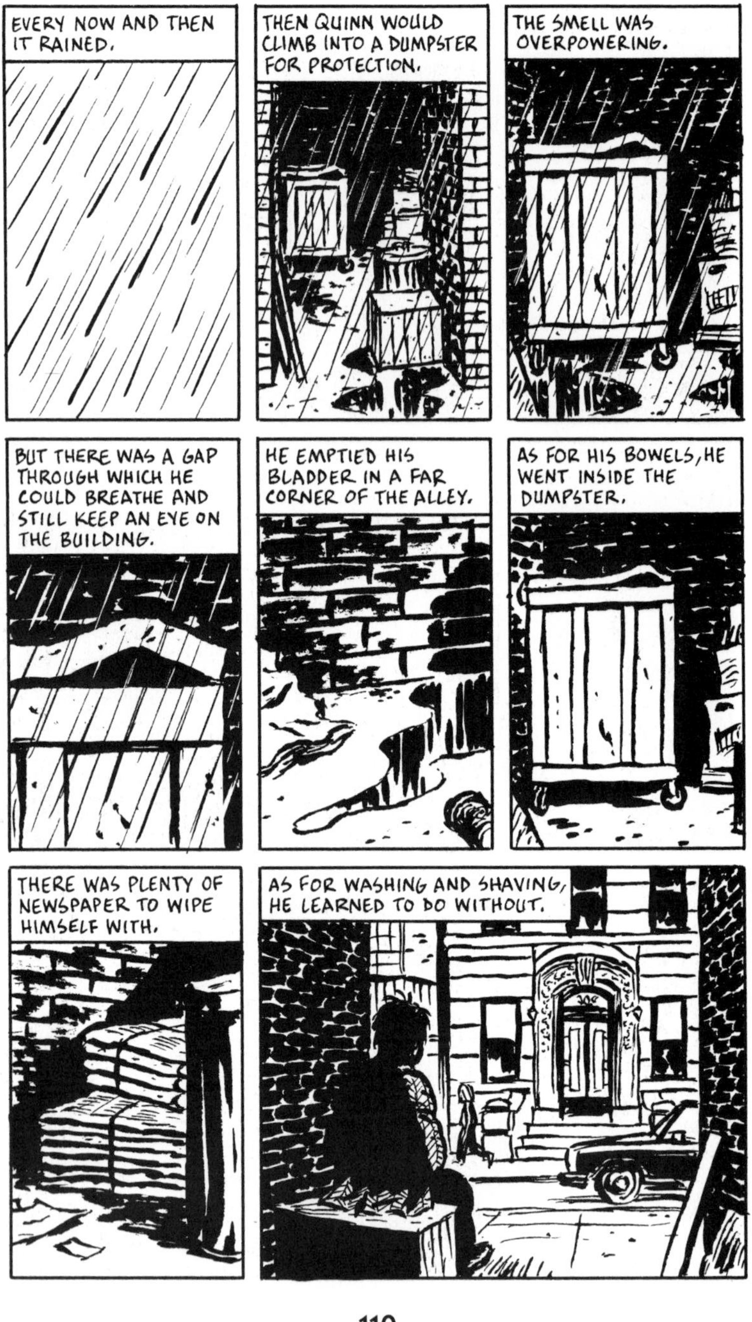
EVERY NOW AND THEN IT RAINED.
THEN QUINN WOULD CLIMB INTO A DUMPSTER FOR PROTECTION.
THE SMELL WAS OVERPOWERING.
BUT THERE WAS A GAP THROUGH WHICH HE COULD BREATHE AND STILL KEEP AN EYE ON THE BUILDING.
HE EMPTIED HIS BLADDER IN A FAR CORNER OF THE ALLEY.
AS FOR HIS BOWELS, HE WENT INSIDE THE DUMPSTER.
THERE WAS PLENTY OF NEWSPAPER TO WIPE HIMSELF WITH.
AS FOR WASHING AND SHAVING, HE LEARNED TO DO WITHOUT.

HOW HE MANAGED TO KEEP HIMSELF HIDDEN IS A MYSTERY.

BUT IT SEEMS THAT NO ONE DISCOVERED HIM.

IT WAS AS THOUGH HE HAD MELTED INTO THE WALLS OF THE CITY.

QUINN HAD ALWAYS THOUGHT OF HIMSELF AS A MAN WHO LIKED TO BE ALONE.

NOW HE BEGAN TO UNDERSTAND THE TRUE NATURE OF SOLITUDE.

AND OF ONE THING HE HAD NO DOUBT: HE WAS FALLING.

AND IF HE WAS FALLING, HOW COULD HE CATCH HIMSELF AS WELL?

WAS IT POSSIBLE TO BE AT THE TOP AND THE BOTTOM AT THE SAME TIME?

IT DID NOT SEEM TO MAKE SENSE.

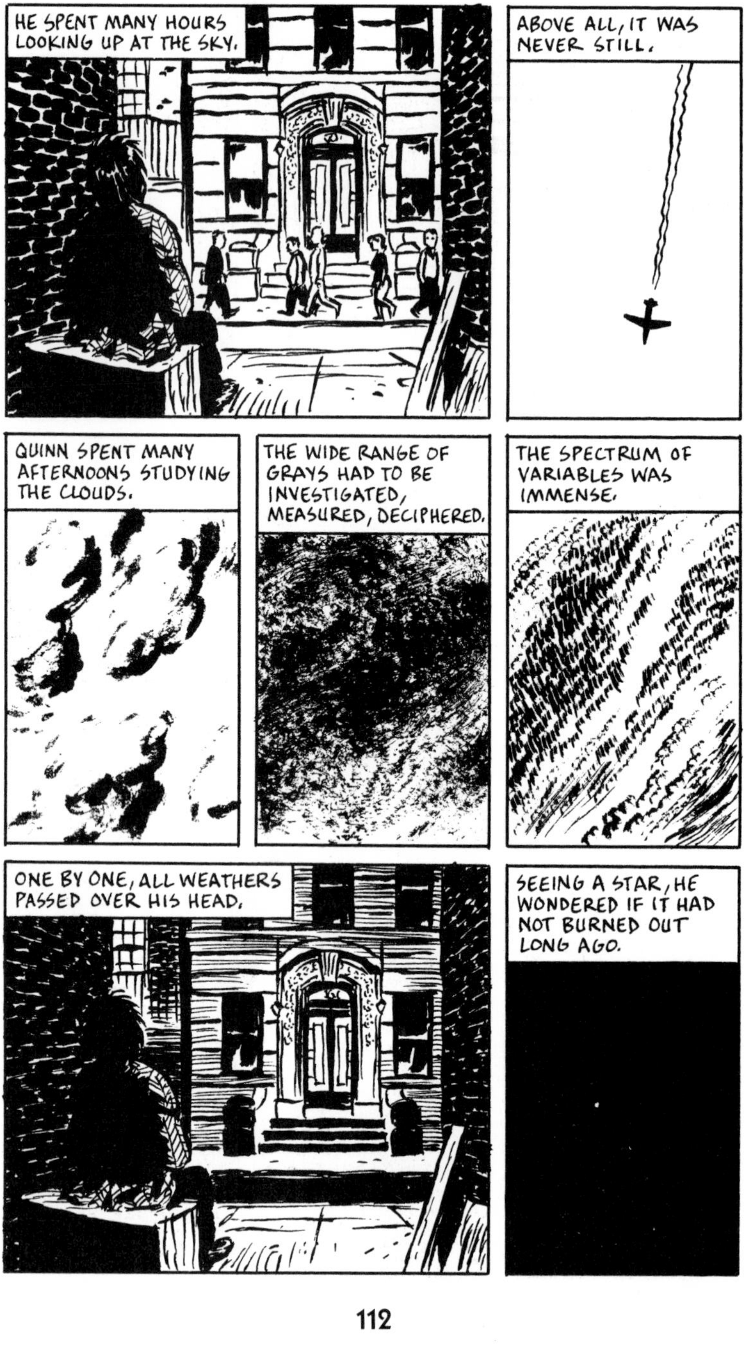
HE SPENT MANY HOURS LOOKING UP AT THE SKY.
ABOVE ALL, IT WAS NEVER STILL.
QUINN SPENT MANY AFTERNOONS STUDYING THE CLOUDS.
THE WIDE RANGE OF GRAYS HAD TO BE INVESTIGATED, MEASURED, DECIPHERED.
THE SPECTRUM OF VARIABLES WAS IMMENSE.
ONE BY ONE, ALL WEATHERS PASSED OVER HIS HEAD.
SEEING A STAR, HE WONDERED IF IT HAD NOT BURNED OUT LONG AGO.

THE DAYS THEREFORE CAME AND WENT.

STILLMAN DID NOT APPEAR.

QUINN'S MONEY RAN OUT AT LAST.

IT WAS SOME TIME IN MID-AUGUST.

HE WAS CERTAIN THAT MONEY HAD ARRIVED FOR HIM.

IT WAS JUST A MATTER OF GOING TO HIS POST OFFICE BOX.

HE COULD BE BACK IN A FEW HOURS.

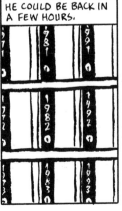

WE WILL NEVER KNOW THE AGONIES HE SUFFERED AT HAVING TO LEAVE HIS SPOT.

113

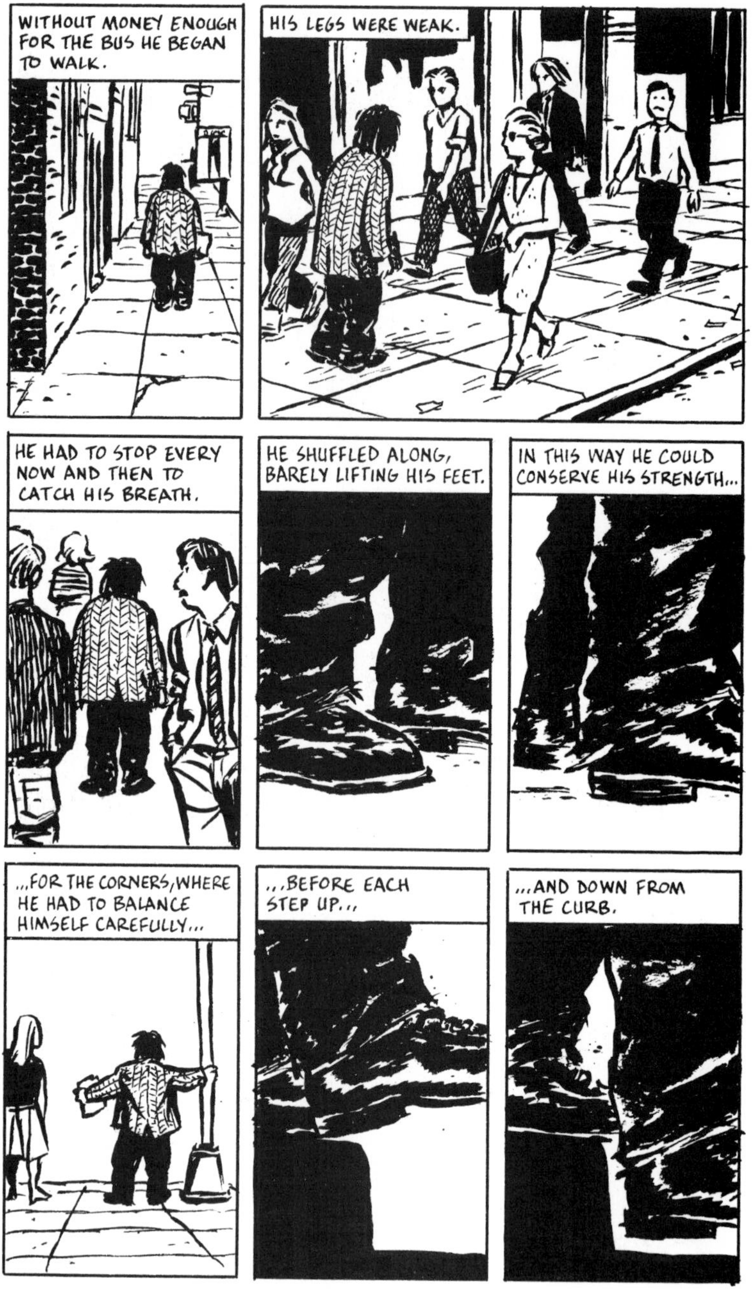
WITHOUT MONEY ENOUGH FOR THE BUS HE BEGAN TO WALK.
HIS LEGS WERE WEAK.
HE HAD TO STOP EVERY NOW AND THEN TO CATCH HIS BREATH.
HE SHUFFLED ALONG, BARELY LIFTING HIS FEET.
IN THIS WAY HE COULD CONSERVE HIS STRENGTH...
...FOR THE CORNERS, WHERE HE HAD TO BALANCE HIMSELF CAREFULLY...
...BEFORE EACH STEP UP...
...AND DOWN FROM THE CURB.

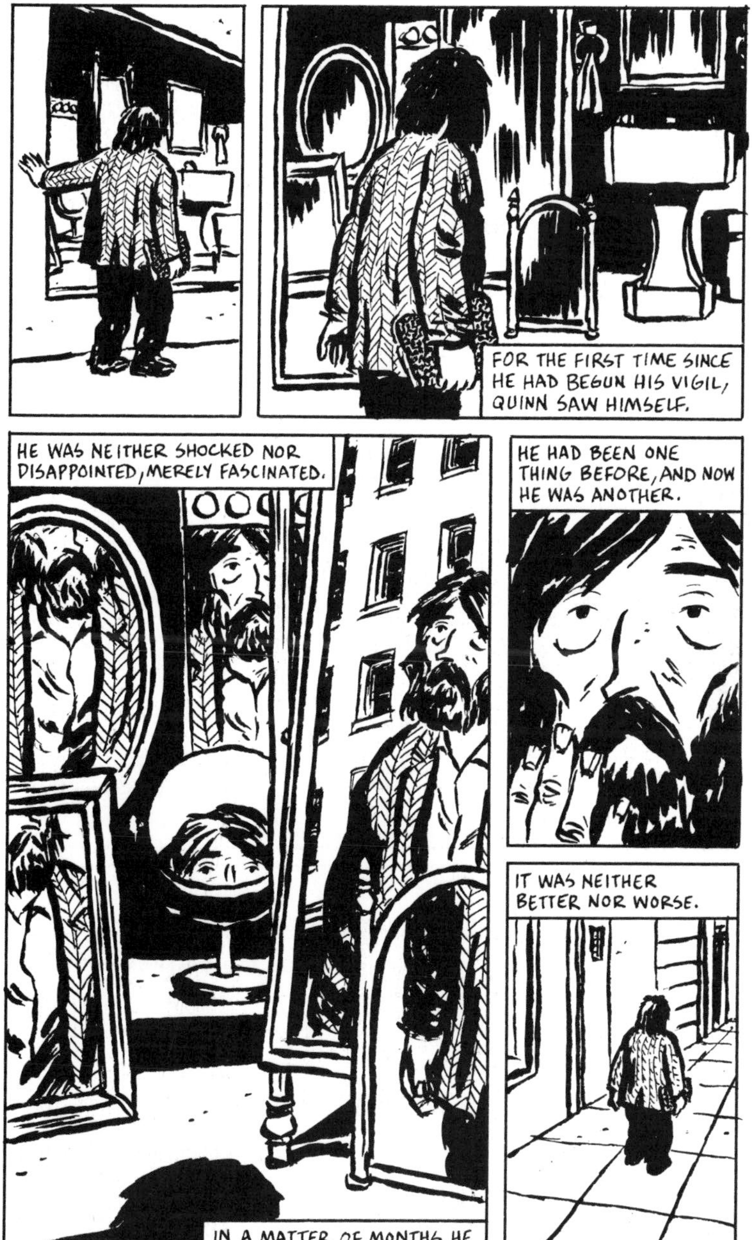
FOR THE FIRST TIME SINCE HE HAD BEGUN HIS VIGIL, QUINN SAW HIMSELF.
HE WAS NEITHER SHOCKED NOR DISAPPOINTED, MERELY FASCINATED.
IN A MATTER OF MONTHS HE HAD BECOME SOMEONE ELSE.
HE HAD BEEN ONE THING BEFORE, AND NOW HE WAS ANOTHER.
IT WAS NEITHER BETTER NOR WORSE.

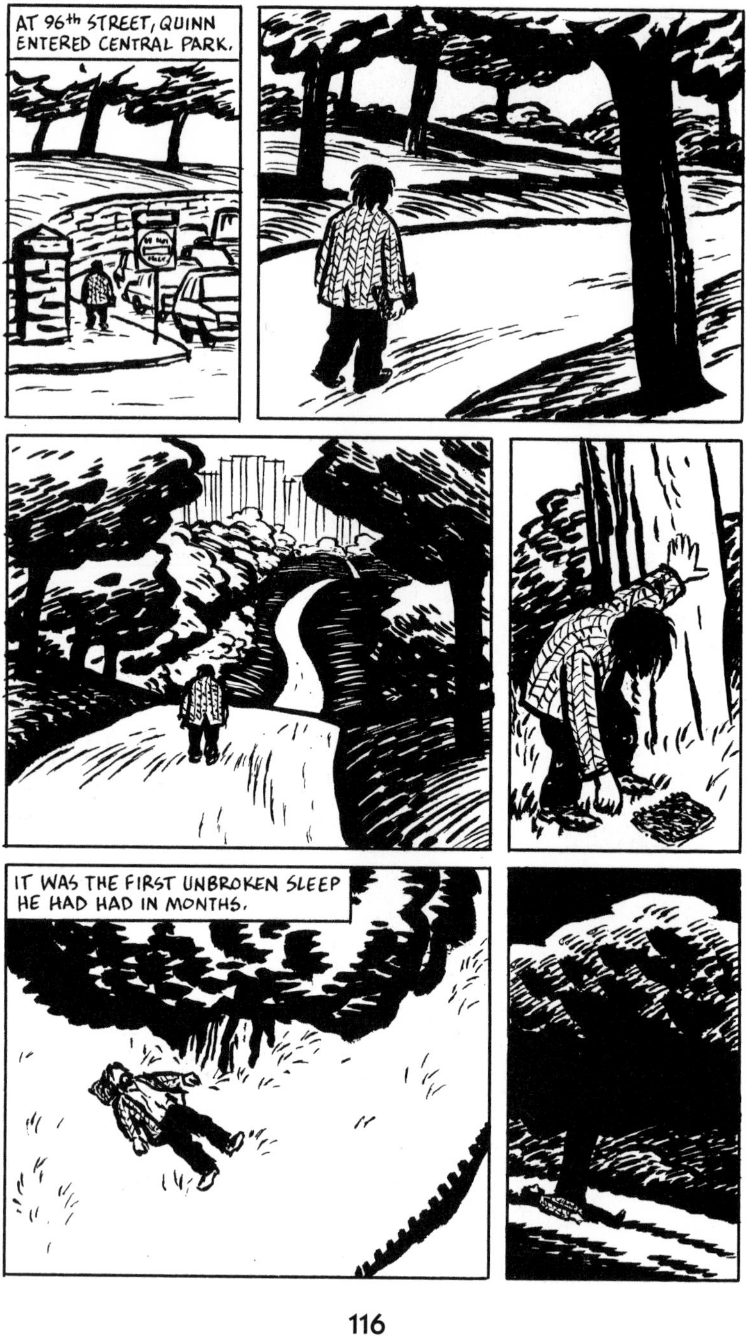
AT 96th STREET, QUINN ENTERED CENTRAL PARK.
IT WAS THE FIRST UNBROKEN SLEEP HE HAD HAD IN MONTHS.

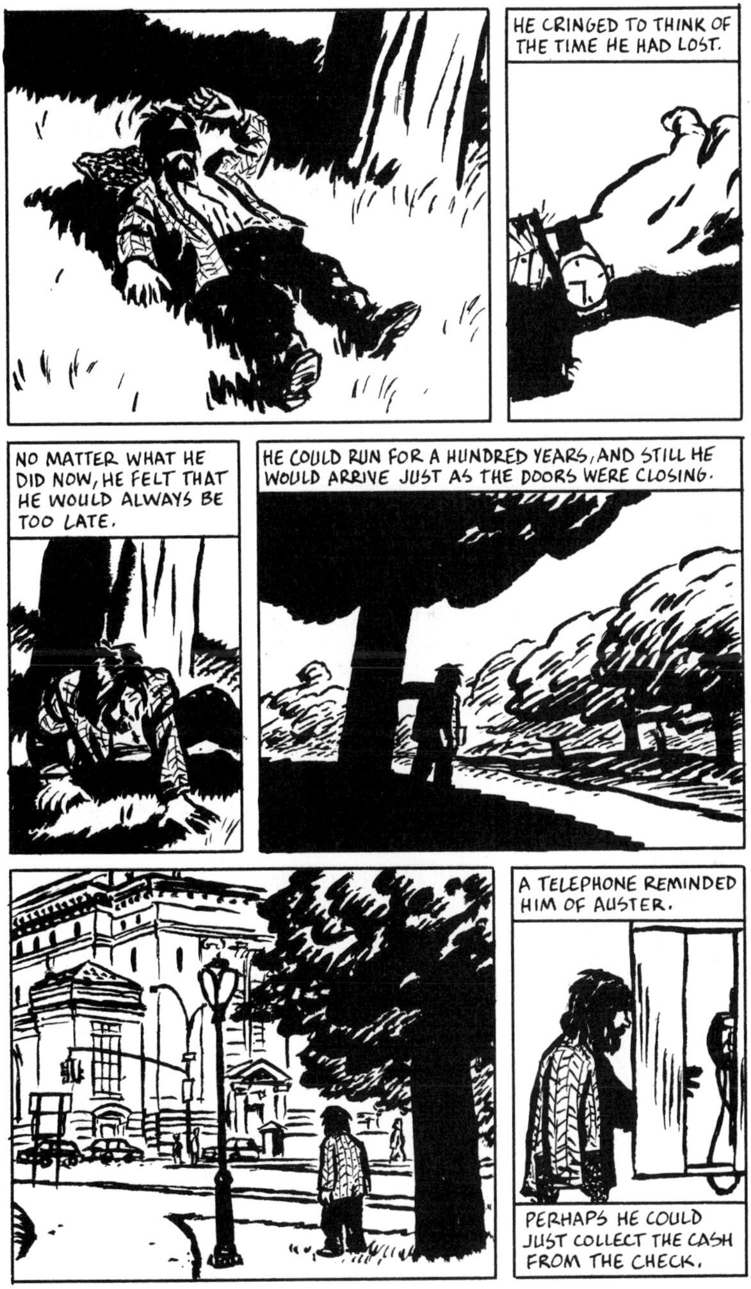
HE CRINGED TO THINK OF THE TIME HE HAD LOST.
NO MATTER WHAT HE DID NOW, HE FELT THAT HE WOULD ALWAYS BE TOO LATE.
HE COULD RUN FOR A HUNDRED YEARS, AND STILL HE WOULD ARRIVE JUST AS THE DOORS WERE CLOSING.
A TELEPHONE REMINDED HIM OF AUSTER.
PERHAPS HE COULD JUST COLLECT THE CASH FROM THE CHECK.

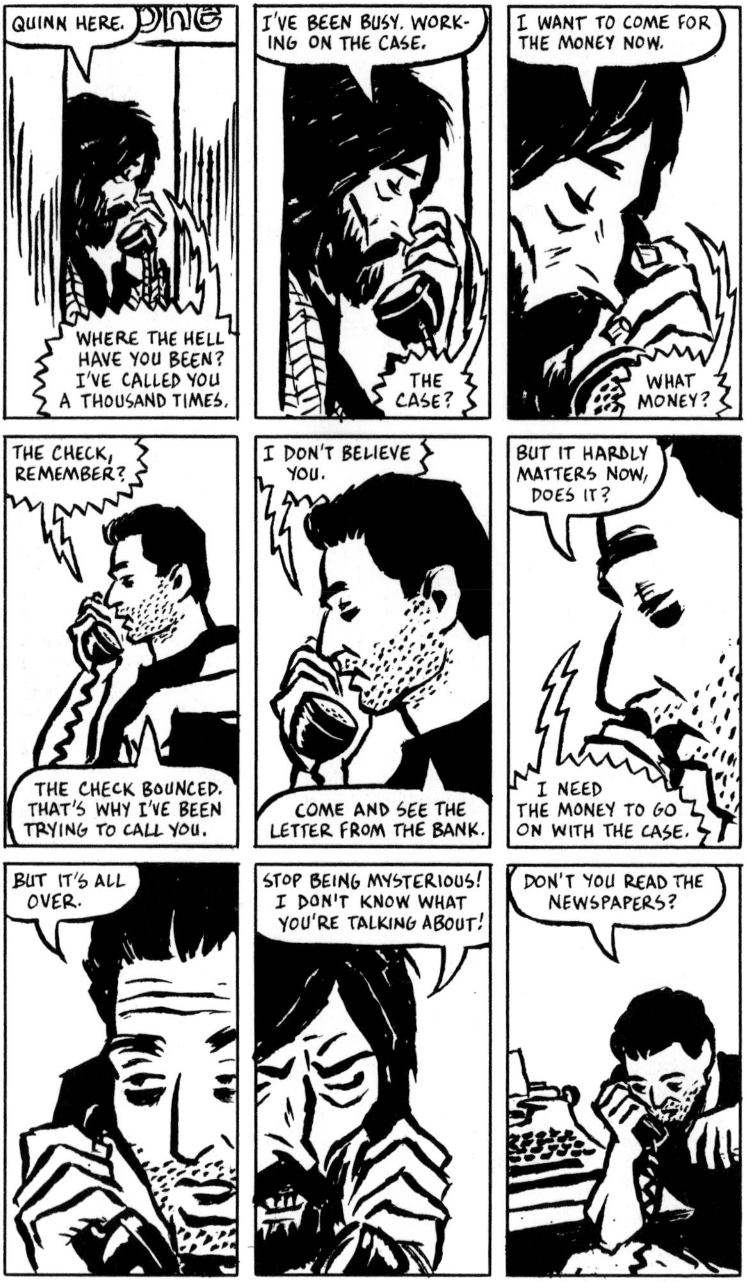
QUINN HERE.
WHERE THE HELL HAVE YOU BEEN? I'VE CALLED YOU A THOUSAND TIMES.
I'VE BEEN BUSY. WORKING ON THE CASE.
THE CASE?
I WANT TO COME FOR THE MONEY NOW.
WHAT MONEY?
THE CHECK, REMEMBER?
THE CHECK BOUNCED. THAT'S WHY I'VE BEEN TRYING TO CALL YOU.
I DON'T BELIEVE YOU.
COME AND SEE THE LETTER FROM THE BANK.
BUT IT HARDLY MATTERS NOW, DOES IT?
I NEED THE MONEY TO GO ON WITH THE CASE.
BUT IT'S ALL OVER.
STOP BEING MYSTERIOUS! I DON'T KNOW WHAT YOU'RE TALKING ABOUT!
DON'T YOU READ THE NEWSPAPERS?

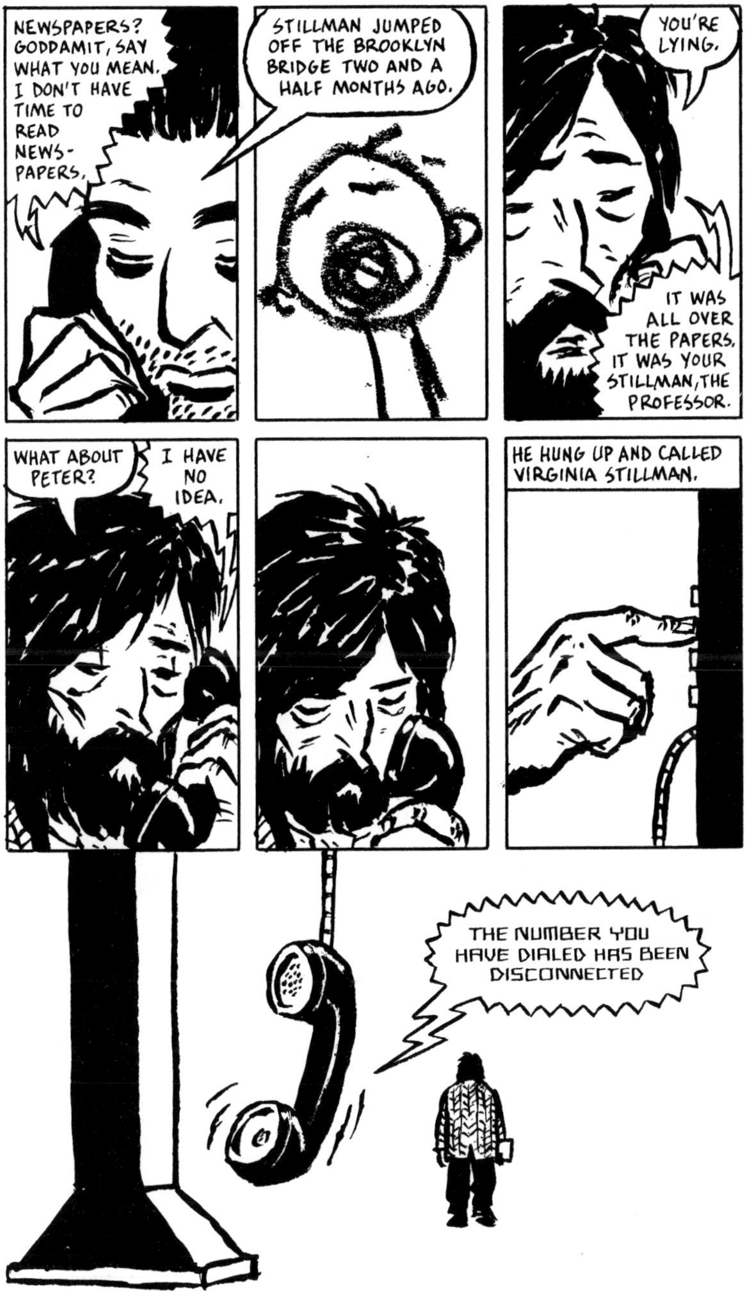
NEWSPAPERS? GODDAMIT, SAY WHAT YOU MEAN. I DON'T HAVE TIME TO READ NEWS-PAPERS.
STILLMAN JUMPED OFF THE BROOKLYN BRIDGE TWO AND A HALF MONTHS AGO.
YOU'RE LYING.
IT WAS ALL OVER THE PAPERS. IT WAS YOUR STILLMAN, THE PROFESSOR.
WHAT ABOUT PETER?
I HAVE NO IDEA.
HE HUNG UP AND CALLED VIRGINIA STILLMAN.
THE NUMBER YOU HAVE DIALED HAS BEEN DISCONNECTED

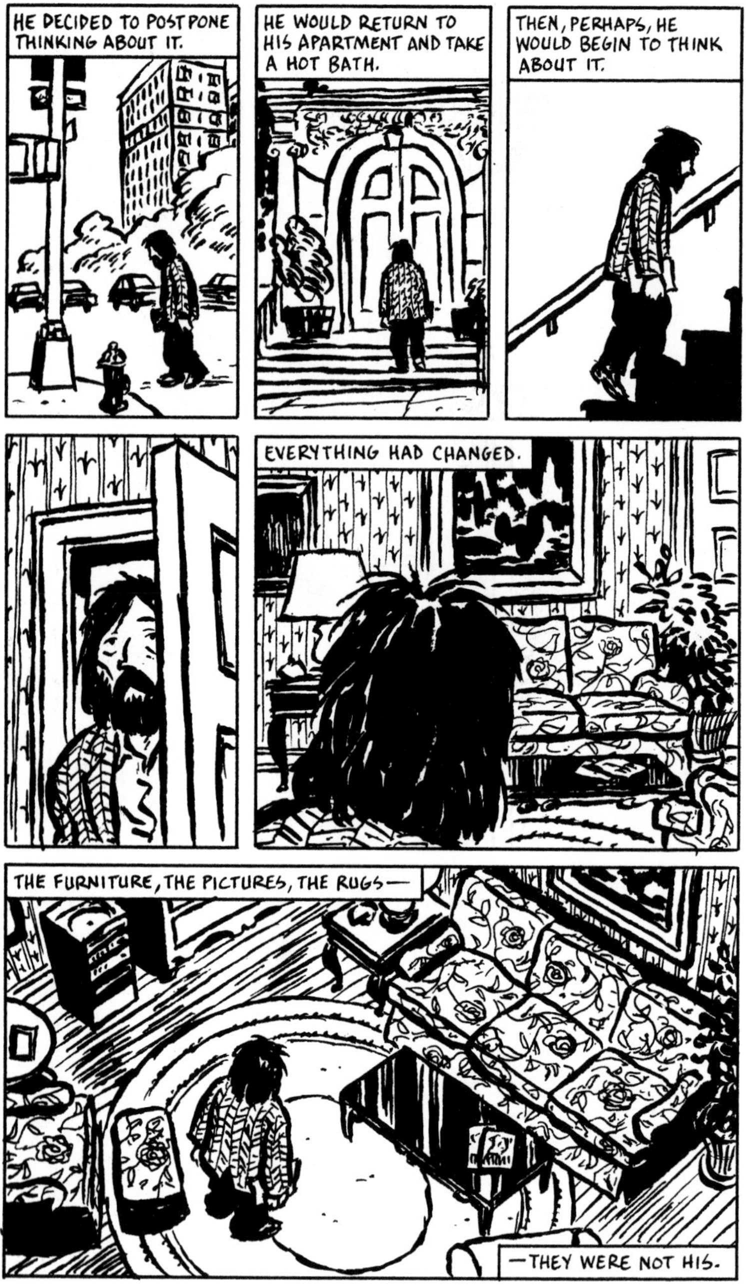
HE DECIDED TO POSTPONE THINKING ABOUT IT.
HE WOULD RETURN TO HIS APARTMENT AND TAKE A HOT BATH.
THEN, PERHAPS, HE WOULD BEGIN TO THINK ABOUT IT.
EVERYTHING HAD CHANGED.
THE FURNITURE, THE PICTURES, THE RUGS—
—THEY WERE NOT HIS.

HIS DESK WAS GONE, HIS BOOKS WERE GONE, THE CHILD DRAWINGS OF HIS DEAD SON WERE GONE.

JANGLE
CLACK

EEEEEEE!

IT TOOK A WHILE TO CALM HER DOWN.

I'VE BEEN LIVING HERE FOR A MONTH. IT'S MY APARTMENT.

BUT I HAVE THE KEY. DOESN'T THAT CONVINCE YOU?

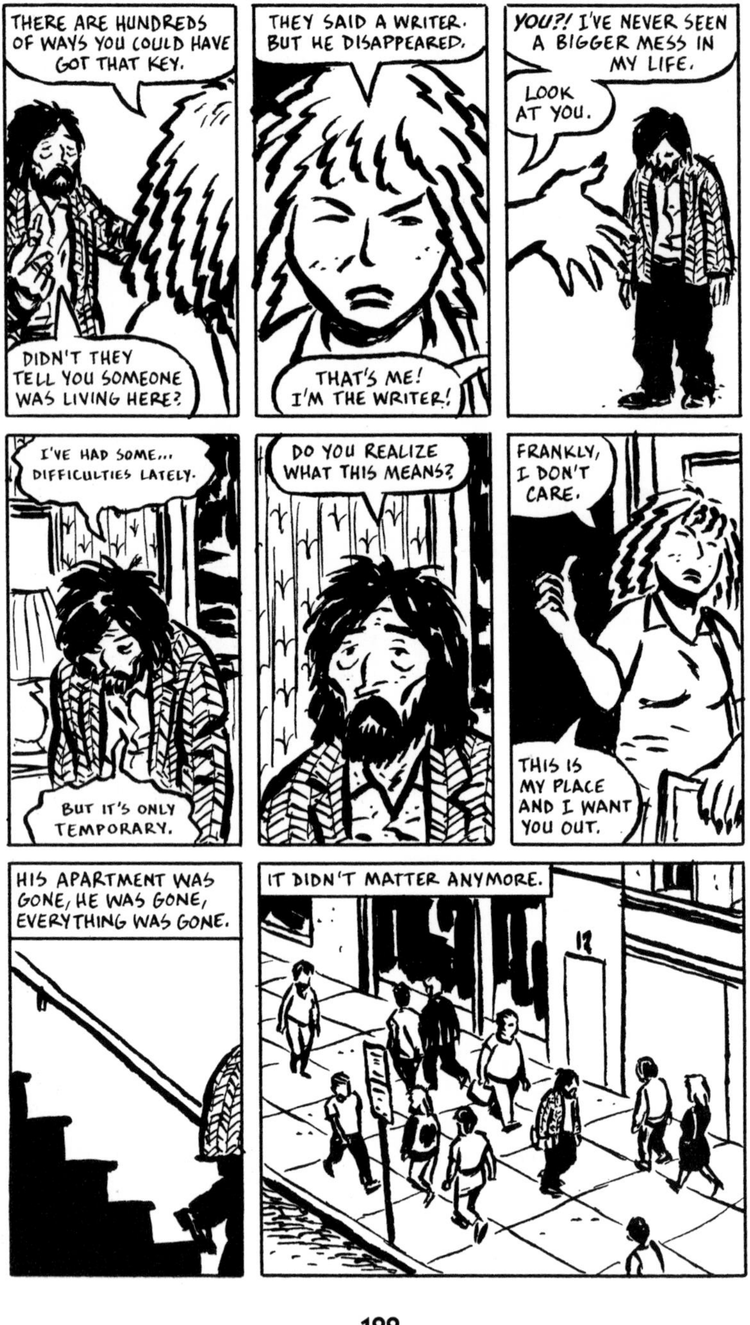
THERE ARE HUNDREDS OF WAYS YOU COULD HAVE GOT THAT KEY.
DIDN'T THEY TELL YOU SOMEONE WAS LIVING HERE?
THEY SAID A WRITER. BUT HE DISAPPEARED.
THAT'S ME! I'M THE WRITER!
YOU?! I'VE NEVER SEEN A BIGGER MESS IN MY LIFE.
LOOK AT YOU.
I'VE HAD SOME... DIFFICULTIES LATELY.
BUT IT'S ONLY TEMPORARY.
DO YOU REALIZE WHAT THIS MEANS?
FRANKLY, I DON'T CARE.
THIS IS MY PLACE AND I WANT YOU OUT.
HIS APARTMENT WAS GONE, HE WAS GONE, EVERYTHING WAS GONE.
IT DIDN'T MATTER ANYMORE.
12

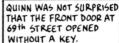

QUINN WAS NOT SURPRISED THAT THE FRONT DOOR AT 69th STREET OPENED WITHOUT A KEY.

NOR WAS HE SURPRISED WHEN HE REACHED THE STILLMANS' APARTMENT...

...THAT THAT DOOR SHOULD BE OPEN AS WELL.

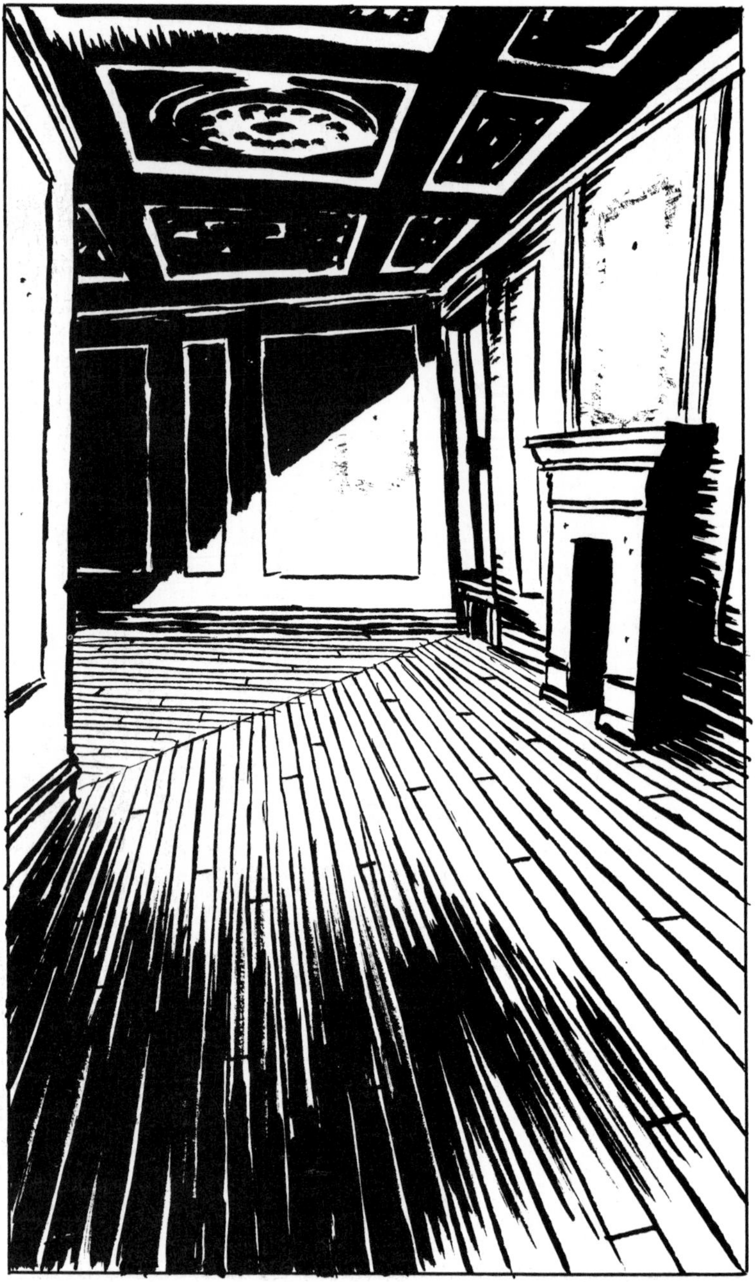

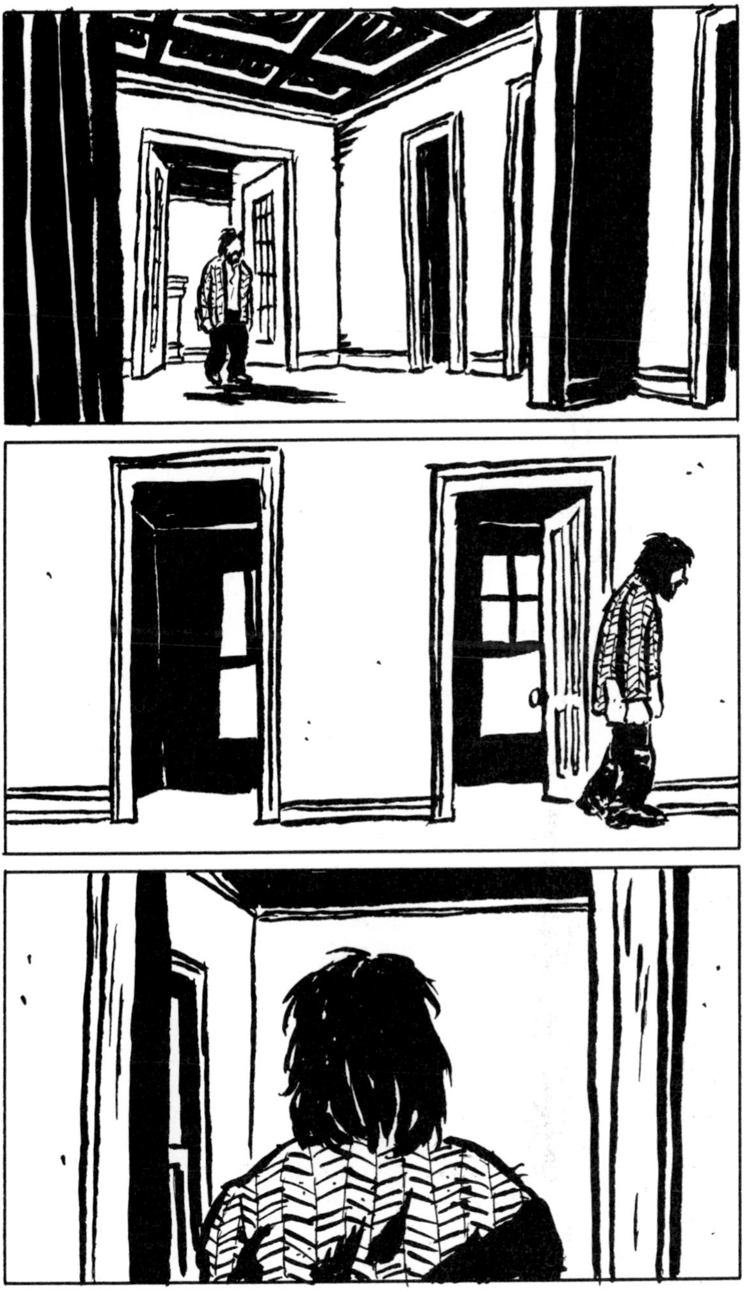

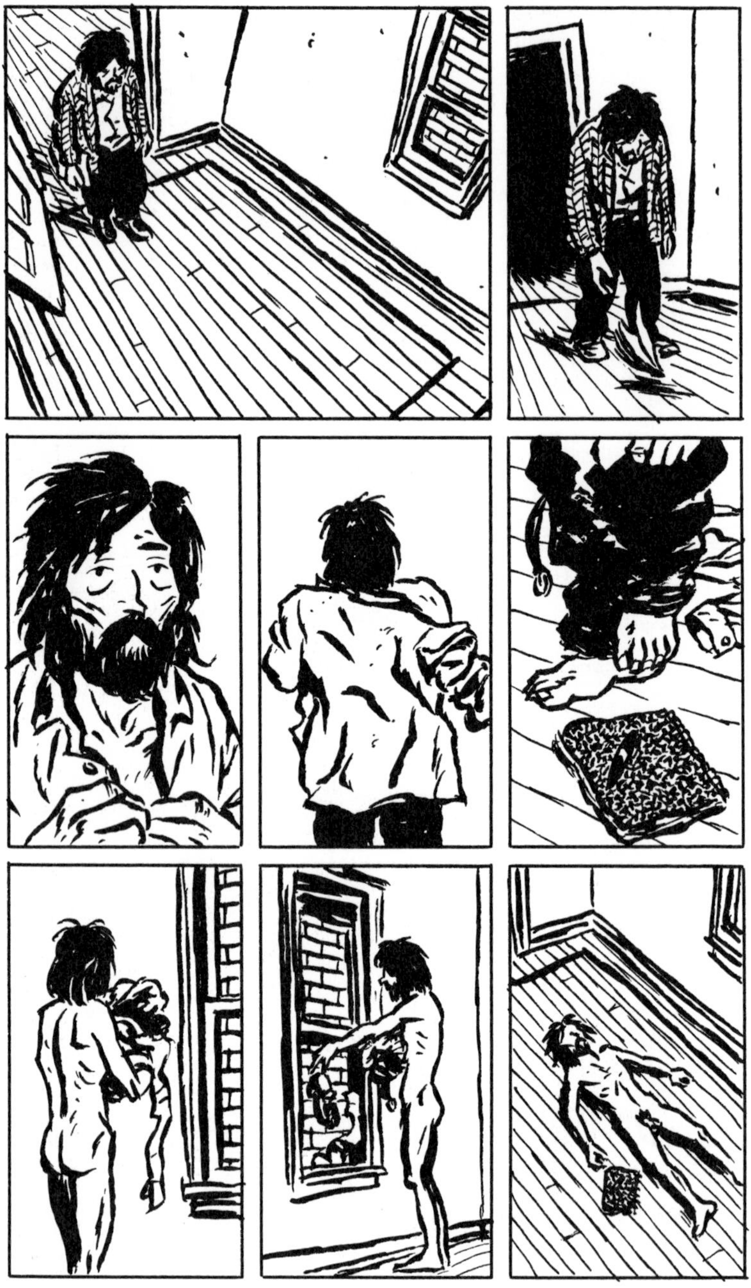

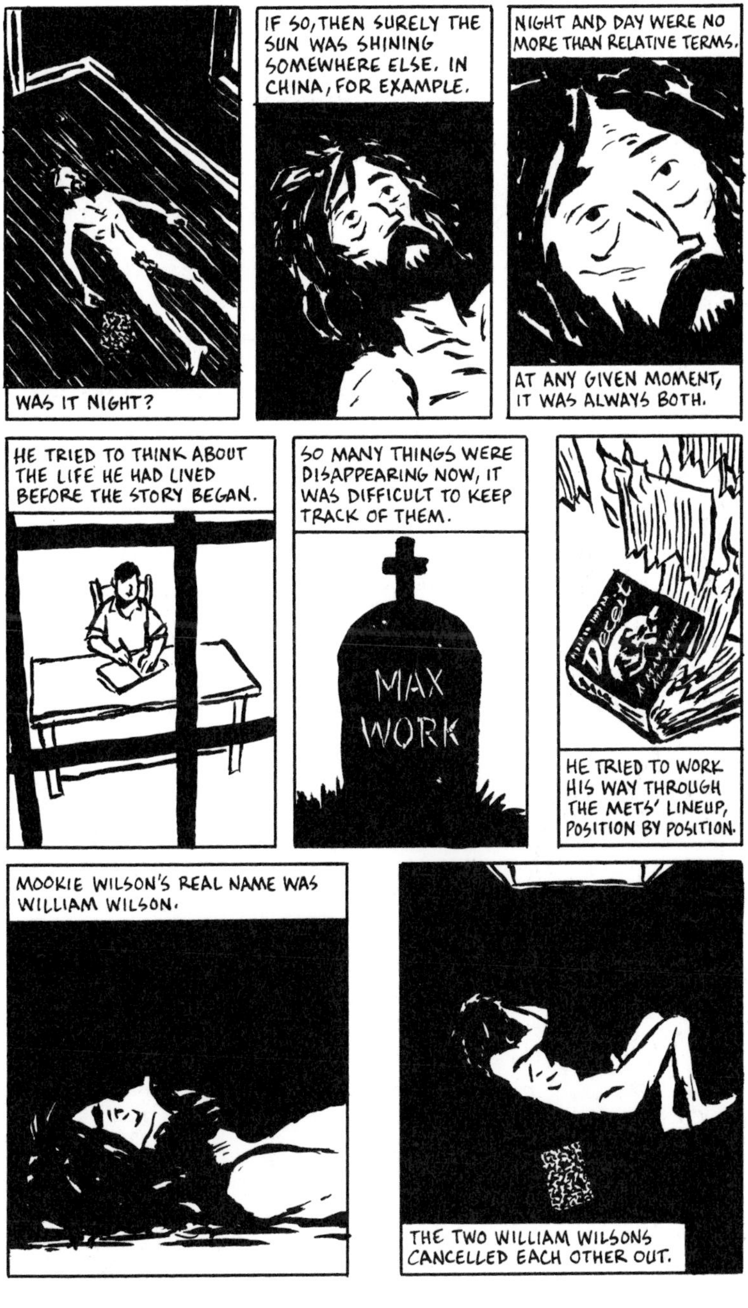
WAS IT NIGHT?
IF SO, THEN SURELY THE SUN WAS SHINING SOMEWHERE ELSE. IN CHINA, FOR EXAMPLE.
NIGHT AND DAY WERE NO MORE THAN RELATIVE TERMS.
AT ANY GIVEN MOMENT, IT WAS ALWAYS BOTH.
HE TRIED TO THINK ABOUT THE LIFE HE HAD LIVED BEFORE THE STORY BEGAN.
SO MANY THINGS WERE DISAPPEARING NOW, IT WAS DIFFICULT TO KEEP TRACK OF THEM.
MAX WORK
Deceit
HE TRIED TO WORK HIS WAY THROUGH THE METS' LINEUP, POSITION BY POSITION.
MOOKIE WILSON'S REAL NAME WAS WILLIAM WILSON.
THE TWO WILLIAM WILSONS CANCELLED EACH OTHER OUT.

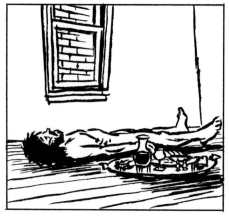

HE WROTE UNTIL IT WAS DARK.

THE THOUGHT OF TURNING ON THE LIGHT DID NOT APPEAL TO HIM.

FOR THE MOST PART, HIS ENTRIES FROM THIS PERIOD CONSISTED OF MARGINAL QUESTIONS CONCERNING THE STILLMAN CASE.

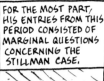

WHY HAD HE NOT BOTHERED TO LOOK IN OLD NEWSPAPERS ABOUT STILLMAN'S ARREST IN 1969?

WHY HAD HE TAKEN AUSTER'S WORD THAT STILLMAN WAS DEAD?

a good egg egg on his to lay an eg as alike as two eggs

WHY HAD DON QUIXOTE NOT WRITTEN BOOKS LIKE THE ONES HE LOVED...

...INSTEAD OF LIVING OUT THEIR ADVENTURES?

WAS THE GIRL IN HIS APARTMENT THE SAME AS THE GIRL IN GRAND CENTRAL?

WAS THE CASE OVER, OR WAS HE STILL WORKING ON IT?

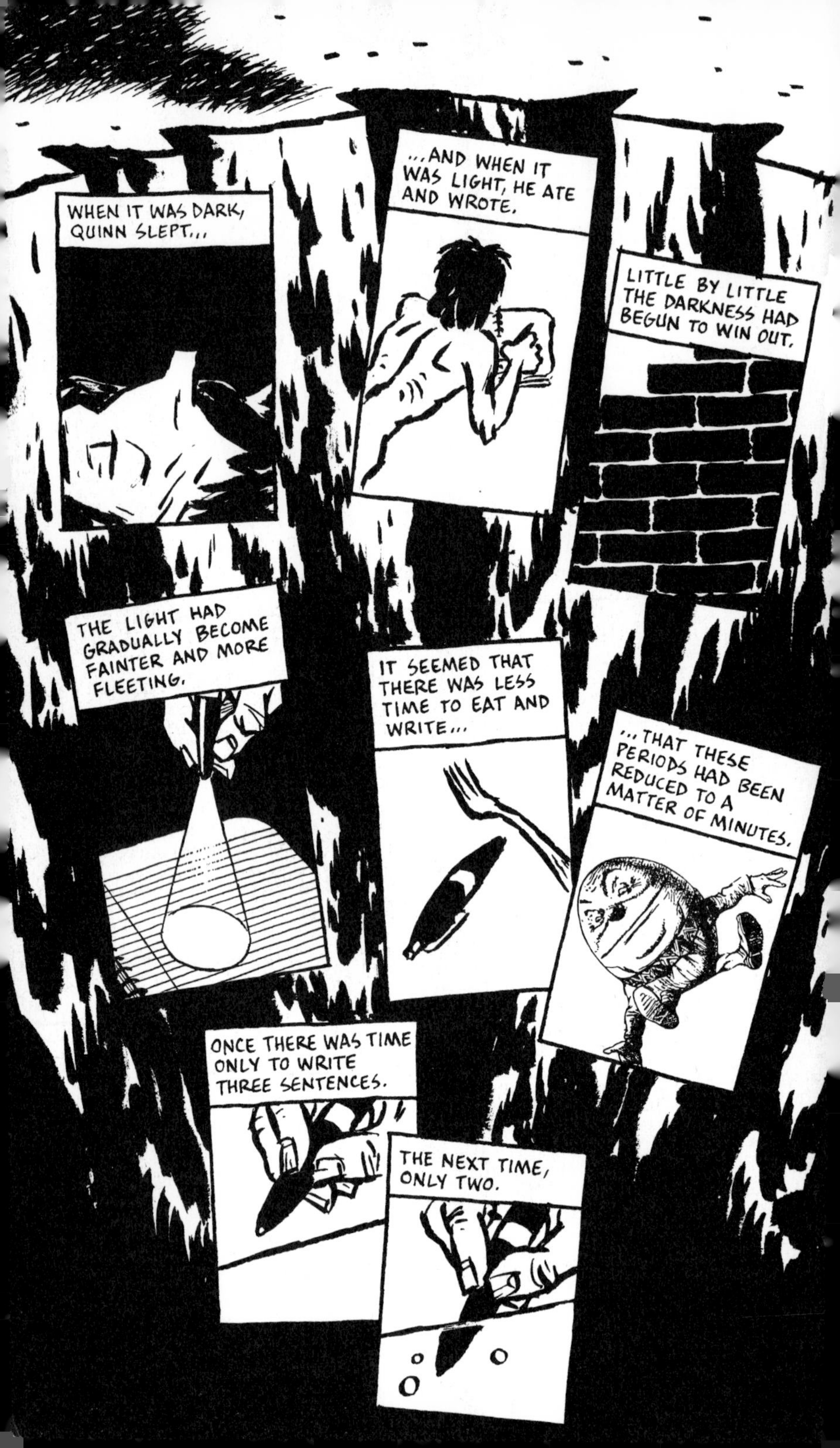

WHEN IT WAS DARK, QUINN SLEPT...
...AND WHEN IT WAS LIGHT, HE ATE AND WROTE.
LITTLE BY LITTLE THE DARKNESS HAD BEGUN TO WIN OUT.
THE LIGHT HAD GRADUALLY BECOME FAINTER AND MORE FLEETING.
IT SEEMED THAT THERE WAS LESS TIME TO EAT AND WRITE...
...THAT THESE PERIODS HAD BEEN REDUCED TO A MATTER OF MINUTES.
ONCE THERE WAS TIME ONLY TO WRITE THREE SENTENCES.
THE NEXT TIME, ONLY TWO.

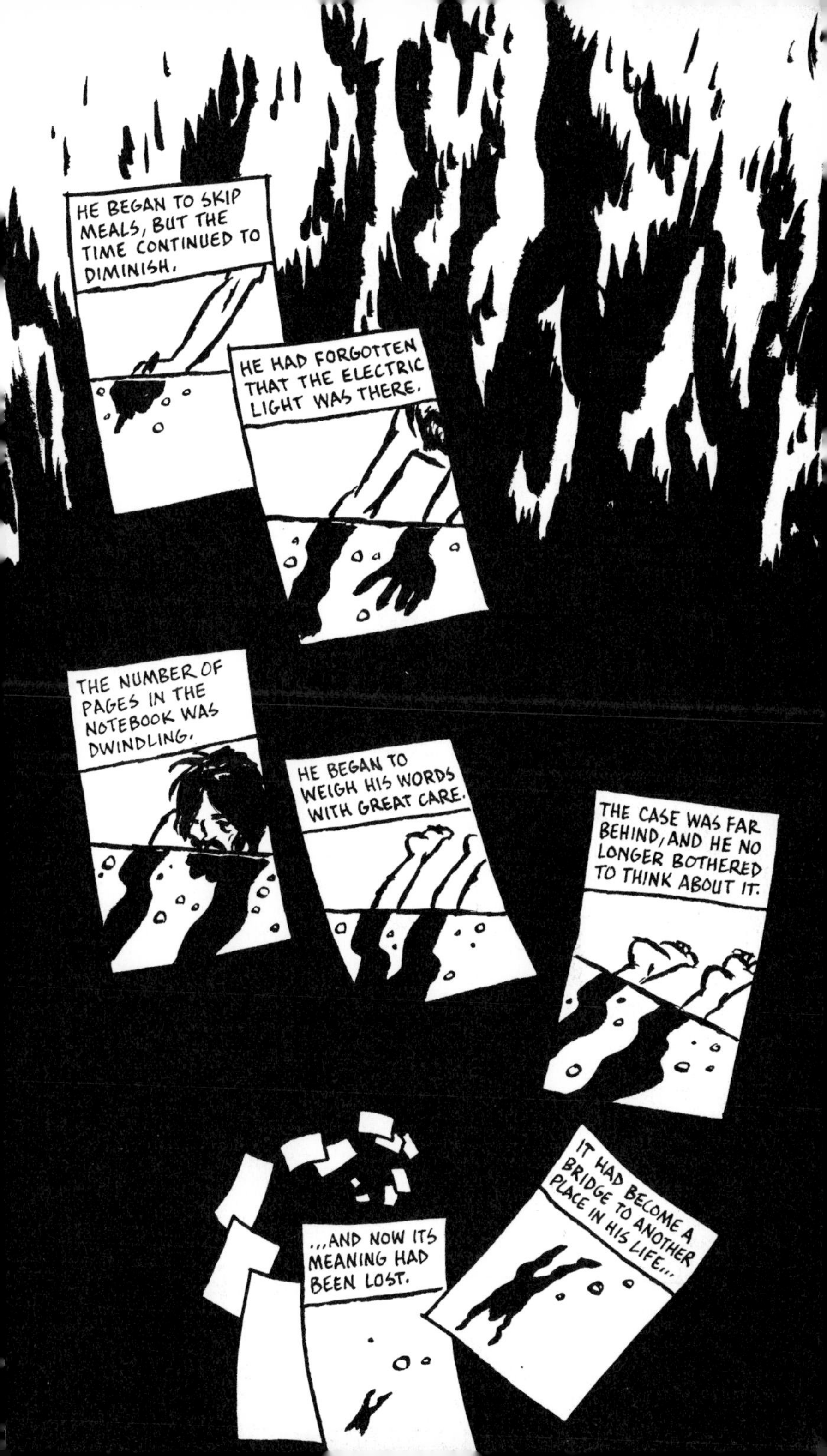
HE BEGAN TO SKIP MEALS, BUT THE TIME CONTINUED TO DIMINISH.
HE HAD FORGOTTEN THAT THE ELECTRIC LIGHT WAS THERE.
THE NUMBER OF PAGES IN THE NOTEBOOK WAS DWINDLING.
HE BEGAN TO WEIGH HIS WORDS WITH GREAT CARE.
THE CASE WAS FAR BEHIND, AND HE NO LONGER BOTHERED TO THINK ABOUT IT.
IT HAD BECOME A BRIDGE TO ANOTHER PLACE IN HIS LIFE...
...AND NOW ITS MEANING HAD BEEN LOST.

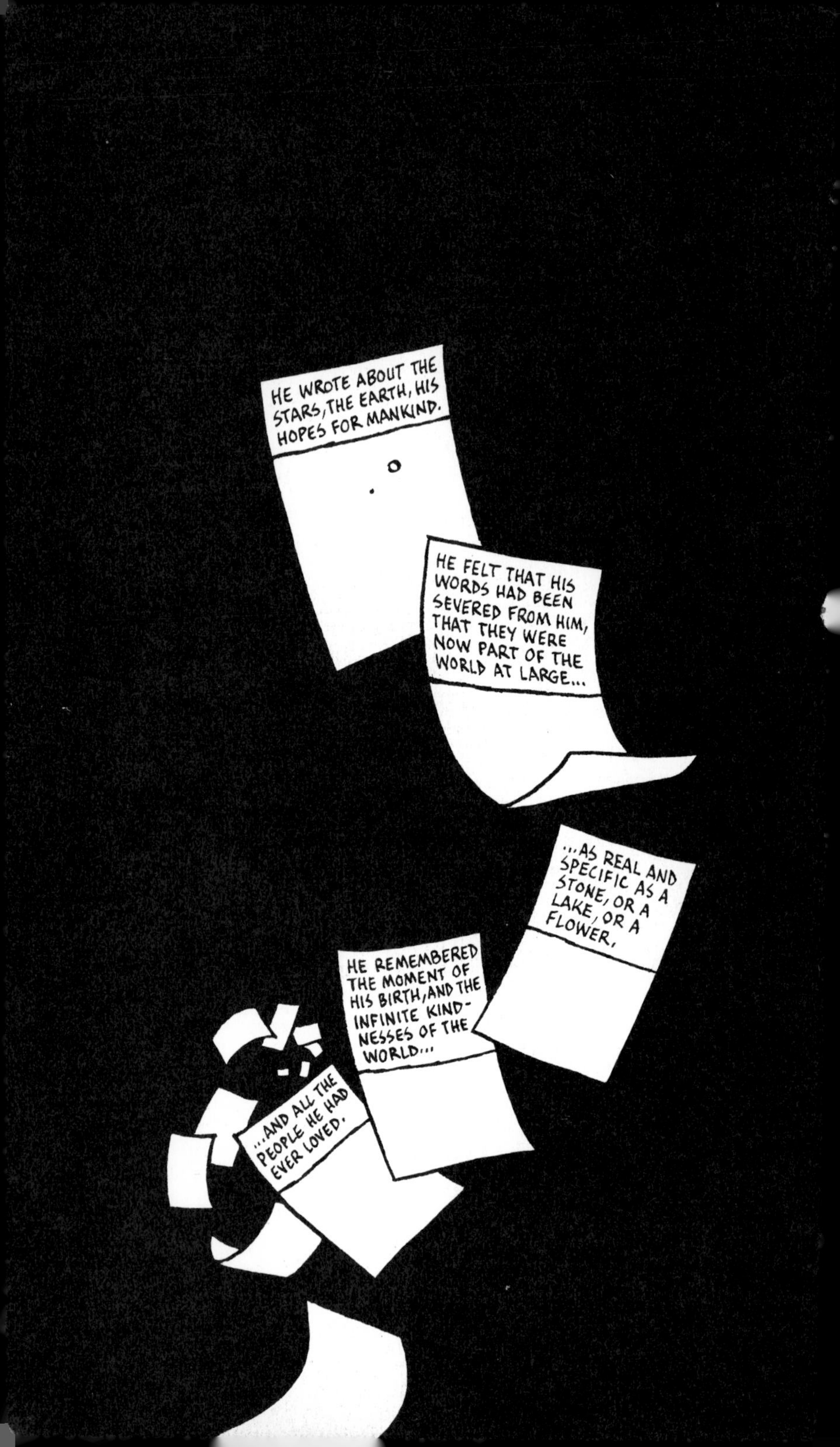
HE WROTE ABOUT THE STARS, THE EARTH, HIS HOPES FOR MANKIND.
HE FELT THAT HIS WORDS HAD BEEN SEVERED FROM HIM, THAT THEY WERE NOW PART OF THE WORLD AT LARGE...
...AS REAL AND SPECIFIC AS A STONE, OR A LAKE, OR A FLOWER.
HE REMEMBERED THE MOMENT OF HIS BIRTH, AND THE INFINITE KINDNESSES OF THE WORLD...
...AND ALL THE PEOPLE HE HAD EVER LOVED.

He wondered if he
had it in him to
write without a
pen, if he could
learn to speak in-
stead, filling the
darkness with his
voice, speaking
the words into the
air, into the walls,
into the city, even
if the light never
came back again.

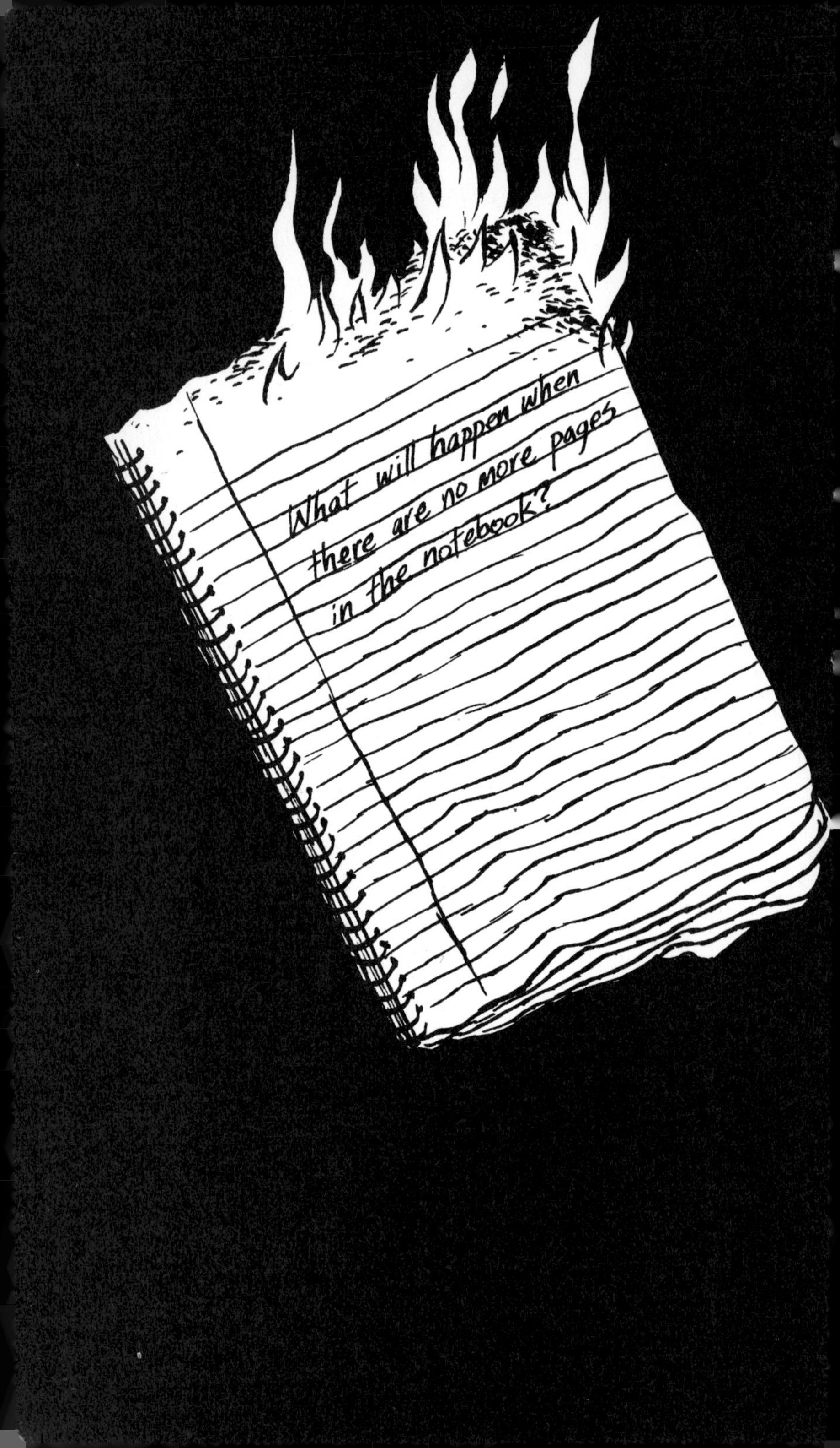
What will happen when
there are no more pages
in the notebook?

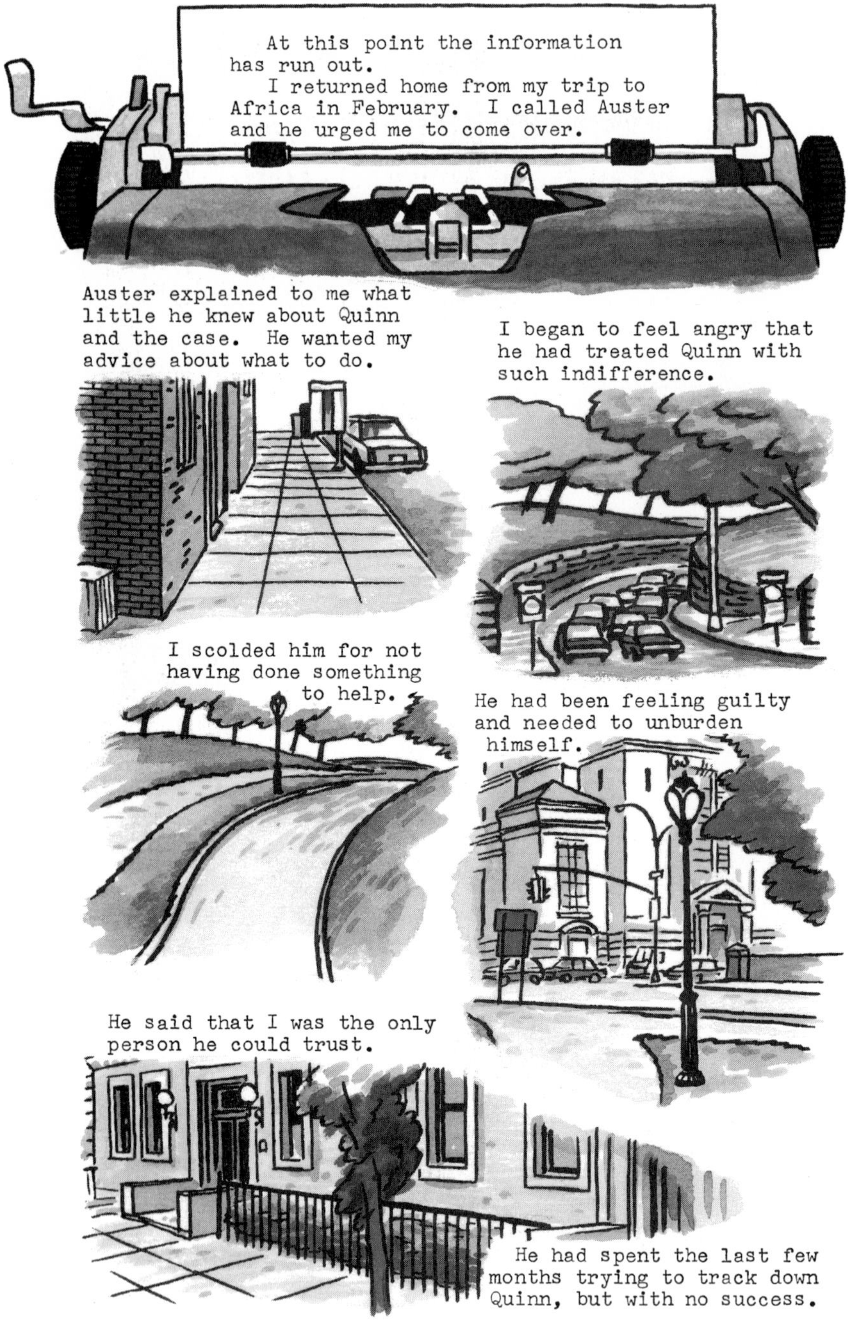
At this point the information has run out.
I returned home from my trip to Africa in February. I called Auster and he urged me to come over.
Auster explained to me what little he knew about Quinn and the case. He wanted my advice about what to do.
I began to feel angry that he had treated Quinn with such indifference.
I scolded him for not having done something to help.
He had been feeling guilty and needed to unburden himself.
He said that I was the only person he could trust.
He had spent the last few months trying to track down Quinn, but with no success.

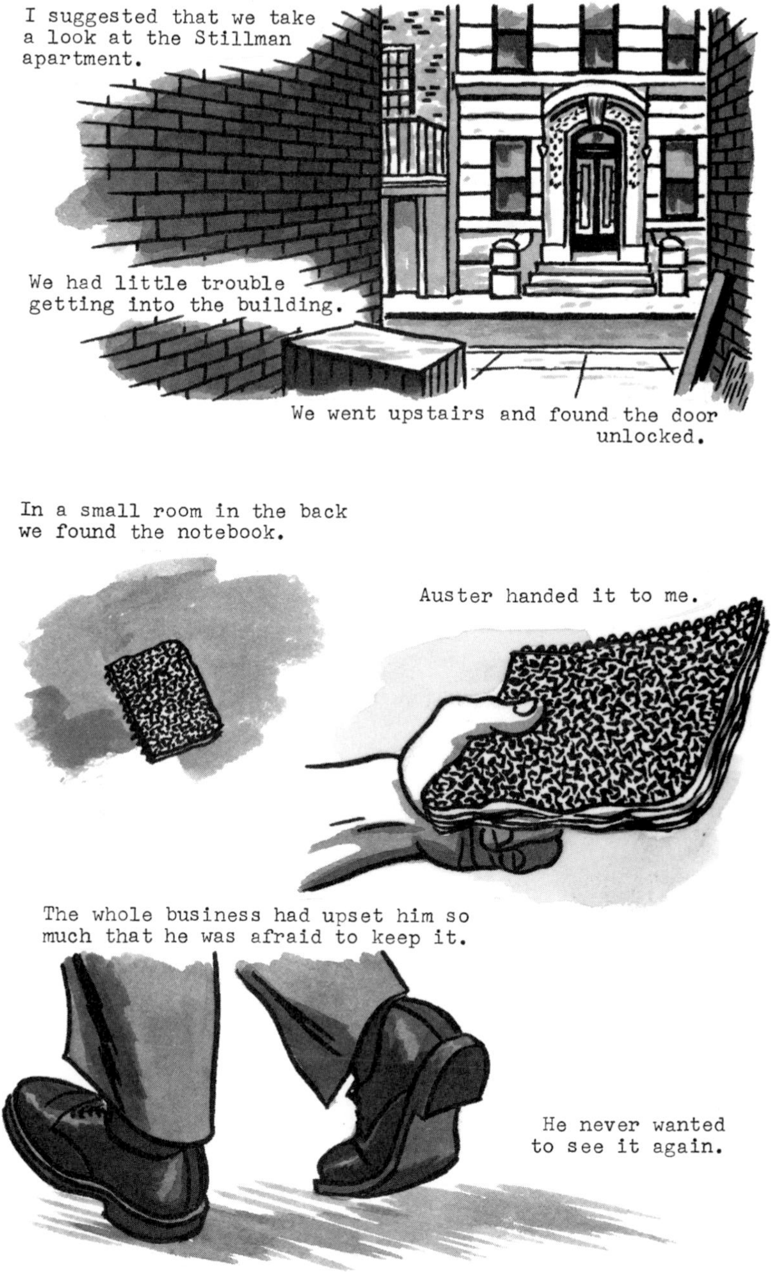
I suggested that we take a look at the Stillman apartment.
We had little trouble getting into the building.
We went upstairs and found the door unlocked.
In a small room in the back we found the notebook.
Auster handed it to me.
The whole business had upset him so much that he was afraid to keep it.
He never wanted to see it again.

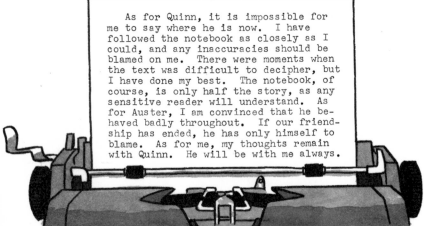

As for Quinn, it is impossible for me to say where he is now. I have followed the notebook as closely as I could, and any inaccuracies should be blamed on me. There were moments when the text was difficult to decipher, but I have done my best. The notebook, of course, is only half the story, as any sensitive reader will understand. As for Auster, I am convinced that he behaved badly throughout. If our friendship has ended, he has only himself to blame. As for me, my thoughts remain with Quinn. He will be with me always.

And wherever he may have disappeared to, I wish him luck.